William M. Rossetti, Richard Clay

A Memoir of Shelley

with a fresh preface

William M. Rossetti, Richard Clay

A Memoir of Shelley
with a fresh preface

ISBN/EAN: 9783337388133

Printed in Europe, USA, Canada, Australia, Japan

Cover: Foto ©Andreas Hilbeck / pixelio.de

More available books at **www.hansebooks.com**

A

MEMOIR OF SHELLEY

(*WITH A FRESH PREFACE*)

BY

WILLIAM MICHAEL ROSSETTI

London

PRINTED FOR THE SHELLEY SOCIETY

BY RICHARD CLAY & SONS, BREAD STREET HILL.

1886

PREFACE.

My thanks are due to Mr. Slark, the present publisher and proprietor of the edition of Shelley's Poems to which the ensuing Memoir forms an introduction, for allowing the Memoir to be issued as one of the publications of the Shelley Society. He handsomely and readily acceded to a request made by Dr. Furnivall to that effect. For me as the author it remains to hope that my fellow-members in the Society will not consider that Dr. Furnivall's zeal and Mr. Slark's liberality were ill bestowed.

The ensuing Memoir was written in 1869, a date when the materials for constructing a Life of Shelley were sparse, slender, and confused, in no small degree : it was first published in 1870. When the edition of Shelley's Poems was about to be reissued, which was done at the beginning of 1878, I revised the Memoir, taking into account any additional materials then accessible. I believe that, both in 1870 and in 1878, the Memoir was not behind the then level of knowledge on the subject. Since 1878 however many further particulars, and not a little controversy more or less warm, have accrued. I could not therefore feel satisfied without once again doing something to make the Memoir presentable to serious and well-grounded students of Shelley's life and writings—persons of the class in whose interest the Shelley Society is founded, and who may be expected to abound in its ranks. I have thus once again gone carefully through my little narrative. As it is printed in stereotype, and the stereotype plates are used for the present reissue, it has not been practicable to alter the actual words of the text ; and the only expedient open to me has been to give a list of those passages or details which need rectification or extension.

This is done in the items of reference which immediately ensue. I have written them with the utmost brevity consistent with clearness ; and shall trust to the reader's candour to distinguish between instances in which actual errors (most of them not avoidable at the time) are corrected, and instances in which the information supplied belongs to a date subsequent to 1877. It is of course true that various other details relating to Shelley have come to light within the same interval of time, some of which might properly figure even in a Memoir so condensed and limited as this. But these I advisedly leave untouched ; restricting myself to the actual contents of the Memoir, and the particulars needed for setting it right.

P. 2. *Percy Bysshe Shelley's descent traced up to Thomas Shelle, in the time of Edward I.* Mr. Forman has published the pedigree which was attested in 1816 by the father and the half-uncle of the poet. It only extends up to Henry Shelley of Worminghurst, who died in 1623. Mr. Jeaffreson has commented with much fulness upon this pedigree ; and has pointed out that it contains no names of more than moderate social standing, and that it does not connect that branch of the Shelley family from which the poet sprang with the older and more aristocratic line. At the same time Mr. Jeaffreson allows that most probably there really was a connexion between the two branches. His observations on these questions of fact appear to be perfectly sound and convincing.

P. 3. *Rev. Theobald Mitchell* should be Michell.

P. 3. *Shelley's grandfather said to have practised as a quack doctor, and owned a mill.* It has been so said, but not correctly. The allegation is really apposite to Shelley's *great*-grandfather.

P. 4. *Two of Shelley's sisters still survive.* One of these two is now dead : the other still, I believe, survives.

P. 7. *Shelley passed to Eton in his fourteenth year*—should be " his twelfth year "—July 1804.

P. 9. *Dr. Keate flogged Shelley liberally.* Dr. Keate was in

1804 the Master of the *Lower* School. Shelley soon quitted the Lower for the Upper School, and Keate became Head Master only at the end of 1809. Probably the statement in the text is inaccurate.

P. 9. *Dr. Lind a tutor at Eton.* I believe this is more than doubtful.

P. 10. *Shelley left Eton some time in* 1809. A mistake. Shelley went from Eton to Oxford in April 1810; then re- turned to Eton, and remained there till the ensuing July.

P. 10. *Harriet Grove daughter of a clergyman.* This is erroneous : the father was a country gentleman.

P. 12. *No reviews of Zastrozzi or of St. Irvyne traced out.* This has ceased to be exactly true.

P. 13. *Miss Grove possibly concerned in the authorship of the Victor and Cazire volume.* Enquirers seem now to be generally agreed that not Miss Grove, but Miss Elizabeth Shelley, had to do with it.

P. 16. *Lieut. Williams said that Shelley looked " of most astonishing genius."* So it stands printed in Trelawny's *Recol- lections :* but I think we ought to re-punctuate the sentence thus : Shelley is certainly a man of most astonishing *genius, in appearance extraordinarily young.*

P. 22. *Shelley's abstract from Hume's Essays printed at Brighton.* Should be Worthing.

P. 28. *Shelley's letter dated 4 July* 1811. I am now convinced, under the guidance of Prof. Dowden, that there is no misprint in this letter, and also no mystery about it. Shelley, an avowed enemy of the legal marriage-bond, simply says that he would have wished Hogg and Elizabeth to unite without marriage, and would wish to act in like manner himself when the time should come.

P. 29. *Shelley eloped with Harriet about the beginning of September* 1811. It was really on one of the latest days of August : the actual Scotch marriage was on the 28th.

P. 33. *De Quincey was another casual acquaintance at Keswick.* I believe this is disputable, or incorrect.

P. 39. *Shelley in the autumn of* 1812 *stayed awhile in Godwin's house.* I understand this is an error.

P. 40. *Suggestion that Daniel Hill may have had something to do with the alleged attempted assassination of Shelley at Tanyrallt.* According to the last information which I have received, I tend more and more to conclude that the alleged attempted assassination was a delusion, or a figment: more a delusion than a figment.

P. 42. *Ianthe Shelley born in Cooke's Hotel, Dover Street.* Mr. Jeaffreson believes that she was really born in Shelley's lodgings in Pimlico: he may probably be right.

P. 43. *Note* 1. The reference should be to p. 153 (not 53).

P. 44. *Mrs. Boinville's daughter Cornelia:* should be "sister."

P. 48. *Harriet Shelley pregnant when Shelley, on* 24 *March* 1814, *remarried her in London: this may have prompted the re-marriage.* The inference is doubtful: the child was only born towards 1 December 1814.

P. 49. *Shelley made a sufficient provision for Harriet after his separation from her.* Mr. Jeaffreson says that, after the death of Shelley's grandfather in January 1815, he allowed Harriet £200 a year.

P. 49. *Letters written by Harriet in moving terms, &c* I understand it would be more correct to say "a letter."

P. 53. *Jane (who adopted instead the name of Claire) Clairmont.* I believe her full christian names were Clara Mary Jane.

P. 54. *Miss Clairmont seldom mentioned in the Memoir, and still living.* Now that Miss Clairmont is dead—she died on 19 March 1879—it may be permissible to say that, in the first form of my Memoir of Shelley, 1870, I gave various details bearing upon the fact of her being the mother of Byron's natural daughter Allegra; but, when the second form of the Memoir was on the eve of publication in 1878, Miss Clairmont asked me to omit any such details. I at once complied. One reference to Allegra, at the close of p. 78, was left in through inadvertence.

P. 55. *Shelley's money-affairs, as consequent on his grandfather's death.* Mr. Jeaffreson is the only writer who has enabled us to understand clearly what Shelley's money-affairs truly were: I say nothing of his inferences, which are unfavourable to Shelley, but of the facts which he details. During the life of the grandfather Shelley was absolute heir (after grandfather and father) to two somewhat considerable estates, which Mr. Jeaffreson conveniently terms A and B. There was also a third estate, C, vastly larger than A and B put together: Shelley could have succeeded to C, if he had consented to the urgencies of his grandfather and father that A, B, and C, should all be put upon one and the same footing of strict entail. Shelley refused, and he and his lost the estate C. One may surmise that Shelley accounted for his refusal upon the same ground which I have set forth in the Memoir, p. 32—a rooted objection, upon principle, to the system of entail: nor can I see any plausible reason why we should suppose that this was not the real ground for a decision so glaringly contrary to his worldly interest. See p. 79 for some further reference to this matter.

P. 58. *The continental trip of Shelley and Mary in* 1816 *probably undertaken as a mere matter of inclination.* This point has been very sharply debated of late years; Mr. Jeaffreson contending with much force that Shelley and Mary consciously seconded Miss Clairmont's scheme for keeping up her amour with Byron. Other disputants say that the contrary can be proved. A neutral enquirer, like myself, awaits production of the proof.

P. 59. *Mrs. Shelley's name applied to Byron, Albè, unexplained.* I think it must mean L. B. [Lord Byron].

P. 66. *Thornton Hunt the most definite among those who have spoken of Harriet Shelley's life after the separation.* Trelawny, in the recast of his *Records,* 1878, was more definite. He felt much sympathy for Harriet: but I am not aware that his sources of information on the subject were in any special degree authentic.

P. 73. *Brougham employed as counsel in Westbrook v. Shelley.* I believe there is no ground for this allegation.

P. 73. *Lord-Chancellor Eldon's judgment delivered in August, not March.* I learn that this is a mistake. March, or thereabouts, is correct.

P. 74. *A clergyman, Dr. Hume.* He was not a clergyman, but an army-doctor, designated by Shelley himself.

P. 74. *Mr. Kendall—uncertain whether he was ever appointed guardian of Shelley's children.* As I now understand the facts, he never was appointed.

P. 79. *Shelley refused to be a yea-and-nay man in the House of Commons, and thereby lost a large fortune.* See above my note upon a passage in p. 55. My observations printed on p. 79 are not quite pertinent to the facts, as established by Mr. Jeaffreson's book. It would appear that Shelley told Hunt that he lost the large fortune, C, by refusing to be a yea-and-nay man in the House of Commons. The primary reason however was that he declined to coöperate in the entailing of that fortune upon himself and his heirs. From Hunt's statement we may not unnaturally infer that, *if* he had thus coöperated, there was a further scheme for returning him to the House of Commons, to be at the beck of the Duke of Norfolk; and that he rejected the parliamentary position along with the entail.

P. 88. *As late as 15th February* 1821—should be 21st March.

P. 91. *Shelley and Mary—discussion as to their mutual affection and satisfaction in married life.* As to this important question the reader should not overlook a letter addressed by Shelley to Mr. Gisborne on 18 June 1822. An extract from it was published by Dr. Garnett in the *Fortnightly Review* for June 1878, and is reproduced in the *Athenæum* for 6 June 1885, review of Mr. Jeaffreson's book.

P. 99. *No trace of Shelley's satire upon satire.* Dr. Garnett has recovered some lines in the heroic metre, relating to Southey &c., which may possibly belong to this satire. I doubt it.

P. 100. *Miss Clairmont may perhaps not have seen Shelley after he quitted Florence.* She *did* see him at Casa Magni: possibly elsewhere also.

P. 114. *The calumny on Shelley, in which the Hoppners were concerned, not clearly defined.* It is now known that the calumny was to the effect that Shelley had at a recent date had a child by Miss Clairmont, which had been consigned to a Foundling-hospital.

P. 116. *Trelawny still happily among us.* He died in August 1881.

P. 120. *Mysterious occurrence on* 23 *June* 1822. The details are not entirely accurate. The affair of "*Siete soddisfatto*" occurred on some day not precisely defined. Shelley was then on the terrace of the Casa Magni, and the Williamses are not mentioned in connexion with this incident. There was *a different* affair on 23 June: a dream or vision which horrified Shelley, who presented himself to Mary, screaming and in a trance of sleep.

P. 121. *Shelley's wraith on* 29 *June.* Byron gave this date: but I believe it ought to be 15 June. Mrs. Williams (apparently no one else) was the person who saw, or fancied that she saw, Shelley.

P. 127. *Question as to the burning of Keats's book.* I understand that in fact the binding of the book was burned.

P. 149. *Shelley's writings in* 1814. We should add Shelley's review of Hogg's *Memoirs of Prince Alexy Haimatoff.*

P. 150. *Shelley's writings in* 1817. Add the fragment of an epistle named *The Elysian Fields,* and the essay *On the Devil and Devils,* both published by Mr. Forman. Date uncertain, but may be towards 1817.

P. 150. *Shelley's letter about Richard Carlile.* Published by Mr. Forman.

P. 150. *Shelley's Lucianic essay identified with the Essay on Devils.* This is disputable. The *Essay on Devils,* as now published, does not embody the argument spoken of by Shelley.

P. 151. *The Shelley Memorials comes nearest to being a complete Life of the Poet.* Of course this can no longer be maintained now that Mr. Jeaffreson's *Real Shelley* has appeared. I should incline to place *The Real Shelley* next after my No. 6. I dissent from the view which it expresses of Shelley's character and career, and I find the work erroneous or defective in some details.   It is however a solid performance, which future biographers cannot ignore.   On various points it throws new and important light : on all sorts of points it is argumentative, and challenges now reflection, and anon refutation.

P. 151. *Trelawny's Recollections.*   This book, in one volume, is now superseded by the fuller *Records*, 1878, in two volumes.

P. 153.   To the list of authorities I should now add (*a*) the book, *Shelley and Mary*, printed but not published in 1882 by Sir Percy and Lady Shelley : scarcely any one has seen it, and I have not seen it ; (*b*) the article in the *Edinburgh Review* founded on (*a*) ; (*c*) Mr. Symonds's Life of Shelley, in the Series *English Men of Letters ;* (*d*) Dr. Garnett's article, *Shelley's Last Days*, in the *Fortnightly Review* for June 1878 ; (*e*) Mr. Froude's article in the *Nineteenth Century* about Shelley, Miss Clairmont, and Byron, arising out of some observations made by Mr. Jeaffreson, and replied to by that gentleman.   The writings of Mr. Forman, who is *the* authority in respect of bibliography, of Miss Blind, of Mr. Hale White, of the late James Thomson (B.V.), and some by myself apart from the present Memoir, may also be named.   Prof. Dowden's great biographical work is expected shortly : it ought to, and I daresay it will, supersede most of the preceding literature on the subject.

W. M. ROSSETTI.

Endsleigh Gardens, London.
March 1886.

MEMOIR OF SHELLEY.

To write the life of Shelley is (if I may trust my own belief) to write the life of the greatest English poet since Milton, or possibly since Shakespeare ; and, as the greatest poet must equal at least the greatest man of any other order, it must also be to write the life of one of the most illustrious personages, of whatever sort, known to these latter ages. And this is peculiarly the case with Shelley, in whom a truly glorious poetic genius was united with, or was one manifestation of, the most transcendent beauty of character,—flecked, indeed, here and there by semi-endearing perversities, or by some manifest practical aberration. However this may be, he commands into love and homage every emotion of the soul and every perception of the mind. To be a Shelley enthusiast has been the privilege of many a man in his youth, and he may esteem himself happy who cherishes the same feeling unblunted into the regions of middle or advanced age. A full and genuine life of the sublime poet remains yet to be written : the materials for it are ripening, but perhaps even yet not entirely matured. Or the facts of his life, intellect, and character might be exhibited in a very interesting manner by a proper collation and reproduction of all his known correspondence, combined with all such passages of his poetical or other works as have a distinct personal bearing. Meanwhile it comes to be my good fortune to write a condensed memoir of Shelley ; a memoir in which I find so many facts and details pressing for record that I feel with reluctance compelled to' leave almost unused those treasures of his own correspondence which would give the inner heart of the story so much better than any biographer can do it. But the full facts—the outer phases of incident—of his life from first to last have never yet been told with the needful combination of sifted and balanced evidence and of ordered method : different authorities give diverse accounts of almost every particular of his career and belongings, and even of his person. Some of these diversities will be discussed or noted as I proceed : and it is more especially with a view to this result of sifting and certifying — as a contribution towards the systematising of materials for a life of Shelley—that I plan this memoir. Brief it necessarily is by the conditions of the case. But I shall endeavour to make it the reverse of loose or vague, and to transmit in it to any future biographer a compact cento of facts, while laying claim to only a moderate amount of exclusive information, and conscious of deficiency as regards fulness of presentation or profound or exhaustive analysis.

I.—DESCENT AND FAMILY.

The Shelleys are an ancient and honourable house. The name has been spelled Shelly and Shellie, as well as Shelley. The arms are sable, a fesse engrailed between three whelk shells or; the motto, Fey e Fidalgia. With these whelk shells legend (or rather Mr. Jefferson Hogg) connects some story of a paladin, Sir Guyon de Shelley, contemporary with Roland and Charlemagne. Him we may leave to the Ariostean region of history, and contemplate with less blinking eyes a Thomas Shelle as lord (in the time of Edward I.) of the manor of Shelley, of Schottis in Nockholt, and of other lands in Kent. There was a Sir Thomas Shelley who fought, and died on the scaffold, in the cause of Richard II.; and a Sir Richard Shelley, Grand Prior of the English language among the Knights of Malta, whose well-proved valour brought him, in extreme old age, to the defence of the island against the Turks in 1565. Somewhat earlier, about the end of the fifteenth century, Edward, the second son of the chief of the house, was settled at Worminghurst Park; his son Henry married a Sackville, and from them descends that branch of the family which has achieved some fleeting distinction in the way of a peerage and a second baronetcy (the first baronetcy, in the older line, dates from 1611), and an eternal distinction in giving birth to the "poet of poets." The name Bysshe came into the family in the sixth generation after Edward Shelley; John Shelley, the then representative of the junior branch, having in 1692 married Helen.

younger daughter and co-heiress of Roger Bysshe of Fen Place. His grandson was Bysshe Shelley, who was born in 1731, and who became the poet's grandfather.

It was in the person of this Bysshe Shelley, and in the year 1806 (nearly fourteen years after the birth of the poet), that the second baronetcy came into the race. Sir Bysshe was then an old man, and the father of two families. By his first wife, Mary Katherine, heiress of the Rev. Theobald Mitchell of Horsham, he had a son, Timothy (the poet's father), and a daughter. By his second wife, Elizabeth Jane Sidney, heiress of Mr. Perry of Penshurst, he had three sons and two daughters. This second family shall not concern us here, further than to say that it inherited from the mother the blood of Sir Philip and other Sidneys,[1] and that the eldest son, John, assumed the name of Shelley-Sidney of Penshurst, was made a baronet, and was the father of Philip Charles Sidney, created Baron De l'Isle and Dudley.

The man who married two heiresses, became a baronet, and founded a second family of sufficient standing to receive a further baronetcy in the first generation and a peerage in the second, was presumably not an altogether commonplace person. If we may trust the memoir-writers, Sir Bysshe Shelley, so far from being commonplace, was decidedly eccentric. He was tall, handsome, and clever; and represented, in the eyes of a younger generation, a gentleman of the old school. His place of birth was Christ Church, Newark in North America; in that country, having no fortune, he is said to have practised as a quack doctor and to have owned a mill. He was penurious, yet spent lavishly upon building Castle Goring, which he left unfinished. A staunch adherent of the Whig house of Norfolk (the prime magnates in his part of the county of Sussex), he earned his baronetcy through that connection. For years before his death, which occurred on the 6th of January 1815, he had lived in retirement at Horsham, not on good terms with his eldest son Timothy, whom he would curse to his face with a will. He left him one of the opulent heirs of the kingdom, £300,000 in the funds and £20,000 per annum being named as the estate of the vigorous old man at his decease. Among several curious incidents of his life the most odd of all[2] is that

---

[1] Percy Shelley himself numbered among his ancestors the great-great-grandfather of Sir Philip Sidney, but not Sir Philip personally.

[2] Medwin's *Life of Shelley*, vol. i. p. 8. I will here say, once for all, that Medwin is an inaccurate writer, and thus save myself the necessity of continually expressing, when I state anything on his authority, a doubt whether it is true or false.

he eloped with both of his English wives; and two of his daughters also eloped. (A rumour was current of an American wife preceding both the English ones; and there is apparently *something* in this story, as a letter from Percy Shelley, dated in January 1812, and seen by myself, exists in M.S., saying that his grandfather behaved very badly to "*three* wives.") Thus elopement was a tradition in the family, which we may bear in mind when another such performance comes to be spoken of— that of the poet. Sir Bysshe had no speculative opinions, unless in the way of negation, and cared nothing for the speculative opinions of others, however extreme : his grandson Percy and he were therefore on terms of mutual tolerance and mutual alienation. The less there was in common between them the less call was there for positive antipathy: a shrug of the shoulders summed up all. Sir Bysshe was indeed on much better terms with his youthful and aspiring grandson and godson than with his own son Timothy. The same letter which I have referred to just above says that Sir Bysshe was "a complete atheist," and built all his hopes on annihilation.

Timothy Shelley was born in September 1753. In 1791 he married Elizabeth, a rare beauty, daughter of Charles Pilfold, Esquire, of Effingham, Surrey, and had by her a family of two sons and five daughters. The eldest child was Percy Bysshe. The sisters (besides a Hellen who died in infancy) were named Elizabeth, Mary, Hellen (thus spelled in the family), and Margaret, and were all noted beauties. The last two still survive. The brother, John, born in March 1806, the youngest of all the family, died in November 1866. The mother was "mild and tolerant, yet narrow-minded;"[1] clever, and even intellectual, but not in the literary, still less the poetical, direction. She is stated to have been an excellent letter-writer.

The believer in Percy Bysshe Shelley naturally conceives a prepossession against the poet's father, with whom he would not or could not agree : but no doubt Sir Timothy had some of the ordinary good qualities of a human being and country gentleman. He was well reputed as a landlord and practical agriculturist, hospitable, kind (though sometimes capricious and violent) in his family and household, proud at first of his illustrious son's talents, and not precisely destitute of literary tastes. The style of his letters, however, shows him to have had no sort of natural or acquired facility, even in the

---

[1] Shelley, in Hogg's *Life*, vol. i. p. 350.

most level forms of writing. This objection (if I may be excused for referring to so small a point) does not extend to *handwriting*: Sir Timothy wrote a capital free clear hand, as perceptible in his franking signature outside some of his son's letters. He had the air of the old school off and on; and has even been described as a disciple of Chesterfield and La Rochefoucauld, though that is not the impression which the general body of evidence concerning him leaves on the mind. He was a christian as so many other people are — a religious indifferentist who acquiesced in what he found established. As a member of Parliament, sitting for the borough of Shoreham, he made no figure, and voted according to his ducal and other party-ties. Creature-comforts and material interests were what he understood; he was fond of self-assertion and pompous interferences, and, like his father, a swearer, and capable of niggardliness, and of considerable oddity of demeanour. Nobody except himself, I believe, ever considered him, during his long life of ninety years, noticeable for any particular talent. That such a person was exceedingly ill-adapted to stand *in loco parentis* to a divine phenomenon like Percy Shelley is flagrantly manifest; but there is nothing nefarious, nor even grossly stupid, in the character whose recorded outlines are sketched above, and we shall do well to enter upon the study of the poet's career without any conviction that he was foredoomed to spiteful or intentional persecution at his father's hands.

Mr. and Mrs. Timothy Shelley were settled at Field Place, near Horsham, Sussex; a mansion ever venerable to posterity, and which remains the property of the present baronet, the poet's son, though not at present in his personal occupation.

II.—BIRTH AND CHILDHOOD.

Percy Bysshe Shelley was born at Field Place on the 4th of August 1792. To mention August 1792 is to carry back one's mind to the overthrow of monarchy in France. On that day, in Paris, the insurrectionary directory of the Federators held a sitting at the Cadran Bleu on the Boulevard, at Bancelin the restaurateur's, to concert measures for a rising : Santerre, Camille Desmoulins, and others, were present.[1] And perhaps the transaction going on in the seclusion of Field Place was of quite co-equal importance to the cause of revolutionary free thought.

The infant received the name of Percy from an aunt distantly

---

[1] Hamel, *Histoire de Robespierre*, vol. ii. p. 362.

connected with the Northumberland family ; Bysshe, as we have
seen, from his grandfather.　He was a beautiful boy, with ring-
lets, deep-blue eyes,[1] a snowy complexion, and exquisitely
formed hands and feet ; in disposition gentle and affectionate.
But of his mere infancy no record remains ; though we may
conceive of him as fondling " the great old snake of Field
Place "—a large ophidian established in the garden of that
mansion, and which, so tradition says, had been known as " the
old snake " three-hundred years before.　Perhaps it had been
wont to fraternize with a dragon which, according to a still
extant pamphlet published in 1612, then haunted St. Leonard's
Forest in the same district.　At last the honoured veteran
was accidentally killed by the gardener in mowing grass : doubtless to the bitter sorrow of Percy, whose curious love of
snakes and serpents, noticeable time after time in his poems,
may probably be traced to this unusual friend of his babbling
years.

At six years of age he was sent to a day-school kept by the
Rev. Mr. Edwards, of Warnham, and began learning Latin
there.　He felt some respect for this his earliest instructor,
and hence in after days for country-clergymen in general : indeed, there is a wondrous anecdote [2] of a momentary *velléité*,
on the part of the then author of *Queen Mab*, to enter the
Church himself.

At the age of ten Percy was transferred to Sion House
School, Brentford, of which Dr. Greenlaw,[3] a Scotchman and
a clerical Doctor of Law, was the principal.　For him also
Shelley was not without a sort of respect, though disgusted
with his coarse jests, and general hardness of mind as well as
discipline.　Here he re-encountered among the pupils Thomas
Medwin, his second cousin on the mother's side, and some
years his senior.　Mostly the boys, numbering about sixty, were
sons of local tradesmen; the system of the house was mean ; the
reception accorded to Shelley by his schoolfellows, and their
subsequent treatment of him, full of taunting and petty persecution (for everything lumpish and sordid had a natural repulsion at contact with Percy Shelley); and his situation was one
of proportional and acute misery.　No distresses are more real

---

[1] So says Miss Shelley (Hellen), and the portrait by Miss Curran gives the same colour.
Mr. Thornton Hunt must be wrong in saying " brown " eyes, and Sir John Rennie not
right in saying " hazel " eyes.
[2] Peacock, *Fraser's Magazine*, 1858, p. 656.
[3] " The Rev. Dr. *Mackintosh*," according to Mr. Middleton = (*Shelley and his
Writings*, vol. i. p. 11).　But I find this name in no other authority.　Middleton had
evidently misread an inscription given by Medwin at p. 22 of his *Life of Shelley*, vol. i.

or more poignant than those of childhood: the man who laughs at them with reason is the very boy who cowered under them, also not without reason. But there dawned one glorious moment in which Percy ceased to be the possible refined weakling, and became the incipient poetical demigod.

 " Thoughts of great deeds were mine, dear friend, when first
  The clouds which wrap this world from youth did pass.
 I do remember well the hour which burst
  My spirit's sleep. A fresh May-dawn it was,
  When I walked forth upon the glittering grass,
 And wept, I knew not why: until there rose
  From the near schoolroom voices that, alas!
 Were but one echo from a world of woes—
The harsh and grating strife of tyrants and of foes.

 " And then I clasped my hands, and looked around;
  But none was near to mock my streaming eyes,
 Which poured their warm drops on the sunny ground.
  So, without shame, I spake:—'I will be wise,
  And just, and free, and mild, if in me lies
 Such power; for I grow weary to behold
  The selfish and the strong still tyrannize
 Without reproach or check.' I then controlled
My tears, my heart grew calm, and I was meek and bold.

 " And from that hour did I with earnest thought
  Heap knowledge from forbidden mines of lore;
 Yet nothing that my tyrants knew or taught
  I cared to learn,—but from that secret store
  Wrought linkèd armour for my soul, before
 It might walk forth to war among mankind." [1]

Shelley was noticeably subject to waking dreams at Sion House, and had at least one fit of somnambulism there, and others at a later date. He was not studious, yet he soon outstripped his companions. With one of these (may it possibly have been John Rennie?) he formed an enthusiastic friendship, which, however, had no sequel in his after years; he has recorded it in a short fragment of an *Essay on Friendship*, written not long before his death. [2]

III.—SHELLEY AT ETON.

He passed to Eton in his fourteenth year, and experienced, from his less uncultured companions there, much the same

---

[1] *Revolt of Islam*, p. 278. Lady Shelley (*Shelley Memorials*, p. 7) cites these verses as applicable to Shelley's sojourn at Eton. The authority of Medwin, however, who expressly refers them to Sion House instead (*Shelley Papers*, p. 3), appears the most conclusive that can be attained; and I think the opening lines would more naturally indicate the earlier period of boyhood.
[2] Hogg, *Life of Shelley*, vol. i. pp. 22–24.

bullying and repulsion that he had endured at Sion House. But the frail, shrinking, and girlish Shelley, the unready boy who joined in no boyish sports from shyness and delicacy combined, was not made to be bullied in sheepish acquiescence. He rose in unquenched indignation against the outrages of the fagging system, and made it "pass him by on the other side." Indeed, it has been said that he got up a conspiracy against fagging; but this, on the testimony of Etonians quoted by Medwin, does not appear to be accurately expressed. The boys would goad him into paroxysms of rage, and then run away from the explosion : he never pursued them, but requited their attentions by assisting them in their tasks. On one occasion, while Shelley was asleep, some of his persecutors blackened his face : on awaking he was wild with horror. " The few who knew him loved him," says a schoolfellow, Mr. Packe. All this corresponds closely with what had previously characterized Shelley at Sion House School, as set forth in the recently published Autobiography of Sir John Rennie, one of his schoolfellows there. Percy was the most remarkable scholar in that academy, and rose high, and he was apt at writing poetry. His excitability was extreme ; and, when teazed by others, he would seize anything—even another little boy—to throw at them. His fancy was always occupied with spirits, fairies, volcanoes, &c. : "in fact, at times he was considered to be almost upon the border of insanity. Yet, with all this, when treated with kindness, he was very amiable, noble, high-spirited, and generous." At Eton, we are informed, he had no liking for the time-honoured "grind" of making Latin verses, and would not "submit to the trammels of the gradus ; " yet his performances in this line availed to procure him prizes. In like manner, though he neglected the regulated school-attendance, he translated half of Pliny's *Natural History.* His money was spent on books, chemical instruments, and acts of liberality. "He used to say that nothing ever delighted him so much as the discovery that there were no *elements* of earth, fire, or water."

The continued activity of Shelley's boyish imagination is best proved by the fact that he had a practical eye for ghosts and fiends : he studied the occult sciences, watched for spectres, conjured the devil, and speculated on a visit to Africa for the purpose of searching out the magic arcana which her dusky populations are noted for. The reading of German books (only in translations as yet) fostered this turn of mind. At home also he would, from very early years, tell tales to his still younger

sisters, peopling the house and grounds with imaginary personages; would narrate curious events which had, or rather had
not, just happened to himself; and would make the girls per-
sonate demons and sprites, while he haled liquid fire in a port-
able stove. No doubt the great turn for chemical experiment
which he developed at Eton, and which became his chief passion there, had as much to do with an impressible fancy, and
with the fact that chemical practice was prohibited to the
schoolboys in their chambers, as with scientific tendencies. He
set fire to a tree on the common by lighting gunpowder with a
burning-glass, and had at Sion House done much the same sort
of thing; and the incautious touching of an electrical machine
in his room at Eton overthrew his tutor, Mr. Bethel, who had
discovered the young rebel "raising the devil" by a blue flame.
The distinction of being one of the dullest men at the school
has been attributed to Mr. Bethel, with whom the future author
of *Epipsychidion* lodged. The rigid Dr. Keate, who became
Head Master in 1809, was at this period, it appears, Master of
the Lower School. He flogged Shelley liberally, and the scape-
grace in return plagued him without stint.

Mysterious and semi-fathomable things happened to Shelley,
either in person or in supposition, throughout his life. One of
these occurred while he was at Eton. The only official person
whom he really liked there was Dr. James Lind, of Windsor, a
physician, chemist, and tutor, and a man of erudition, who
superintended the youth's scientific studies. "He loved me,"
said Shelley, " and I never shall forget our long talks, where he
breathed the spirit of the kindest tolerance and the purest wisdom." He furnished the prototype of the old sage who releases
Laon from the tower-prison, in the *Revolt of Islam*, and of Zon-
oras in *Prince Athanase*. Shelley, having been attacked by a
fever which affected the brain, was about to be sent to a private
madhouse by his father—so at least he overheard, or learned
from a servant [1]—when Dr. Lind posted to Field Place at the
dismayed patient's request, cured him, and dispelled the paternal
purpose. Another story told by Shelley,[2] and doubted by the
recipient of the information, is that the immediate cause of his

---

[1] Compare the not entirely identical accounts in Hogg, *Life of Shelley*, vol. i. p. 32,
and in the *Shelley Memorials*, pp. 9, 10. Apparently the whole affair of the madhouse
was one of the poet's delusions.

[2] Peacock in *Fraser's Magazine*, 1858, p. 647. The story is told also, with some degree
of variation, by Mr. Thornton Hunt (*Atlantic Monthly*, February 1863, p. 192). He
says that Shelley, in the course of his general resistance to the senior scholars and
school-customs, was dared to pin a companion's hand to the table with a fork, and
did so.

quitting Eton was that, in one of his fits of rage at some boyish persecutor, he struck a penknife through the offender's hand. According to his own account, this was his third Etonian catastrophe; he had been twice before expelled, but re-admitted at his father's instance. The fact that he finally left Eton some time in 1808, a long interval before his going to Oxford in the autumn of 1810, suggests that he really was withdrawn from the former place with some degree of abruptness, for there is nothing to show that this interval was devoted to preparing for the university.

Immediately after leaving Eton (if not possibly before that event) he had managed to fall in love—which was indeed a feat almost certain to be achieved by a youth of such a disposition. In the summer of 1809 (*ætatis* sixteen or seventeen) he fell captive to his very charming young cousin Harriet Grove, who, with her brother, was on a visit to Field Place. She was the daughter of a clergyman, and was of the same age as Percy, and a good deal like him in face. She returned his affection, engaged or semi-engaged herself to him, and corresponded with him on returning to her home in Wiltshire.

Many further details might be given of Shelley's stay at Eton, did space admit. The one remaining fact essential to be noted is that he went there by the name not only of " Mad Shelley," but also of " Shelley the Atheist." This sounds like an important indication of the early and extreme development of Shelley's speculative opinions; and I think it would be unsafe to reject it as such altogether, though Mr. Hogg affirms that the name of atheist was bestowed at Eton upon any boy specially distinguished for setting the authorities at defiance, whether or not he entertained any opinion at all on the question of Deity. In Shelley's case, the title is said to have come to him in virtue of the firing of the tree, already alluded to. Something may also possibly have been due to the fact that he was known among his schoolfellows for a habit of " cursing his father and the king." And here I will take leave to say that this, so far as his father was concerned, was simply a vile and detestable practice, learned partly from the venerable Sir Bysshe, and partly from the equally venerable Dr. Lind;[1] and indeed that the poet's animus in regard to his father (for whom nevertheless he had had some affection in quite early years) was in various details derogatory to his character, intellect, and common sense.

---

[1] *I.e.*, if Mr. Hogg's account is to be implicitly accepted; but I understand there are fair grounds for dubiety, as regards both Dr. Lind and Sir Bysshe Shelley.

I think it the least excusable trait which has to be recorded of so great and loveable a man. Not long after leaving Eton, Shelley was asked to repeat the cursing process; which, after saying he had left it off, he finally consented to do, " and delivered, with vehemence and animation, a string of execrations, greatly resembling in its absurdity a papal anathema: the fulmination soon terminated in a hearty laugh." [1] Of course, the whole thing was the freak of a schoolboy; but there are some freaks which neither schoolboys nor other persons are tolerated in—as the bestowal upon a father of such nicknames as "Old Buck" and "Killjoy."

IV.—EARLIEST WRITINGS.

Percy Shelley was an uncommon sort of boy, appetent of knowledge (such as suited his own taste), and very rapid in acquiring it, and with impulses and characteristics indicative of genius. He is said to have learned the classical languages as if by intuition—his memory, which was always an excellent one for all sorts of things, retaining whatever he once learned. Still, it does not appear that he as yet exhibited any exceptional originating aptitude or precocity of mind : and certainly, if we look to his earliest writings, such as are preserved in our Appendix, the suggestions which they yield to us are not those of a great capacity or a premature gift—but on the contrary of very shallow incentives puffing up feeble faculties into meaningless forms of self-expression. The child who wrote the *Verses on a Cat*, at perhaps eight or nine years of age, was indeed a ready and sprightly versifier, superior to his years; but, from this simple and pleasing outpouring of a child, we sink down, in the following compositions lasting up to and beyond Shelley's departure from Oxford, into the inflated balderdash of a boy, unmarked either by right perceptions, by any genuine direction of taste, or by promising execution. There is facility of a certain kind : one has heard of such a thing as fatal facility.   Probably the verses preserved are but a small minority of what Shelley wrote in these opening years.   At one time—precise boyish age and subject unknown—he and his sister Elizabeth secretly wrote a play, and sent it to Mathews the comedian; who returned it, opining that " it would not do for acting."   Presumably not. Another considerable attempt was *The Wandering Jew*, which he wrote together with Medwin about 1809 ; next to no remains

---

[1] Hogg, *Life of Shelley* vol. i. p. 138.

of Shelley's section of it are now accessible, but a safe instinct certifies us that it was nonsense.

A true curiosity of literature is Shelley's first published book, the novel named *Zastrozzi*—one of "a great many" (so says Lady Shelley) which he composed about this time. He wrote it at the age of sixteen, with some co-operation (it is stated) from Miss Grove—which however I should doubt, having regard to dates. It is a wild story of a virtuous Verezzi, persecuted and ruined by the effervescent passion of a "guilty siren," Matilda Contessa de Laurentini, in league with a mysterious and dark-browed Zastrozzi, who has, in chapter the last, a family grudge to clear off. A deep-buried romance named *Zofloya, or the Moor* [1] (there is great force of suggestion in the letter Z), is recorded to have been the model of *Zastrozzi*. A curiosity of literature this novel would be, if merely on the ground of its authorship, and of its gorgeous absurdity; but, when we learn that there was actually a publisher in human form, Mr. Robinson of Paternoster Row, to pay £40 or so for the privilege of publishing it, thus furnishing forth "a magnificent banquet [not of the Barmecide class] given to eight friends" by the Etonian romancist, and that human reviewers were capable of criticizing it, and deprecating its supposed immoralities [2] (which are in fact few or none), *Zastrozzi* glides from a curiosity into a phenomenon of literature. There is a delicious reserve of tone in the terms which Shelley used a few years later, 10th January 1812, in forwarding his two novels to the philosopher Godwin : [3] "From a reader, I became a writer of romances. [4] Before the age of seventeen I had published two, *St. Irvyne* and *Zastrozzi*, each of which, though quite uncharacteristic of me as now I am, yet serves to mark the state of my mind at the period of their composition. I shall desire them to be sent to you : do not, however, consider this as any obligation to yourself to misapply your valuable time." If Godwin did misapply his valuable time, and read *Zastrozzi*, he must have been a sight for the gods and the glorified spirit of Mary Wollstonecraft during that process.

---

[1] Mr. Swinburne has seen and looked through a copy of *Zofloya*.

[2] So it is said ; but I believe no Shelleyite of the present day has ever lighted upon any review of *Zastrozzi*, nor yet of *St. Irvyne* (see p. 19).

[3] Hogg's *Life of Shelley*, vol. ii. p. 55. Shelley is wrong in saying *St. Irvyne* (whatever may have been the case with *Zastrozzi*) was published before he had attained seventeen years of age ; it came out in December 1810, when the author was past eighteen. This is not the only instance in which he understated his age, whether through negligence of mind or possibly with a spice of coxcombry.

[4] From an expression in a letter of Shelley's dated 10th December 1812 (*Shelley Memorials*, p. 45), it appears that he had by then ceased to be "a reader of romances." But he did not entirely exclude them from his after perusal.

The only purpose which *Zastrozzi* can serve at the present day—except to raise a hearty laugh—is to furnish a few indications how far Shelley's anti-christian opinions had been developed at that early date. We must, however, remember that some portions of the romance are ascribed to Miss Grove's authorship. The wicked Zastrozzi, we find, is in one passage an unbeliever in immortality, for which he is distinctly reprobated by the correct-minded author : further on he is not a total unbeliever, but over-page figures as an atheist. Materialism and atheism are denounced by the narrator at a later stage, and there is a passage, in the ordinary religious tone, concerning divine mercy consequent upon repentance. Thus nothing but orthodoxy, though toying on the verge of the atheistic precipice, attaches to Shelley from the investigation of the bad characters of his novel. But the virtuous though "infatuated" Verezzi yields a less respectable Shelleyan result: he dares to think that " love like ours wants not the vain ties of human laws," or in plain English the marriage-ceremony.

Nobody now will or ought to read *Zastrozzi* save as a curious study conducive to an exact knowledge of Shelley : nobody *can* read his first volume of verse, for it has entirely disappeared from human ken.[1] At some time in the year 1810 Shelley called upon a London publisher, Stockdale, and asked to be assisted out of a hobble, as he had commissioned a Horsham printer to strike off 1480 copies (!) of a volume of poems, for which, as he now found, he was unable to pay. Stockdale consented that the book should be transferred to himself; and it was soon announced in the *Morning Chronicle* of 18th September 1810, under the name of *Original Poetry by Victor and Cazire*, and was published in due course. There really was a second author, besides Shelley ; namely, his sister Elizabeth, if Mr. Barnett Smith is correctly informed. But lo! when the book was out, it was found to embody productions by a third author, and then one of considerable name, and

---

[1] What is known on this subject is due to Mr. Garnett : see his article in *Macmillan's Magazine*, June 1860, *Shelley in Pall Mall*. He has kindly informed me moreover that a gentleman connected with the Shelley family says that Percy "wrote and printed *another* book of verse about the same time. He could not remember the title, but thought a copy might still be in existence."

" Quis desiderio sit modus aut pudor
Tam cari capitis ? "

Perhaps this other book of verse is the *Poetical Essay on the Existing State of Things* to which Mr. D. F. MacCarthy (in his book, *Shelley's Early Life*) first called attention, but of which no copy is yet forthcoming.—Mr. J. R. P. Kirby (of Great Russell Street) has discovered a review of the volume by Victor and Cazire. It is in a publication named *The Poetical Register, and Repository of Fugitive Poetry* (vol. viii. 1810-11), and treats the book with disdain, doubtless well deserved. It does not raise any question as to plagiarism.

much admired by Shelley, Matthew Gregory Lewis, the author of *The Monk* and of *Tales of Terror;* Victor, or Cazire, or both of them, had been making free with the sepulchral stock-in-trade of that potent necromancer. Shelley withdrew the volume from circulation after a hundred copies or so had got about; and no one has set eyes on it since. One can but speculate on the question whether Shelley was himself in fault in this matter, or whether he had been duped by his coadjutor. There was certainly some tendency to secretiveness in his early literary attempts; and it may be doubted whether the Etonian scatter-brain would have seen much harm in appropriating stanzas or whole compositions from Lewis if they fell in with his notions—or indeed whether he had ever perceived or pondered the meaning of the word copyright. Stockdale, at any rate, does not seem to have considered himself aggrieved by Shelley, as he soon after undertook the publishing of *St. Irvyne;* in fact, after some serious squabbles during their business-connexion, and in the face of an unpaid bill, he continued enthusiastic as to the young author's character and honour.

Even the poems in the volume by "Victor and Cazire" were perhaps not the earliest printed by Shelley. It seems that "many of his fugitive pieces" were struck off by "a printer at Horsham, named Phillips." This may, I suppose, have been going on in 1810 mostly, but possibly also in 1809. Sir Bysshe Shelley was in the habit of paying the printer. [1]

V.—SHELLEY AT OXFORD.

Meagre indeed must be our account of Shelley at Oxford in comparison with the inimitable treasury of anecdote which Mr. Hogg wrote under the same title, and finally incorporated in his *Life of Shelley.* [2]

Towards the middle or end of October 1810, Shelley went to University College, Oxford, where his father also had been

---

[1] These details are given in a narrative, *A Newspaper Editor's Reminiscences*, published in *Fraser's Magazine*: see the number for June 1841. The writer, at first a corresponding clerk in the house of Ackermann the print-seller, and afterwards a country journalist, was on familiar terms with Shelley during some portion of his Oxford career, and for several months after his expulsion. The intimacy lasted, according to the writer himself, "three years:" this would take us on to about December 1813, and must, I think, be overstated. See note, p. 31.

[2] The aroma of personal knowledge and affection, along with the keen zest of a *raconteur* who enjoys every oddity, and reinforces it in the telling, impart a peculiar charm to those Oxford reminiscences—and indeed, spite of its many flaws and perversities, to the whole *Life*, the suppression of whose concluding portion defrauds the admirers of Shelley of their just perquisites. That the conclusion exists in MS. has been affirmed to me as a known fact: also that it does *not* exist. The worst flaw of all is that letters of Shelley given in Hogg's *Life* are garbled and misdated. Even apart from special information, one can discern that they are jumbled together without any care or guidance to the reader

educated; and he at once became acquainted, at the College dinner-table, with Mr. Thomas Jefferson Hogg, a fellow-student in the same College, and of much the same age. This gentleman belonged to a family of high Tories living at Norton near Stockton-on-Tees, and was destined for the conveyancing branch of law, having besides the prospect of a competent fortune. We can trace in his book the character of a robust *bon vivant* and man of society, with a great contempt for bores and crotchet-mongers of all sorts, and a generally sardonic or cynical turn, the antipodes of anything "gushing" or any revolutionary idealism, tempered however by a deep respect for the forms and monuments of intellect consecrated by experience. That an acute mind of this calibre should at once have accepted Shelley as a beautiful soul and heaven-born genius, and should have been inspired with a warm enthusiasm for him, such as neither radical divergences of view, nor early and final separation, nor subsequent long lapse of time, could avail to bedim, speaks as strongly as anything for the poet's intellectual and personal fascination. It is difficult to say why the author of *Zastrozzi* should have been a considerable figure in the eyes of a young Oxford Tory of a literary turn, or rather it can only be accounted for on the ground of his admirable qualities, ascertained by immediate experience : such, at any rate, he was, and the event proved how thoroughly well Mr. Hogg read between the lines.

Shelley, now growing up towards man's estate, was strong, active, and tall (nearly 5 feet 11), though slight, narrow-chested, and with a kind of stoop :[1] his bones, joints, and extremities, were large; his complexion red and white, but easily tanned and freckled by exposure ; his features small, not regular save the mouth, and in some sort feminine — but with a certain seraphic look, and infinite play of expression. The side-face was not strong, and the nose very slightly turned up.[2] His head was quite uncommonly small, covered with abundant wavy

---

[1] "Less a stoop," says Mr. Thornton Hunt, "than a peculiar mode of holding the head and shoulders; the face thrown a little forward, and the shoulders slightly elevated."

[2] Mr. Peacock (*Fraser's Magazine*, 1860, p. 103) points out that, in this respect, the ordinary portraits are not correct. A head of the painter Antonio Leisman, in the Uffizi Gallery at Florence, reminds him of Shelley. This is a dark-complexioned face, looking out, with a vivid and rather startled look, from under a broad-leaved hat. Mr. Trelawny (*Recollections*, p. viii.) considers that the portrait of which he gives a lithograph (and this edition an engraving), and which was painted by Clint from a water-colour by Lieutenant Williams now lost, and from the oil-portrait by Miss Curran, is the only likeness of any decided value. According to Mr. Thornton Hunt, the portraits are particularly imperfect; and the "ordinarily received miniature [engraving?] resembles Shelley about as much as a lady in a book of fashions resembles real women." This gentleman says, however, that the features are not unlike

hair, dark-brown and of a wild growth; his eyes were prominent, very open and fixed, hardly ever so much as winking:
"stag-eyes" is the picturesque epithet for them which I have
frequently heard Mr. Trelawny employ.[1]   He looked "preter-
naturally intelligent," or (as Lieutenant Williams said at a later
date) "of most astonishing genius."[2] His gestures were abrupt,
yet often graceful; his clothes good, but carelessly worn. He
was a finished gentleman, and, as Mr. Hogg emphatically puts
it, "a ladies' man"—the elect of dames and damsels. And
certainly Shelley repaid this preference without stint; for nothing is more manifest throughout his life and writings than the
intense love he entertained for the feminine nature in its ideal,
and in many approximate realizations of that ideal, and the
delight with which he hailed any symptoms of superiority of
intellect or faculty in women. I think he stands next to Shakespeare among great poets in love of the female character. His
voice was peculiar, and Mr. Hogg found it at first "excruci-
ating;" Mr. Peacock, "discordant;" Captain Medwin, "a
cracked soprano;" Mr. Thornton Hunt, "a high natural
counter-tenor," comparable to the Lancashire tone of speech.
Its unpleasant quality, however, is ignored altogether by some
authorities : and others, while admitting it, say that, although
disagreeable when the poet was excited, the voice was of varied
modulation, and, in reading poetry, not only good but wonderfully effective. His dominant passion at this time was argument, and his favourite recreation a country-ramble. He was
also now and henceforward an insatiable reader, occupying
himself with books sometimes as much as sixteen hours out
of the twenty-four, and under all circumstances of locality or
environment. His diet was of the simplest, tending already
strongly towards vegetarianism, which in the sequel (from the
beginning of March, 1812) he adopted absolutely, and per-
severed in for long periods of time together, though not without breaks now and then. Bread was his staple food ; with
water and tea to drink, and occasionally wine—but he could
scarcely be reckoned among wine-drinkers at all, and sometimes totally rejected that beverage, and spirits (it may be said)
invariably.

Omitting a host of other details (without which, however, no
true picture can be given of Shelley in his supreme capacities,
varied traits, and numerous peculiarities), a few words must

---

[1] Medwin says that Shelley was very near-sighted ; Trelawny does not now remember
nor believe it.   [2] Trelawny, *Recollections*, p. 12.

here be said regarding his health. He considered himself a
permanent and grievous invalid, of a consumptive habit, and
afflicted by nervous and spasmodic attacks ; he said also that
he had ruined his health at Eton by swallowing in a fit of
amorous dejection[1] arsenic or some mineral poison. Another
account (which I find in no Shelleyan writer save Mr. Thornton Hunt[2]) is that "Shelley himself ascribed the injury from
which he suffered to a pressure of the assassin's knee upon him
in the struggle" which he had had to wage with a mysterious
assailant at Tanyrallt in 1813, and of which more anon. At
one time, towards the end of that same year, Shelley had a
fancy, no doubt a baseless one, that he was about to be visited
with elephantiasis. Hogg, in his caustic way, makes light of all
these statements and alarms ; but it is, I think, only too abun-
dantly clear from the evidence that such of them as related to
facts, not inferences, to an actual and not a prospective state of
body, were perfectly true. Mrs. Shelley speaks of her husband
as a martyr to ill-health all his life, and suffering constant pain;
and other eye-witnesses testify to spasms which made him roll
on the ground in agony, though without losing his gentleness
of temper, which induced a deleterious and lifelong use of
opium (especially towards 1812), and which continually threatened to end fatally. Medwin, who thinks the disease must
eventually have thus ended, speaks of it as nephritis, and of
lithotomy as a dangerous remedy that might have been, but
never was, tried; Trelawny regards "occasional spasms" as the
only complaint, but without discussing their origin or extenuat-
ing their severity, and he intimates that the poet's long fasts
brought on the attacks. The usual remedies adopted on the
exigency of the moment were cold water and friction with the
hand. Nothing is clearer from Shelley's own correspondence
than that he was often tantalized by intervals of what he considered improved health, and perpetually thrown back again,
and that he "suffered much of many physicians." Hogg, who
was only in the way of seeing Shelley in his very early manhood, may not unnaturally have thought his complaints of ill-
health belied by the buoyant energies and activities of youth ;
but we shall surely have a very false conception of Shelley's
life, in its course from week to week and from year to year, if

---

[1] Hogg gives this detail in one passage (vol. ii. p 332). Miss Shelley says that her
brother used to speak of the arsenic-swallowing as an accident, and Hogg himself says the
same elsewhere.
[2] *Atlantic Monthly*, p. 185.

we believe that Hogg came to a right conclusion, and that the poet, spite of his own repeated assertions, and those of persons who were constantly about him, lived in a condition of moderate physical comfort, instead of ever-recurring and often poignant suffering. The shadow of death was upon him oftener than once or twice, and the blight of pain, even when it dispersed, was ever in prospect. Mr. Trelawny, however, informs me that Shelley's health had, within the last few months of his life, during which he was less solitary than for some years preceding, improved so conspicuously that there was a good prospect of his living to an advanced age. The physician, Vaccà, whom Trelawny consulted on the subject after the poet's death, did not confirm the notion that the malady was of a nephritic character.

When he first went to Oxford, Shelley's tastes were chiefly for metaphysics, poetry, and chemistry ; the last he gradually slackened in, and at last dropped, and for mathematics he never showed any aptitude, though we find that he and his second wife were proposing to engage in this study together in 1820, and perhaps did so. As regards chemistry also, his taste still so far lingered that, at the end of 1811, in Keswick, he excited remark by experiments with hydrogen in his garden. A vivid flame was seen which alarmed the villagers; and his landlord gave Shelley notice to quit. "As his love of intellectual pursuits was vehement, and the vigour of his genius almost celestial, so were the purity and sanctity of his life most conspicuous." This is the testimony of Mr. Hogg ; and, as he and Shelley became at once, and continued during their joint residence at Oxford, inseparable companions, no better evidence on the point can be attained or desired. It is true that Mr. Hogg, reporting a conversation with Mr. Shelley senior which took place very soon after the young men had left Oxford,[1] sets forth that he acquiesced in the paternal suspicion that Percy must be "rather wild," and the context is such as would naturally suggest that "wild" here signifies "rakish" ; but, looking to Mr. Hogg's other statements on that subject, we must conclude that he only meant "harebrained" or "unmanageable." Mrs. Shelley speaks of Percy in the same strain, but with much less authority, as being "of the purest habits in morals" when he left Oxford ; and so say other biographers,

---

expressly or tacitly. But here again Mr. Thornton Hunt[1] is an exception. "Accident has made me aware of facts which give me to understand that, in passing through the usual curriculum of a college-life in all its paths, Shelley did not go scatheless; but that, in tampering with venal pleasures, his health was seriously and not transiently injured. The effect was far greater on his mind than on his body."

Shelley's next printed book, *St. Irvyne, or the Rosicrucian, by a Gentleman of the University of Oxford,* was published towards the middle of December 1810, on the author's own account. It is stated to have shared the fate of *Zastrozzi* in being a good deal noticed by the press, and not to the advantage of its moral tone. This novel is even greater nonsense than *Zastrozzi,* and the truncated confusion and unmeaning of its close exceed anything that the sane reader could anticipate: to talk of its being either moral or immoral is proportionately out of place, although a certain inflammability of temperament may be traced in it. Though only published at the end of 1810, *St. Irvyne* appears to have been written in 1809; for a letter from Shelley to Godwin, dated 10th January 1812, says that he had been acquainted with the *Political Justice* of that author more than two years, and that *St. Irvyne* was composed before that period. The heroine's name, Megalena di Metastasio, is the most rememberable thing in this romance: her "symmetrical form," and the "sofa" on which she or somebody is sinking ever and anon, may also linger awhile on the memory, when "the gigantic Ginotti" with his elixir of life, "the guilty Wolfstein," and other fantoccini, have gone the way of all dolls. Godwin's *St. Leon* is reported to be mainly chargeable with the sin of procreating *St. Irvyne.* The atmosphere of absurdity which envelopes one while the book itself is in question clears aside when we learn that, to the credit of the reading public, *St. Irvyne* was quite a failure. The author had to confess, in August 1811, that he could not pay the bill of the

---

[1] This gentleman, being then a mere child, was known to Shelley in England; and, when a boy, saw him for two or three days in Italy. His reminiscences are interesting, and should be read by all Shelleyites; but of course, on such a question as Shelley's morals at Oxford, he has no *personal* testimony to give. The phrase which he uses, "Accident has made me aware of facts" &c., seems to point to some real discovery: if such there be it needed not to be bolstered up by giving to the passage in *Epipsychidion* (vol. ii. p.357) which begins—

"There, one whose voice was venomed melody,"

an interpretation in accordance with this supposed discovery. The interpretation appears to me both servilely literal and forced; and, though I have felt bound not to suppress Mr. Hunt's statement, I cannot profess to attach, as the case stands, much weight to it.

publisher Stockdale;[1] and, with the daring unteachableness of
youth, he suggested whether the copyright of a series of Moral
and Metaphysical Essays might not do in lieu of pounds ster-
ling. The bill, however, remained unpaid, and also the Essays
unpublished. But I am anticipating.

Much about the same time that *St. Irvyne* appealed from
London to an irresponsive public (indeed I think it must have
been rather before than after[2]), the author was making a less
unsuccessful literary venture in Oxford. One day he showed
Hogg some poems he was about to publish anonymously :
Hogg read them, and expressed, with true friendliness and
obviously correct judgment, the opinion that they were not
good enough. Shelley returning to the charge, his Mentor observed that the verses ought only to be issued as burlesques,
if at all ; and made a few alterations in them the more clearly
to bring out their extravagances. The idea pleased Shelley—
a strong evidence of his substantial good sense and freedom
from pettish vanity ; the two friends set to work together,
introducing a greater and greater amount of absurdity into
the verses ; and Hogg started the notion of attributing them
on the title-page to one Margaret Nicholson, a washerwoman
who, having in a mad fit attempted the life of George the
Third, was then passing the remainder of her days in a lunatic
asylum. The Oxonians, however, chose to number her among
the defunct, and to invent a nephew of hers, John Fitzvictor,
as editor of her "Posthumous Fragments." The printer, Mr.
Munday, who was to have issued the serious poems at Shelley's
cost, finding them withdrawn and the burlesques substituted,
was so taken with the idea that he volunteered for the risk of
publication himself; and the book appeared forthwith,—a very
thin volume, but luxurious in paper and type. The general
tone of it is a glorifying of revolutionary personages and sentiments—carried out in a spirit which the least acute reader perceives to be excessive, but which one might hardly, were it not
for the explanations offered by Mr. Hogg, recognize as wilfully
burlesqued. The poems, indeed, had a considerable success
among Oxford men, with whom tall talk about liberty was a
fashion ; they were accepted as the genuine and slightly *exalté*
but not precisely incongruous outpouring of an untutored

---

[1] A MS. journal of Dr. Polidori, *penes me*, says that the amount of the debt was about
£100. Mr. Stockdale rated it at £300, "principal and interest."
[2] *St. Irvyne* was published on or just before 20th December 1810 ; and the title-page of
Margaret Nicholson bears the date 1810. A facsimile reprint of the latter volume was
issued lately, an edition of but few copies.

faculty. The true author or authors remained unsuspected, and had a right to chuckle over so daring and undetected an experiment on academic credulity. Beyond the circle of university men the book probably never went.

Shelley appears to have published anonymously, during his studentship in Oxford, yet another volume of verse, now untraceable. It was named *A Poetical Essay on the Existing State of Things;* and the profits of sale were assigned to the benefit of an Irish patriot and journalist, Mr. Peter Finnerty, then incarcerated in Lincoln Castle. It was stated in print, in 1812, presumably on Shelley's own authority, that the profits amounted to nearly £100; an allegation which, considering the various circumstances of the case, and especially the total oblivion which has overtaken the poem, rather taxes one's powers of belief. [1]

"Stupendous felicity,"[2] along with next to no supervision or guidance, was the lot of Shelley and Hogg at Oxford—so the latter informs us. That career and that felicity were rapidly approaching their term. Shelley had been initiated by Dr. Lind into a habit of corresponding under some pseudonym with a number of people personally unknown to him on a variety of subjects—at first scientific, then metaphysical, moral, or what not. One of the persons he addressed was Felicia

[1] We are indebted to Mr. MacCarthy for the discovery of the facts which go to prove the existence of the *Poetical Essay* (See *Shelley's Early Life*, pp. 3, 100, &c.) The evidence may be thus briefly summarized:—

(1.) During Shelley's sojourn in Dublin, in 1812, a newspaper, the *Dublin Weekly Messenger*, of 7th March, contained the following statement, written probably by the young poet's acquaintance, Mr. John Lawless:—"Mr. Shelley, commiserating the sufferngs of our distinguished countryman, Mr. Finnerty, whose exertions in the cause of political freedom he much admired, wrote a very beautiful poem, the profits of the sale of which, we understand from undoubted authority, Mr. Shelley remitted to Mr. Finnerty. We have heard they amounted to nearly an hundred pounds."

(2.) The poem was advertised for publication as follows, in the *Oxford University and City Herald* for 9th March 1811:—"Just published, price two shillings, *A Poetical Essay on the Existing State of Things*, by a Gentleman of the University of Oxford. For assisting to maintain in prison Mr. Peter Finnerty, imprisoned for a libel. London: sold by B. Crosby & Co., and all other booksellers. 1811." A quotation from Southey's *Curse of Kehama* was added in the advertisement.

(3.) (Observed by myself, and published in *The Academy* for 19th December 1874.) A work published in 1838, named *A Diary Illustrative of the Times of George IV.*, contains the following statement, written on 15th March 1811 by a fellow-student of Shelley at Oxford, known (as I have since been apprised) to be Mr. Kirkpatrick Sharpe:—"A Mr. Shelley, of University College, . . . hath published what he terms the *Posthumous Poems* [of Margaret Nicholson], printed for the benefit of Mr. Peter Finnerty. . . . Shelley's last exhibition is a poem on the state of public affairs." The context clearly indicates that the last-named "poem" is not the same thing as the "*Posthumous Poems.*" Whether *both* were really published for the benefit of Finnerty may be questioned: probably Mr. Sharpe was not accurately informed on this point.

Considering the bearing of these items of evidence, the one upon the other, it is difficult to doubt that a composition named *A Poetical Essay on the Existing State of Things* was actually published, and that the author of it was Shelley. Mr. MacCarthy has searched for a copy high and low, but has not as yet discovered one.

[2] The letters published by Hogg show, however, that Shelley had, during his Oxford time, much mental suffering in connection with Miss Grove.—See p. 26.

Browne, afterwards Mrs. Hemans, whose first volume of poems had attracted his admiration. He retained at Oxford the habit he had formed at Eton. In the course of their studies, Shelley and Hogg had made an abstract from Hume's Essays ; a portion of which abstract Shelley got printed at Brighton early in 1811, and, in keeping up his speculative correspondence on questions of theology, was wont to enclose it in his letter, using it as a nucleus for further discussion. He would in fact profess to have come casually across the paper, and to be unable to refute its arguments : it was headed *The Necessity of Atheism*, and ended with a Q.E.D. It is reprinted, either verbatim or substantially, in the notes to *Queen Mab* (pp. 229–231). Such is the general purport of what Hogg says concerning this audacious pamphlet : but I think that he clearly pares the thing down rather too close, and that Shelley circulated his syllabus less with a view to mere convenience as a disputant, and more because he believed in and meant to champion the arguments it contained, than Mr. Hogg is willing to admit. Else why did he republish it in *Queen Mab*, with implied and indisputable adhesion to its terms ? In this case as in others the honestest and boldest course is also the safest ; and we shall do well to understand once for all that Percy Shelley had as good a right to form and expound his opinions on theology as the Archbishop of Canterbury had to his. Certainly Shelley differed from the Archbishop, and from several other students of and speculators on the subject, past and present ; but, as there was no obligation on him to agree with all or any of them, so is there nothing to be explained away or toned down when we find that in fact he dissented. Except indeed that any man of mature years and reflection will admit that Shelley, aged eighteen and a half, showed a certain amount of youthful presumption in obtruding upon other people, known to be of a contrary and even bitterly contrary opinion, his then notions on subjects unfathomable by either himself or them. Shelley did not avow the authorship of *The Necessity of Atheism*, but neither did he take any great pains to conceal it ; he circulated the production among the college authorities—and it has even been said that he sent it to the Bench of Bishops with his name,[1] but that is transparently improbable or impossible.

On the 25th of March 1811 Shelley was summoned before the authorities, "our Master and two or three of the Fellows ; "

---

[1] Medwin, *Conversations with Byron*, p. 385.

the pamphlet was produced to him; and he was required to declare whether or not he had written it. A tutor of a different college is supposed to have denounced him. He asked why such a question was put. The Master simply repeated his former enquiry, and Shelley declined to answer it, insisting that it lay with his accusers to bring the charge home to him if they could. "Then you are expelled," replied the Master; "and I desire you will quit the college early to-morrow morning at the latest." A regular sentence of expulsion, ready-written, under the seal of the college (the university was not directly concerned in the act), was then handed to him, and he departed. This is the substance of the account which Shelley gave to Hogg immediately after the event: to Peacock, at a later date, he said that he had made a defence, or denial of jurisdiction, in due elocutionary form, and (what is singular) he produced an Oxford newspaper containing the speech. The probability is that he (or else Hogg) used the license of a Thucydides or a Livy; and, not having delivered the oration at the time, invented it afterwards, and furnished the newspaper with the entire report. There is yet another account of the matter. This purports that the interrogator, after sternly denouncing *The Necessity of Atheism*, suggested to Shelley, with more of good-nature than of uprightness, to disavow it, and no harm would ensue to him. Shelley, however, replied, "I *did* write the work," and absolutely refused to make any recantation; and thereupon his expulsion ensued.[1]

Percy was greatly agitated and distressed when he narrated the case to Hogg, although he appears almost directly afterwards to have consoled himself with the distinction of martyrdom. The warmth of Hogg's feelings and friendship appeared conspicuously on this occasion. He wrote a short note to the Master and Fellows, demurring to their decision; was forthwith summoned to appear; was asked whether *he* had written the atheistic pamphlet (a question which could hardly have been put, had Shelley already confessed the authorship); declined to reply, on the general ground of self-respect and resistance to browbeating; and was himself also expelled by a ready-written document. "The alleged offence was a contumacious refusal

---

[1] This is the statement made by Shelley himself to the "Newspaper Editor" (see p. 14), according to that writer. He avowedly speaks only from memory, and at a distance of about thirty years from the event; but he adds that he is confident of being correct, as Shelley's narrative made a strong impression on him, and had in the interim been frequently repeated by the Editor to others.

to disavow the imputed publication." On the following morning the two young men left Oxford.

Strong language has been used in condemnation of the
college authorities; but he who, on the broad ground of freedom
of opinion, claims latitude of thought and action for the atheist
Shelley, will not deny the same to the christian regulators of
University College, Oxford. It appears to me clear that
Shelley, known to be the author of *The Necessity of Atheism*,
and refusing to recant, could not be allowed to remain a
member of the college: a mild measure would have been to
rusticate him, and to expel him was nothing extraordinarily
harsh. The necessary subordination of a pupil to his teachers,
moreover, makes it difficult to conclude that the authorities had
no sort of right to require Shelley to affirm whether or not he
had written the pamphlet; or that his refusal to say yes or no
(if indeed he *did* refuse, as seems most probable) barred, in
the absence of direct evidence against him, all further action
on the part of the college. So far for the substance of what
the authorities did : the manner is a different thing. All we
know about the manner is what Shelley and Hogg respectively
say of that which happened to themselves. If we could—
which we cannot—assume these *ex parte* statements to be final
and incapable of correction in detail, we should have to say
that the manner was overbearing and precipitate, and probably
it was so in very deed; and, as regards Hogg, there seems to
have been no fair ground either for the severe sentence or for
the summary procedure.

VI.—SHELLEY MARRIES HARRIET WESTBROOK.

Shelley and Hogg came up to London, and took lodgings at
No. 15 Poland Street, Oxford Street. At the end of about a
month Hogg left for York, where he studied with a convey-
ancer. Of course consternation reigned in Field Place at the
news of the expulsion. His father offered Percy a qualified
sort of forgiveness, on condition that he should reside at Field
Place, drop all intercourse with Hogg for a while, and place
himself under the control and instructions of some gentleman
to be named by paternal authority. The precise answer
returned is not on record; but the terms of capitulation failed
—chiefly, it would seem, because unrestrained correspondence
by letter between the two young men was their *sine quâ non ;*
and Percy, greatly to his concern, was excluded from his
natural home, and left without any definite means of support.

His sisters, for whom he had always shown much brotherly affection, mitigated his embarrassments by saving up pocket-money, and transmitting it to him; and he managed to rub on somehow. It was probably about this time that Shelley, with exquisite audacity, wrote to the Rev. Rowland Hill in an assumed name, proposing to preach to his congregation at Surrey Chapel. The eminent divine did not reply.

A young girl named Harriet Westbrook, a fellow-pupil of the Misses Shelley at a school at Clapham,[1] was in the habit of bringing round to Percy their sisterly remittances. She was not, however, altogether unknown to Shelley even before his expulsion from Oxford; he saw her first in January 1811, having taken her a present from his sister Mary, and a letter of introduction. This was at any rate as early as the 11th of that month, for he then ordered a copy of *St. Irvyne* to be sent to her at her father's address, 10 Chapel Street, Grosvenor Square.[2]

Harriet was a charming girl, even a beauty; beauty enough to be designated for the part of Venus in some school *fête champêtre*—"with a complexion brilliant in pink and white, with hair quite like a poet's dream, and Bysshe's peculiar admiration," colour light brown. She was small and delicately made, and was now nearly or quite sixteen. Her father, Mr. John Westbrook, had been a hotel-keeper, and had for some years past retired from the business, with competent means. His house of entertainment, a place of some fashionable resort, was named "The Mount Street Coffee-house," but was in fact a tavern. He looked Jewish; and both aspect and character co-operated in procuring him the nickname of "Jew Westbrook." The mother was a nonentity. Besides Harriet, there was an unmarried sister, perhaps nearly twice as old, named Eliza; with dark eyes, dark and much-brushed hair, marks of the smallpox, and meagre figure. She also had a Jewish aspect.

Shelley's first flame for his cousin Miss Grove was now

---

[1] Clapham, according to Shelley; Brompton, according to Lady Shelley; Wandsworth, according to Mr. Hogg; Balham Hill, according to Mr. Middleton, who terms the establishment "a second-rate boarding-school." Mr. MacCarthy has fixed the precise locality. The school was named Church House, facing Trinity Church, Clapham Common: the site is now occupied by Nelson Terrace. Mrs. Fenning was the school mistress. As everything however remotely connected with Shelley is contested, even such a point as the spelling of Harriet's name has had its pros and cons. Perhaps a business-letter from Shelley (Medwin, *Life*, vol. i. p. 373) may be taken as conclusive: "The maiden name is Harriett Westbrook, with two t's—Harrie*tt*." Hogg, however, is positive that she habitually *signed* only one t; and, as that spelling is adopted by other writers, Shelley himself included, I also adhere to it.

[2] This is the number, 10, given in Shelley's letter. Elsewhere it is 23 Chapel Street. and that is probably correct.

flickering in the socket. He indeed retained his love for her, and still did retain it for at any rate a month or two to come. But her father, though he had not interdicted the match, was not in favour of it; she herself had been raising objections to the lover's increasingly sceptical opinions;[1] and somewhere about August of this year[2] she was the bride of another man— a gentleman of property, and inevitably "a clod of earth" in Shelley's eyes. His letters addressed to Mr. Hogg, towards this time of supense and dereliction, expatiate much on his wounded feelings, the atrocities of intolerance, his suicidal proclivities, and the like—and indeed the family did perceive these proclivities to be to some extent real, and used to watch him anxiously when he went out with dog and gun.[3] One cannot, however, lay very much stress on his letters of the period in question. They are flighty, scattered, and excitable, in an extreme degree; and lend themselves equally to the supposition that he was thrown off his balance by all sorts of things, or that he overdid in words every passing matter that affected him. That he felt keenly at the time the loss of his beautiful cousin will be believed by every one who reflects on the character and constitution of the youth, and the probabilities of the case: but the biographers who *will* have it that this proved a lifelong sorrow to him are probably indulging themselves in applying to Shelley one of the pet resources of the memoir-writing tribe. No doubt, however, his disappointment with Miss Grove may have precipitated his dallyings or entanglements with Miss Harriet Westbrook.

Harriet was not only delightful to look at, but altogether most agreeable. She dressed with exquisite neatness and propriety; her voice was pleasant, and her speech cordial; her spirits were cheerful, and her manners good. She was well educated; a constant and agreeable reader; adequately accom-

---

[1] "She abhors me as a sceptic—as what *she* was before!" (Letter of Shelley, 3rd January 1811, in Hogg's *Life*, vol. i. p. 156).

[2] This date is named to me on good authority and very positively as being about correct: moreover, Lady Shelley says (*Shelley Memorials*, p. 13) that Miss Grove made another choice *after* her cousin's expulsion from Oxford. If this is correct, there is something strangely wrong about a letter of Shelley's published by Hogg under the date of 11th January 1811, in which the marriage of Miss Grove is announced as a fact already accomplished. From various points in connexion with that letter, and others amid which it is inserted, I find it extremely difficult to suppose that there has been, in this instance, any serious misdating on Hogg's part, and cannot account for the discrepancy. Possibly Shelley, in saying "She is married," meant, "She is *engaged* to be married, and the marriage is certain to ensue."

[3] I find no hint of any sporting habits of Shelley in after life. He seems, however, to have done some fishing with Williams in the Bay of Lerici—Letter of Williams, 4th May 1822, in the *Essays and Letters*, vol. ii. p. 282. In the notes to *Queen Mab* he speaks of "the brutal pleasures of the chase."

plished in music. She had great fortitude, if it should not rather be called insensibility, of temperament.[1] Perfectly frank in character and manner, she became under Shelley's guidance perfectly "unprejudiced" in mind. This, however, took some while : Harriet was a Methodist in bringing-up, and felt at first a lively horror at learning that he was an atheist. In process of time, ethical ideas had a considerable attraction for her, religious ideas none at all. So far she seemed excellently fitted both to acquire and to retain a hold upon Shelley's affections. Yet there was in reality a fatal deficiency. When we have summed-up all Harriet's attractions and merits—and they were neither few nor unsubstantial—we find that we have described at best a sweet young creature qualified to adorn any ordinary position in life ; we have not described a poet's ideal, but only the simulacrum and external imitation of such. Depth of character or of mind—a real distinctive personality of whatever sort —was not included among Harriet Westbrook's qualifications. There was indeed no absolute reason why the void should make itself painfully felt ; but, once felt by so ardent and penetrating a nature as Shelley's, it remained, neither to be filled nor forgotten—an aching void, a craving and persecuting want. Harriet was beautiful, amiable, good, accommodating, affectionate ; but—deadly and at last unevadeable discovery—she was commonplace.

Shelley was not ever deeply nor even impulsively in love with Harriet ; he never wooed her to be his.[2] He visited at her father's house, and took pleasure in inducing upon her mental faculties something that might be regarded as conformity to his own daring and fervent tone of opinion ; he escorted her back to school towards the end of April after an illness which had laid her up ; lent a ready ear to tales, more or less genuine, of domestic coercion and incompatibilities. And it is easily open to conjecture that the family, though they may have done nothing underhand or entrapping, seconded to the utmost of their power any uncertain chances of a possible alliance with the grandson and eventual heir of a very wealthy baronet.

The letters of Shelley show that he was now eagerly bent upon promoting a match between Mr. Hogg and his eldest

---

[1] See, in Hogg, vol. ii. p. 509, the account of her impassive demeanour during a surgical operation performed on her infant daughter Ianthe.
[2] I can affirm this with certainty, having read and transcribed a letter from Shelley to Miss Hitchener (see p. 38), written almost directly after his marriage : here he gives a somewhat detailed account of his acquaintance with Harriet, and her ultimate and spontaneous avowal of her love for him.

sister Elizabeth. She also wrote verses, of which some speci-
mens, far from good, are preserved, and she painted besides :
her mental gifts impressed him intermittently, but at times
strongly ; at other times he gave her up as a victim of conven-
tionality and prejudice.[1] The project, however, resulted in
nothing—Shelley's advocacy being no doubt a minus quantity
under the circumstances ; and Elizabeth died unmarried in
1831. By the middle of May the inconvenient son was re-
admitted to Field Place, and came to an arrangement with his
father, under which he was to receive an allowance of £200 per
annum, with liberty to choose his own place of abode. His
maternal uncle Captain Pilfold, residing at Cuckfield, a naval
officer who had seen service under Nelson at the Nile and Tra-
falgar, exerted a conciliatory influence ; he stands out indeed
as a very pleasant figure amid the various family complications
which Percy's erratic course gave rise to. The latter next,
from about the beginning of July, paid a visit of two or three
weeks to his cousin Mr. Thomas Grove, at Cwm Elan, Rhayader, in Radnorshire.

There was a commotion now in the Westbrook household ;
and Shelley was made a party to it—not, it might seem, without
steady female manipulation. The details appear in print, in
letters addressed by Shelley to Hogg from Cwm Elan, undated,
and seemingly misplaced in the printing. Presumably they
were written towards the middle or end of July.[2]

During Shelley's stay at Cwm Elan, Eliza and Harriet Westbrook were going to a house of their father at Aberystwith.
Percy expected to meet them there, the father having invited
him. The letter printed next after the one which names this
fact contains the following passage :—" Your jokes on Harriet
Westbrook amuse me. It is a common error for people to
fancy others in their own situation ; but, if I know anything
about love, I am *not* in love. I have heard from the West-

---

[1] One of his letters, dated 4th July 1811, printed by Hogg (vol. i. p. 411), claims attentive pondering by the student of Shelley's life. A very grave conjecture might be, and has
been, built upon its terms ; but I suspect that, owing to Hogg's slovenly editorship, there
is a serious misprint in it, and shall leave it without further comment. This course I
adopt not because the question raised is "painful," for that I consider no adequate
ground for biographic reticence in the case of so important a man as Shelley ; but because the document which raises the question is unsafe—and one cannot afford to rummage
cupboards for skeletons, if a strong presumption exists that the skeletons themselves are
only plaster of Paris.
[2] Lady Shelley (*Shelley Memorials*, p. 22) refers to two of these letters, and says she
is "not able to guarantee" their authenticity. No doubt Lady Shelley speaks advisedly : but a biographer who knows nothing to the contrary must accept as genuine
letters printed by Hogg as having been addressed to himself, and by himself received
at the date of the transactions.

brooks, both of whom I highly esteem." The next following letter is momentous. "I shall certainly come to York, but Harriet Westbrook will decide whether now or in three weeks. Her father has persecuted her in a most horrible way by endeavouring to compel her to go to school. She asked my advice. . . . I advised her to resist. She wrote to say that resistance was useless, but that she would fly with me; and threw herself upon my protection. We shall have £200 a-year; when we find it run short, we must live, I suppose, upon love. Gratitude and admiration, all demand that I should love her for ever. We shall see you at York. I will hear your arguments for matrimonialism, by which I am now almost convinced." The upshot was that Shelley returned to London, where he lodged with his cousin, Mr. Grove, a surgeon; and about the beginning of September 1811, after some half-dozen stolen interviews with Harriet, eloped with her from her father's house.[1] He had been much moved by finding her pining, and suffering in health; and learning from her own lips that love for him was the cause. They went off straight to Edinburgh, and there became man and wife according to the law of Scotland.

Thus the advances, immediately leading to elopement, came from Harriet to Shelley, and not from Shelley to Harriet. It might even appear that Harriet (a school-girl of sixteen, hardly more than a child, and lately philosophized out of the ordinary standard of propriety) was ready to be Shelley's mistress,[2] and professedly—not perhaps in truth—aspired to nothing higher; and that it was solely the poet's strong sense of honour which induced him, and this in the teeth of some pet theories of his own, to make her at once his wife.[3] Conse-

[1] I do not find the exact date stated: it was apparently the first week in September: see Hogg, *Life*, vol. i. p. 425. Mr. C. H. Grove, who saw Shelley and Harriet off from London, confirms the month (vol. ii. p. 554).
[2] So at least I interpret the phrase "threw herself upon my protection"; which phrase, however, we must in fairness recollect, is at the utmost Shelley's summing-up of Harriet's expressions, and not the *ipsissima verba* of Harriet herself.
[3] The MS. diary of Dr. Polidori, written while he was in habits of daily intercourse with the Shelleys on the shores of the Lake of Geneva in 1816 (30th May) makes a noticeable statement which, though certainly not to be accepted as conclusive, deserves to be borne in mind. The primary likelihood is that the diarist made his jotting direct from what he had heard Shelley say—or at farthest from what Byron reported to him as said by Shelley.—"Gone through much misery, thinking he was dying. Married a girl for the mere sake of letting her have the jointure that would accrue to her. Recovered. Found he could not agree. Separated." The more obvious motive for marrying—that of avoiding obloquy to the woman, and impediments in any future effort to do good—is distinctly put forward in a letter of Shelley to Godwin, 28th January 1812 (Hogg, vol. ii. pp. 63–4), and in other letters that I have seen, in which Shelley treats the whole affair as natural and right, save only the act of formal marriage—a truckling to custom which needs and receives reiterated apology. The statement of Dr. Polidori that the poet in early youth expected a very short lease of life is fully confirmed by a remark made by Mrs. Shelley (p. 250) relative to *Queen Mab*, and the period, 1812–13, when it was written. "Ill-health made him believe that his race would soon be run; that a year or two was all he had of life."

quently, instead of pulling long faces or shaking middle-aged
heads over this escapade of a youth just nineteen years of
age, we shall do much better to regard it as a beautiful example
of chivalry shining through juvenility; or, if the calculating
habit is still strong upon us, we may compute what percentage
of faultlessly christian young heirs of opulent baronets would
have acted like the atheist Shelley, and married a retired hotel-
keeper's daughter obtainable as a mistress. To deny that the
act was foolish would be absurd under any circumstances, and
doubly so when we reflect upon the ultimate issue of it to
Shelley and Harriet themselves : let us then distinctly recognize that it was foolish, and no less distinctly that it was
noble.

VII.—MARRIED LIFE WITH HARRIET.

The bridegroom and bride took groundfloor lodgings in
George Street, Edinburgh, a handsome house on the left side
of the recently built street, and were soon joined there by Hogg.
The poet had borrowed £25 from Mr. Medwin (his connection
by marriage, a solicitor at Horsham, and father of his schoolfellow and subsequent biographer), but without letting him into
the secret of the approaching elopement : he was expecting also
to receive £75 at the end of the week. All supplies from his
father were now cut off. But Mr. Westbrook made some
allowance to the young couple, which has been stated at £200
per annum. Besides this, Shelley raised money on his expectations from time to time; and must be viewed as now living in
a state of permanent embarrassment—not far removed, however,
from a modest sufficiency, save at moments of exceptional
pressure. In a letter of 5th July 1812 he speaks of himself
as having an income of £400 per annum from his relatives.

In October [1] Hogg returned to York, and the Shelleys accompanied him : they all three took lodgings with some dingy
milliners of advanced age—the Misses Dancer, in Coney Street.
Bysshe (he was designated by this name in his own family, and
as yet by Harriet) went soon afterwards to London and Cuckfield to negotiate with his father.

I suppose it may have been somewhere towards this time
that an incident occurred, worth recording as an evidence of
the vehement irritation which Shelley, now and again, felt
and showed against the christian religion; although it should

---

[1] Hogg gives the date as "the end of October": I believe it was really the beginning
of that month, or perhaps the end of September.

be understood that he was mostly not less mild than firm as a disputant. Trelawny, when he knew Shelley some years afterwards, perceived that nothing whatever could rouse him into an ebullition of intemperate anger : reason held her own against every impulse of passion. The writer of *A Newspaper Editor's Reminiscences*[1] informs us that he called one day to see Shelley at Field Place; found that he was not in; and was received by his father—at first rather gruffly, but, on explaining the orthodoxy and moral rectitude of his sentiments, with hearty good-will. The Editor next proceeded to the Swan Inn, Horsham : Shelley was there, and they had a talk together. The conversation took a discursive range over natural philosophy, politics, and social institutions. Finally, Shelley charged the evils of society upon christianity, and urged his friend to co-operate in schemes to "reform it altogether." Opposition ensued, and roused Bysshe to indignation. "His eyes flashed fire; his words rolled forth with the impetuosity of a mountain-torrent ; and even attitude aided the manifestation of passion." At last, "'Have your own way, mad fool!' exclaimed Shelley; and, taking his hat, he quitted the room."[2]

The efforts at an arrangement with his father failed. For the while, nothing could mollify the offended parent, and the poet returned to York : but towards the beginning of 1812 the allowance of £200 was renewed, accompanied by a gracious

---

[1] See Note, p. 14. The Newspaper Editor is exceedingly lax in some matters, and most especially in dates. He says that his first acquaintance with Shelley occurred when the latter was "at Oxford," though temporarily on a visit to London. As Shelley first went to Oxford in October 1810, and was expelled on 25th March 1811, we may suppose the introduction to have taken place towards December 1810. The incident which we are now considering—the outburst of Shelley against christianity—"severed" (so says the Newspaper Editor) "a friendship of three years' standing": if so, its date would be towards December 1813. But it is certain that Shelley was not at that period "passing much of his time at Horsham," within the immediate cognizance of his father. Further, the Newspaper Editor informs us that, after a lapse of seven months and more —say ten months—from Shelley's outburst, he heard of the "elopement" (so he terms it) of Miss Hitchener with Shelley to Wales—the Editor being manifestly quite unconscious that Shelley was then already married to Harriet. Now Miss Hitchener was a visitor with the Shelleys from about July to November 1812. If we reckon ten months backwards from July 1812, we come to September (or October) 1811 ; and I am inclined to suppose that the interview with Shelley may in fact have taken place towards that time. If so, the personal acquaintance of the Editor with Shelley can have lasted barely one year, instead of three. However, I feel very uncertain as to the true date of the interview.

[2] The Newspaper Editor gives the conversation at some length ; and says that it is reproduced "from notes which I made a few days afterwards." Six months later he received a letter from Shelley, proposing, as an experiment in unsophisticated human nature, to bring up two girls in solitude, from the age of four or five. The Editor (who remained unaware, even in 1841, that Shelley was at the time a married man) remonstrated, and the project was dropped : though why dropped by a married man, in consequence of remonstrances pertinent only as addressed to an unmarried man, is not over clear.

message from Mr. Shelley senior "that his sole reason for so doing was to prevent his cheating strangers." This meagre but convenient result closed a series of attempts at coming to terms, in the course of which Bysshe gave a noble proof of his ideal purity of principle. About the beginning of December Captain Pilfold told him of a meditated proposal, from his father and grandfather, of an immediate income for him of £2000 per annum (Shelley wrote of it as a capital fund of £120,000), on condition that he would entail the estate on his eldest son, or, in default of issue, on his younger brother John. This Shelley rejected, not only with peremptory decision, but with consuming indignation. That *he* should be supposed capable of entailing all this "command over labour" upon a possible fool or scoundrel !

Meantime, and just before his return to York, Miss Westbrook had arrived there as pre-arranged, and had taken possession of the establishment, and especially of Harriet, who had always been much under her control, and looked up to her with a long-confirmed habit of trustful and almost daughterly affection. Besides, she was wholly destitute of housewifery. Shelley found himself at once an infinitesimal quantity ; Harriet was a cipher, and Hogg a zero. Eliza Westbrook, over-ruling everything that everybody else wanted to do, solicitous for Harriet's hitherto unapparent nerves, dominating her by the terrible query "What would Miss Warne say?"—and brushing her own harsh but glossy black hair for hours in her bedroom—is an inimitable portrait limned by the equally skilful and ruthless hand of Mr. Hogg. That she may have meant well he allows ; and more than this will not readily be conceded by the reader who regards Shelley, and his comfort and proper position in his own house, as of somewhat more consequence than the managing and fussing propensities of this mature spinster.[1] Her undisputed function as regulator of the household expenditure appears in the small fact that, when she was soon afterwards with the Shelleys in Dublin, Eliza kept the common stock of money in a blind corner of her dress, and told it out as occasion required.

About the beginning of November, Shelley, with his wife and sister-in-law (the latter probably supplying the funds on this occasion), went off to Keswick, in the Lake-country of Cumberland : scenery and economy both attracted him thither. They

---

[1] Miss Westbrook married eventually, I am informed.

also wished to lose sight for a while of Hogg, who (as appears at length in an unpublished correspondence which has passed through my hands) had, during Shelley's recent absence from York, made advances to Harriet which she regarded, and it might seem not without some reason, as an attempt at seduction. The excerpt which Hogg gives from a writing of Shelley's, forming (according to the biographer) part of a variation of Göthe's *Werther*, is in fact, I am fully convinced, a portion of the severe remonstrances which the poet addressed to Hogg himself on this occasion. The Shelley party took at Keswick a small furnished house, Chesnut Cottage, at a rent of thirty shillings a week, which was afterwards reduced. The Duke of Norfolk (through whom Shelley had already tried to make terms with his father) invited all three to Greystoke, and did his best, in a kindly and handsome spirit, to promote their comfort. Southey also called upon Shelley; and they met— to use the elder poet's own phrase—"upon terms, not of friendship indeed, but of mutual good-will." Southey admired Shelley's talents at this time, and believed his heart to be kind and generous. The writings of the future Laureate, as likewise of Wordsworth and Coleridge, and Landor's *Gebir*, were among those for which Shelley, in early youth, had a particular predilection : of the older English poetry he then knew very little. By the time of his sojourn in Cumberland, however, Shelley had come to regard Southey—not as yet Wordsworth—as guilty of tergiversation, and this feeling increased into indignant disgust, before his departure, in consequence of some fulsome adulation of George the Third which the author of *Wat Tyler* had just been publishing : but in personal intercourse Shelley prized him, and could even, soon after their first meeting, speak of him as "a great man." De Quincey was another casual acquaintance at Keswick. Here the Shelleys and Miss Westbrook remained till the beginning of February 1812.[1] Bysshe could not be long anywhere without having an adventure of some sort. Accordingly, to accept his own account contained in a letter of 26th January, a robbery had just then been attempted on his person, and he was only saved from undefined ill-consequences by happening to fall *within* the limits of his house. The same letter mentions that he had been taking

---

[1] I have seen a letter of Shelley's, written from Keswick, inscribed outside "Single sheet, by God," for every postman to read. He had had reason to consider himself overcharged by the post under the old regulations concerning single or double sheets. This is exquisitely Shelleyan.

laudanum medicinally—a practice which he had then very recently begun ; possibly in this instance—and not in this one alone—the laudanum and the idea of the perilous adventure may have been connected as cause and effect.

From Keswick, on the 3rd of January, Shelley began one of his wonted volunteered correspondences—this time with the eminent publicist and novelist William Godwin. Soon before leaving Eton he had read that author's *Political Justice;* and he looked upon the book as having exercised an important influence on his character, rousing him from merely romantic notions, and showing that he had duties to perform. Shelley was now, spite of some dissuasion from Godwin (who evidently responded to his letters in a friendly and judicious spirit, though the answers are not on record), meditating a journey to Dublin, with a view to furthering Catholic Emancipation and the Repeal of the Union ; he had already prepared an address to the Irish people. He was also writing (as one of his printed letters expresses it) " An Enquiry into the Causes of the Failure of the French Revolution to benefit Mankind." From other sources of information I learn that this was in fact a tale or novel, by name *Hubert Cauvin:* he had written about two hundred pages of it by the 2nd of January, but in all probability it was never finished. One of his assertions to Godwin regarding his father is very startling. " My father . . . wished to induce me by poverty to accept of some commission in a distant regiment ; and, in the interim of my absence, to prosecute the pamphlet [*The Necessity of Atheism*], that a process of outlawry might make the estates, on his death, devolve to my younger brother." He speaks of it as an entailed estate of £6000 per annum ; of this, it seems, the fee-simple vested, upon his father's death, in Shelley, who could dispose of it by will,—and, besides the entailed estate, there was other property to a similar amount which could be cut off from Percy. From his statement above quoted, we may perhaps assume, as a fact in Shelley's career, that his father, after the Oxford *esclandre*, had wished him to enter the army; but for the rest Hogg's terse observation is indisputable. " It is only in a dream that the prosecution, outlawry, and devolution of the estate, could find a place. . . . It would have been too large a requisition upon the reader's credulity to ask him to credit them in the father of Zastrozzi or of St. Irvyne." Fortunately for himself, Hogg had probably not read *St. Irvyne*, or he would have found that that name designates a locality, and not a man.

The Irish project, at any rate, was "not all a dream." Shelley arrived in Dublin, with Harriet and Eliza, on the 12th of February 1812, after a tedious and stormy voyage which had driven them to the North of Ireland. His address was 7 Lower Sackville Street, and afterwards 17 Grafton Street. He at once issued, with his name, his *Address to the Irish People*—a mean-looking pamphlet of twenty-two pages, for which, it appears, no publisher would venture to be responsible. The edition was 1500 copies. Shelley pitched his diction in a purposely low key, to suit his readers; the tone is juvenile as well as commonplace, but does not tend to advocating any forcible or illegal acts—on the contrary, there are the usual tritenesses about the violence which destroyed the French Revolution, and which should on no account be imitated by the Irish patriots, about a peaceful progress towards perfectibility, and the like. The pamphlet had a considerable sale, and met with some newspaper eulogy. It was Shelley's custom to throw copies from his balcony to passers-by who looked "likely" recipients, and to distribute the pamphlet in the street: on one occasion, walking out with Harriet, he popped a copy into a lady's hood, making his bride "almost die of laughing." The *Address* was followed by another pamphlet, of eighteen pages—*Proposals for an Association of those Philanthropists who, convinced of the inadequacy of the moral and political state of Ireland to produce benefits which are nevertheless attainable, are willing to unite to accomplish its Regeneration. By Percy B. Shelly.* Here again the youthful agitator thought he had guarded against the dangers and disadvantages of associations (much enforced by Godwin) by providing for the publicity of meetings, and the optional secession of members. Nothing, however, save total abandonment of the Irish scheme, could satisfy the author of *Political Justice:* so, about the middle of March, Shelley, who most sincerely reverenced Godwin from afar, withdrew his pamphlets, and prepared to retire from the scene and field of Hibernian politics, profoundly moved by the misery and ignorance he had witnessed in Dublin. Meanwhile he had attended in person at least one political meeting, an "Aggregate Meeting of the Roman Catholics," on the 28th of February, in Fishamble Street Theatre ; and here he spoke at length in the presence of O'Connell and other celebrities.[1] Shelley was

---

[1] This speech is to be found in the *Dublin Evening Post* for 29th February 1812. An article by Mr. MacCarthy, published in *The Nation* (Dublin) in 1846, was the best account of Shelley's stay in Ireland, prior to the issue of the same writer's work, *Shelley's Early Life*, which constitutes a very detailed monograph of the Dublin episode.

truly impressive in discussion, or in grave and elevated conversation : Medwin says, " In eloquence he surpassed all men I have ever conversed with," and, according to Trelawny, " he left the conviction on the minds of his audience that, however great he was as a poet, he was greater as an orator." Even " his *ordinary* conversation is akin to poetry," says the loving Lieutenant Williams. But it is probable that in this instance in Dublin he did not greatly shine as a speaker. Chief Baron Woulfe recollected his speaking "at a meeting of the Catholic Board " (no doubt the same occasion), pausing now and anon, and delivering his slow sentences as so many disconnected aphorisms. His speech, however, was very well received by the audience, except one portion of it touching on religious matters, which was greeted with hisses. On the whole, his experiences did not augment his Irish enthusiasm ; neither did personal intercourse with the renowned Mr. Curran, for whom Godwin had sent him a letter of introduction, and whom he found a sufficiently prurient and buffoon-like old gentleman —qualities always and peculiarly distasteful to Shelley. In after years, an obscene story, or ribaldry of set purpose, would suffice to make him rise from his chair, and leave the room. He stayed in Dublin long enough, it would seem, to find that his absence would be a convenience to the governing powers ; long enough also to begin, with Mr. John Lawless, a voluminous History of Ireland, of which 250 pages had been printed by the 20th of March. He had likewise had a project of taking a share in a newspaper. Lawless's *Compendium of the History of Ireland*, published in 1814, embodies, no doubt, some of Shelley's work.

On the 7th of April the Shelleys and Eliza left Dublin.[1] They ranged about North and South Wales in search of a residence ; paused at and again left a " haunted " house at Nant-Gwillt, near Rhayader ; flitted through Cwm Elan ; and at last, from about the end of June, settled down for a short while at Lymouth in North Devonshire. They had a small unpretending cottage in a beautiful locality.

Shelley brought with him from Dublin a paper of his composition termed *Declaration of Rights ;* various copies of which

---

[1] Medwin (*Life*, vol. i. p. 177, and *Shelley Papers*) gives an account, self-contradictory in more respects than one, of a storm on this return-journey, and of the exertions of Shelley, who did much to save the vessel, and its crew of three. In my edition of 1870 I pointed out some grounds for disbelieving the story ; and Mr. MacCarthy has since detailed others which cast so much discredit on it that I think it can no longer be tolerated in Shelleyan biography.

had been seized at Holyhead, while on postal transit, in March of this year, and had become at that time the subject of some correspondence between the Post Office and the Home Office. The *Declaration* consists of thirty-one axioms, in favour of absolute control by the commissioning body, the nation at large, over its delegates, the government; advocating also unlimited freedom of opinion and of expression, the abolition of war, and so on. The opening proposition is "Government has no rights." The document is not wanting either in generous largeness of purpose, or in pointed expression. Its author made a practice of enclosing this broadsheet, and another on which was printed his poem of *The Devil's Walk*, in carefully secured boxes or bottles, which he dropped into the sea, hoping that somebody would pick them up, and that his ideas would thus peacefully germinate in congenial or impressible minds, and prepare the millennium in a regenerated country. Shelley, no doubt, considered this an ingenious device; but possibly even he was struck with a sense of its being in some degree unpractical. He next took a bolder step. On the 19th of August an Irish servant whom he had brought from Dublin, Daniel Hill (or more properly Healey), was found in the neighbouring town of Barnstaple, distributing and posting up, by his master's order, copies of the *Declaration of Rights*, and carrying about him *The Devil's Walk*. He was arrested, brought before the mayor on a charge of publishing and dispersing printed papers not bearing the printer's name, convicted in penalties amounting to £200, and, in default of payment, committed to the borough jail for six months. The Town-clerk of Barnstaple consulted the Home Office, then under the direction of Lord Sidmouth, on this matter; the postmaster of the same town also communicated regarding it with the Postmaster-general, Lord Chichester; and instructions were given for watching Shelley's proceedings. The result was that the latter found it apposite to disappear from Lymouth with his household. At the end of August they left. Godwin, after much urging, came down on the 18th of September to pay them a visit, only to find they had vanished. His sympathies and intellectual curiosity had been greatly excited by the letters Shelley had addressed to him.

At Lymouth Bysshe had two boyish hobbies, not heretofore recorded by his biographers. He would blow soap-bubbles from the hill-slope before Mrs. Hooper's lodging-house, where he resided. He would also cut out paper, and stick it on pasteboard, thus manufacturing a kind of balloon, to which he then fastened a stick or straw : this appendage he fired, and watched his balloon intently as it floated away, rising higher and higher, and gradually fanned by the wind into a full blaze. Mrs. Hooper dreaded a descent of the fire-balloon upon her own or some neighbouring thatch ; but this never actually occurred, the wind wafting the frail structure along cliffs on the opposite shore.[1]

The next and rather less brief sojourn was at Tanyrallt, near Tremadoc in Carnarvonshire, where Shelley hired a commodious cottage or country-house belonging to a gentleman named Madocks, who was engaged on extensive works for reclaiming land from the sea—several thousand acres. Here, and at Lymouth previously, Shelley, with his usual unreflecting enthusiasm of good-will, received an additional inmate—Miss Elizabeth Hitchener. This lady was a deist and republican, who kept a school in Sussex, at Hurstpierpoint, and whom Shelley invited away from the sphere of her operations to aid him in emancipating the human race. He was possessed with an enormous admiration of Miss Hitchener's independence of mind—an admiration which, indeed, for some months before and after his elopement with Harriet, exceeded all bounds of proportion and sound judgment. It is to be presumed that he supported her at Tanyrallt, and he certainly subsidized her afterwards : for, as "the Brown Demon" (such is the sole title which this estimable person used to obtain in printed Shelleyan records) proved sovereignly distasteful to Eliza, and hence to Harriet and Shelley himself, the connection was severed in November of this same year, and Shelley felt bound to indemnify her to some extent for her damaged prospects. This was not now from love ; for he disposes of the Brown Demon in one monumental sentence—"What would hell be, were such a woman in heaven?" A much more signal instance of his splendid generosity and public large-heartedness occurred about the same time. An uncommonly high tide broke through the embankment of Mr. Madocks's earthworks, to the great dismay and peril of the cottagers. Shelley went about personally soliciting subscriptions (a task which was likely to be especially unpleasant to him, as his letters speak of his neighbours as being in a high degree bigoted and prejudiced), and himself headed the

---

[1] Miss Mathilde Blind learned these and other entertaining particulars, in the summer of 1871, from Mrs. Blackmore, a worthy old woman then aged eighty-two, who had been servant at the lodging-house when Shelley was there, and who remembers him and his ways with much predilection. In justice to Daniel Hill, it may be added that she believes in his thorough faithfulness and devotion to Shelley. Mrs. Blackmore died at a recent date.

list with £500—much more than a year's precarious income. He also hurried up to London, which he reached on the 4th of October, to push the subscription there, and had the satisfaction of saving the work. Here, after a long interval, he again saw Hogg, who was now studying in the Temple, and he treated him apparently with absolute adherence to the gracious maxim "forgive and forget": here also he made Godwin's personal acquaintance, and stayed awhile in his house. A letter of the 19th of February 1813, written to Mr. Hookham the publisher, after the poet's return to Tanyrallt, marks another act of genuine liberality, though only on a small scale. He was "boiling with indignation" at the tyrannical sentence of fine and imprisonment (£1000 and two years) passed upon Leigh Hunt and his brother John for an alleged libel[1] on the Prince Regent printed in the *Examiner;* and he proposed a public subscription to pay-off the fine, and sent for the purpose £20, which appears to have been about all the ready money he had at the time even for his own requirements. The Hunts honourably declined to avail themselves of the proposal, and of a subsequent offer of £100 from Shelley during their imprisonment. This was not the first time that Shelley had had something to do with Leigh Hunt; for, on the occasion of the failure of a previous Government prosecution against the *Examiner,* he had written from Oxford (2nd March 1811), without any personal acquaintance, "to submit to his consideration a scheme of mutual safety and mutual indemnification for men of public spirit and principle." By the date of the sentence for libel he had met Hunt, but not on an intimate footing.

The residence at Tanyrallt came to an end in a startling and mysterious manner. On the 26th of February the Irish servant Daniel Hill reached the dwelling of the family, his six months' term of imprisonment having just expired. During the night of the same day an attempt to assassinate Shelley in his own house was made, or was supposed or alleged to have been made. For some unexplained reason, Shelley, on retiring to

---

[1] There is nothing like understanding and attending to the *facts* of a case, whichever direction they may bear in. It has often been said that the attack made by Leigh Hunt upon the Prince Regent was some slight affair of ridicule or depreciation; calling him "a fat Adonis of *sixty*," according to Hogg. This is quite untrue: the assault was as virulent as it was well-deserved. One phrase no doubt is "that . . . this 'Adonis in loveliness, was a corpulent gentleman of *fifty*"; but (besides other severities) the very next sentence has anything but a bantering tone :—"In short, that this 'delightful, blissful, wise, pleasurable, honourable, virtuous, true, and immortal Prince' was a violator of his words, a libertine over head and ears in debt and disgrace, a despiser of domestic ties, the companion of gamblers and demireps, a man who has just closed half a century without one single claim on the gratitude of his country or the respect of posterity."

bed that night, had expected to have occasion for pistols, and
had loaded a brace: possibly the arrival of Daniel had revived
in his mind the idea of Government *surveillance* and persecution. Hearing a noise in one of the parlours, he got out of
bed with his pistols, and saw a man who fired upon him. A
struggle ensued, in which Shelley twice returned the fire, with
dubious result: the ruffian, vowing outrage and murder on
Eliza and Harriet, ran away. But he returned about three
hours afterwards, and shot through Shelley's night-gown and
the window-curtain : another struggle ensued, with sword and
pistols : Daniel arrived, and the assassin again made off. Such
is the account given by Harriet in a letter to Mr. Hookham,
who had been implored to send funds to enable the Shelleys
to quit their Cambrian Castle Dangerous, and retreat to
Dublin.[1]

The Shelleys went to "the solicitor-general of the county,"
and had an investigation set on foot. No trace could ever be
found of the assassin. The Shelleyan theory was that a certain
Mr. Leeson,[2] a man whom they avoided as "malignant and
cruel to the greatest degree," was at the bottom of the affair.
The Leesonian and irreverent theory was at least as tenable
primâ facie —viz., " that it was a tale of Mr. Shelley's to impose
upon the neighbouring shopkeepers, that he might leave the
country without paying his bills." People in general, along
with Messrs. Hogg, Madocks, and Peacock, and Mr. Browning among later analysts, have disbelieved the story, and attributed it to an excited imagination, or nerves unstrung by
laudanum : Hogg suggests that Daniel may possibly have had
something to do with it. This presumption had hitherto been
a mere conjecture ; but the facts recently ascertained regarding
Daniel's imprisonment[3] seem to lend it no inconsiderable degree
of plausibility. It is fairly surmisable that Daniel might have
entertained revengeful feelings against Shelley, and might have
concocted a plan either for simply frightening him, or for mal-
treating him and robbing the house as well. If he really was
at the bottom of the affair, he must, according to the details
narrated by Harriet, have had a confederate ; and some one of

---

[1] A preliminary brief and agitated letter from Shelley to Hookham is dated 3rd March in
Hogg's *Life*—in the *Shelley Memorials* it is given without any date. I think " 3rd
March " must be incorrect ; for it seems clear the missive was despatched immediately
after the event, and, if so, on 27th February.
[2] This is the correct name : in Hogg's *Life* it is Luson.
[3] These facts have been traced out through certain documents preserved in the Record
Office, and published, with some remarks of my own, in the *Fortnightly Review* for
January 1871.

the jail-birds who had lately formed his society might have been readily available for such a purpose. Or some such rascal might, even without Daniel's privity, have heard from him details sufficiently suggestive of such an enterprise on his own account. In either of these cases, the offender, being a perfect stranger in the district, would be the more likely to remain untracked. If, on the contrary, we incline to disbelief of the alleged facts, we may find something confirmatory in the nocturnal conditions : the night was one of rain, and "wind as loud as thunder," which may have started in Shelley's perturbed brain the notion of pistol-snappings : it is a fact, however, that *some* pistol was really fired. Another point (hardly hitherto dwelt on) is that Shelley *expected*, on going to bed, to need his firearms : if the expectation was a mere fantasy, the subsequent assumed actual need of them may have been the same. But Lady Shelley and Mr. Thornton Hunt discover no ground for scepticism : " Miss Westbrook was also in the house at the time, and often, in after years, related the circumstance as a frightful fact." [1] This last evidence is of great weight, and must, even were there nothing else to be pleaded on the same side, give us pause before we dismiss the whole story as delusive. Miss Westbrook became one of Shelley's bitterest enemies, and certainly would not, out of any consideration for him, have upheld "in after years" his account of the matter. But it is conceivable that, having at first committed herself to a figment, she found it impossible afterwards, for her own sake if not for Shelley's, to recant. Here I must leave this still debateable mystery.

A short stay in Mr. Lawless's house, No. 35 Great Cuffe Street, Dublin, preceded a tour to Killarney, uniting enjoyment with discomfort—more satisfactory at any rate to the Shelleys and Miss Westbrook than to Hogg, who, arriving in Dublin by invitation, learned that they had left for the lake-trip. And, when Shelley and Harriet (in brief respite from Eliza, who remained at Killarney) returned on purpose to the Cork Hotel, Dublin, on the 31st of March, Hogg had started back to London. These little incidents may stand as a sample of the hurried and unconcerted movements in which Shelley was continually engaging. The spouses left Dublin again about the 4th of April ; and why they had ever gone thither, unless to be far from Tanyrallt, or as a stage towards a holiday at Killarney,

---

[1] *Shelley Memorials*, p. 56.

is not apparent. They reached the house ot Mr. Westbrook
in Chapel Street in May. Eliza soon joined them in London,
where they took to living in hotels for a while ; but she was
apparently not just at present a fixed member of their household. Daniel Hill now quitted their service ; being still, in
Harriet's eyes, a model of fidelity. They afterwards lodged in
Halfmoon Street ; seeing much of Hogg, and of other society,
including some literary acquaintances—nothing of Shelley's own
relatives. Somewhere about this time, but presumably a little
later, Shelley indulged his wife in a whim to set-up a carriage ;
and the culpable extravagance was very near sending him to
prison for debt.

On or about the 28th of June Harriet was delivered of her
first child, Ianthe Eliza,[1] at Cooke's Hotel, Dover Street : it
was a very easy confinement. There was some blemish in one
of Ianthe's eyes ; her mother did not nurse her, but handed her
over to the cares of a wet-nurse whom Shelley disliked ; and
Eliza, whom he was now getting to loathe, was continually
hovering and busying herself (no doubt with genuine good-feel-
ing) about the infant. These circumstances were all vexatious
to Shelley, and it has even been said that he exhibited no
interest in the baby ; but this is distinctly disproved by Mr.
Peacock. "He was extremely fond of it, and would walk up
and down a room with it in his arms for a long time together,
singing to it a monotonous melody of his own making, which
ran on the repetition of a word of his own coining. His song
was 'Yáhmani, Yáhmani, Yáhmani, Yáhmani.' It did not
please *me ;* but, what was more important, it pleased the child,
and lulled it when it was fretful. Shelley was extremely fond
of his children : he was pre-eminently an affectionate father."
In later years we read of his playing for hours with his last
child Percy on the floor. Mr. Trelawny, however, tells me
that (at least within his experience) Shelley was not "fond of
children," in the ordinary sense of the term : they obtained
little notice from him.

VIII.—QUEEN MAB.

Among the various writings of Shelley which I have hitherto
had occasion to mention—and there were many besides—the
only one having any moderate degree of literary merit is the
Necessity of Atheism. We have next to contemplate him as a
poet taking a certain actual rank among poets ; no high rank

---

[1] The lady who became Mrs. Esdaile, and died in June 1876.

as yet, but still one which is not to be ignored. The poem of *Queen Mab* places him in this position. He began this work in the spring or summer of 1812, subsequent to his first return from Ireland:[1] it was finished in February 1813, after which he compiled the lengthy notes. He had at first thought of publishing it; but eventually limited himself to a private edition of 250 copies, for which he bespoke fine paper, thinking that, though the aristocrats would not read it themselves, "it was probable their sons and daughters would." Shelley sent copies to many writers of the day—to Byron among others. The thorough genuineness of his character and feelings appears in the fact that, in transmitting *Queen Mab* to the all-famous author of *Childe Harold*, Shelley wrote a letter detailing all the accusations he had heard against him, and saying that, if these were not true, he would like to make his acquaintance.[2] The letter, however, did not reach Byron, though the book did, and was read by him with some admiration. Indeed, it produced a certain general sensation and impression, within the limits of its circulation. It was first pirated in 1821.

For the speculative qualities of *Queen Mab* and its notes I have to refer the reader to the book itself; only further observing that, while it is declaredly atheistic in the ordinary sense, and highly hostile to theologic christianity, it has also a certain element of pantheism, and is decidedly not the writing of a self-consistent materialist, or disbeliever in spirit as something other than a function of body. The ardour of Shelley for his own beliefs, and his unreasoning youthfulness of self-confidence, made him actually imagine that such a performance as *Queen Mab* was capable of producing a change in the ideas and practices of society. He seems to have retained notions of this sort up to the year 1816 or 1817, when he became both less sanguine and less aggressive—never less nobly and enthusiastically self-devoted. As to the poetical merits of *Queen Mab*, I think the ordinary run of criticism is at fault. Some writers go to the ridiculous excess of speaking of it as not only a grand

---

[1] So says Shelley in a letter quoted in the *Shelley Memorials*, p. 39. But there may be some nucleus of truth in Medwin's assertion (*Life*, vol. i. p. 53) that the poem had been begun, as a mere imaginative effusion, as early as about the autumn of 1809, and that it was only after his expulsion from Oxford that Shelley continued it into an attack on religious and other systems.

[2] Moore's *Life of Byron*, vol. ii. p. 22. Moore states this distinctly as a fact; but there is another story (Medwin, *Life of Shelley*, vol. i. p. 237), that Shelley, on reaching Sécheron in 1816, wrote to Byron detailing the accusations made against Shelley himself, and saying that he, if Byron disbelieved them, would like to become known to him. I should incline to suppose this the true version of the story, but that I find no sort of confirmation of it in Dr. Polidori's MS. journal.

poem, but actually the masterpiece of its author; and even those who stop far short of this expatiate in loose talk about its splendid ideal passages, gorgeous elemental imagery, and the like. The fact is that *Queen Mab* is a juvenile production in the fullest sense of the term—as nobody knew better than Shelley himself a few years afterwards; and furthermore (unless I am much mistaken) the *most* juvenile and unremarkable section of it is the ideal one. The part which has some considerable amount of promise, and even of positive merit at times, is the declamatory part—the passages of flexible and sonorous blank verse in which Shelley boils over against kings or priests, or the present misery of the world of man, and in acclaiming augury of an æra of regeneration. These passages, with all their obvious literary crudities and imperfections, are in their way of real mark, and not easily to be overmatched by other poetic writing of that least readable sort, the didactic-declamatory.

The reader will observe that the name Shelley bestowed on his first-born daughter, Ianthe, is the same which he had already appropriated to the mortal heroine of his poem.

IX.—HARRIET SHELLEY AND MARY GODWIN.

Shelley's next removal was into a quiet street in Pimlico, for the more especial purpose of being near the Boinville family, with whom he had become intimate. Mrs. Boinville (or Madame de Boinville, widow of a French *émigré*) was a lady past middle age, but more than commonly young in general appearance, save for her snow-white hair : hence Shelley named her Maimuna, after a personage in Southey's *Thalaba*. He regarded her as "the most admirable specimen of a human being he had ever seen," though "it was hardly possible for a person of the extreme subtlety and delicacy of Mrs. Boinville's understanding and affections to be quite sincere and constant." She had a daughter, Cornelia, married to Mr. Newton, a vegetarian enthusiast whose views had a considerable influence at this time upon Shelley—as testified in the notes to *Queen Mab*. The society that he met at Mrs. Boinville's was of the free-thinking and levelling kind, and included no doubt its full proportion of crotchet-mongers and pretenders : it was highly distasteful to Hogg, and after a while not altogether congenial to Shelley himself, supremely free as he was from any feeling of exclusiveness or social disdain.

He was now in pecuniary straits,[1] with no resources beyond the £200 from his father; and, with a view to economy, he retreated, before the end of July, to a small cottage named High Elms, at Bracknell in Berkshire, where the Newtons, with their family of five children, stayed with him awhile.

It was probably in the summer of 1813[2] that Shelley saw his birthplace for the last time. He walked down from Bracknell to Horsham, at his mother's request, his father and the three youngest children being then absent from Field Place. A very youthful military officer named Kennedy was on a visit there at the time; and, as Bysshe's advent was a secret, the two used to interchange costumes whenever the prodigal son walked out. Captain Kennedy has noted down his impressions of Shelley in a few paragraphs full of good feeling and much to the purpose. Let us appropriate one detail. "I never met a man who so immediately won upon me. The generosity of his disposition and utter unselfishness imposed upon him the necessity of strict self-denial in personal comforts: consequently he was obliged to be most economical in his dress. He one day asked us how we liked his coat, the only one he had brought with him: we said it was very nice, it looked as if new. 'Well,' said he, 'it is an old black coat which I have had done up, and smartened with metal buttons and a velvet collar.'"

In August Shelley came of age, "and his first act was to marry Harriet over again in an Episcopal Chapel in Edinburgh."[3] They were accompanied by Mr. Thomas Love Peacock.[4] This gentleman had been known to Shelley just before the latter went to Tanyrallt: Mrs. Newton describes him in 1813 as "a cold scholar, who, I think, has neither taste nor feeling." But Mrs. Newton may have regarded with some prejudice a gentleman who, seconded by Harriet,

[1] See two important letters, from Mr. Shelley senr., 26th May 1813, and from Percy Shelley a few days later, published in *Notes and Queries*, 2nd ser., vol. vi. p. 405. The father, learning that Percy (whom he addresses as "My dear boy") has not changed his speculative opinions, finally declines all further communication; and the poet (addressing the Duke of Norfolk) spiritedly says: "I am not so degraded and miserable a slave as publicly to disavow an opinion which I believe to be true."
[2] The date given by Hogg is "the beginning of the summer of 1814." Lady Shelley, who reproduces the letter printed by Hogg, says "1813," and must, I think, be right.
[3] This detail, which I give in the words of an informant exceedingly unlikely to be mistaken, has never hitherto been recorded; and the journey to Edinburgh had passed as being one of Shelley's motiveless and costly freaks.
[4] Perhaps it was now that Shelley saw Matlock. A letter to Mr. Peacock (22nd July 1816) shows that he had been there at *some* time, and, it might be inferred, in Peacock's company.

laughed heartily at the intellectual nostrum-vendors who abounded in the Newtonian regions. At any rate, Shelley, who, at one time of unprosperous fortune to Mr. Peacock, made him an allowance of £100 a year, continued, as long as he remained in England, to see him with predilection, and kept up with him from Italy a correspondence equally friendly and interesting. He valued his abilities highly, and relished the peculiar tone of witty causticity and badinage in action evidenced in such works as *Nightmare Abbey*, in which the character of Scythrop presents some traits of Shelley, and was so understood by himself.

About the end of 1813 Shelley was back in London; and early in 1814 he published *A Refutation of Deism*, a dialogue between Eusebes and Theosophus in 101 pages. The object of the author is to show that there is no tenable medium path between christianity and atheism, coupled with an ironical upholding of the former.

Hitherto nothing appears in the documents of Shelley's life to show that he was on other than affectionate and pleasant terms with Harriet. We find in his published letters the following expressions :—"My wife is the partner of my thoughts and feelings" (28th January 1812). "I am a young man, not of age, and have been married for a year to a woman younger than myself. Love seems inclined to stay in the prison" (August 1812). "How is Harriet 'a fine lady'? You indirectly accuse her in your letter of this offence—to me the most unpardonable of all. The ease and simplicity of her habits, the unassuming plainness of her address, the uncalculated connection of her thought and speech, have ever formed, in my eyes, her greatest charms; and none of these are compatible with fashionable life, or the attempted assumption of its vulgar and noisy *éclat*. You have a prejudice to contend with, in making me a convert to this last opinion of yours, which, so long as I have a living and daily witness to its futility before me, I fear will be unsurmountable" (to Fanny Godwin, 10th December 1812). "Harriet is very happy as we are, and I am very happy" (27th December 1812). "When I come home to Harriet, I am the happiest of the happy" (7th February 1813). Mrs. Newton writes to Hogg, 21st October 1813 : "The lady whose welfare must be so important in your estimation [Harriet] was, as usual, very blooming and very happy during the whole of our residence at Bracknell." The dedication to *Queen Mab* may also be accepted as evidence of affection; though (as I have before remarked) I find nothing to show that Shelley ever had a passion for Harriet—was ever thoroughly "in love" with her. But this satisfactory condition of things was now rapidly changing and vanishing. It appears that some estrangements had occurred between Shelley and his wife towards the end of 1813; she had yielded to the suggestions of interested persons, and importuned him to act in ways repugnant to his feelings and convictions, and conjugal quarrels ensued.[1] When they returned to London, Shelley had evidently lost the pleasure he previously took in watching Harriet's studies in Latin and otherwise: (she had, by December 1812, been brought on as far as reading many of Horace's Odes). During the spring of 1814 he was much at Bracknell: staying at Mrs. Boinville's house there, without Harriet, from about the middle of February to the middle of March. His letter of the 16th of March to Mr. Hogg shows that by this time his domestic discomforts were grave indeed, at least in his own eyes, and were hurrying towards a crisis. "I have escaped, in the society of all that philosophy and friendship combine, from the dismaying solitude of myself. . . . My heart sickens at the view of that necessity which will quickly divide me from the delightful tranquillity of this happy home—for it has become my home. . . . Eliza is still with us—not here; but will be with me when the infinite malice of destiny forces me to depart. . . . I have sometimes forgotten that I am not an inmate of this delightful home—that a time will come which will cast me again into the boundless ocean of abhorred society."[2] One reads such passages, and looks forward to the rapidly approaching result, with a sensation of pain; for he must have a hard heart who, after perusing the accounts of Harriet given by Hogg and Peacock from personal knowledge, has not a kindly sympathy for her, and a reluctance to contemplate her as parted from her husband and her better self.

The first incident that now comes before us looks like the direct reverse of separation. On the 24th of March 1814 Shelley and Harriet were remarried at St. George's, Hanover Square, in order to obviate any doubts as to the validity of the previous marriage according to the rites of the Church of

---

[1] This is the statement of Mr. Thornton Hunt. The date, "towards the end of 1813," appears in the *Shelley Memorials.* It has been vigorously controverted by Mr. Peacock; but he does not seem to me to have *disproved* it, and one is left to suppose that Lady Shelley speaks from documentary or other solid evidence.

[2] "Abhorred society" means, I think, not the society of Harriet, nor even of Eliza, but general or miscellaneous society.

Scotland.[1]   The fact is that Harriet was again pregnant; and, though there seems to be no real question of any sort as to the binding force of the previous marriage, Shelley may have thought it prudent to make assurance doubly sure for the possible heir to his name and claims.   A letter of his dated 21st October 1811 shows that, even at that early date, he was proposing to remarry in England within a month or so.   His intention, as expressed in the letter in question, was to settle £700 a year on Harriet in the event of his death.

He saw Mary Wollstonecraft Godwin soon after this renewed marriage—perhaps towards the middle or close of May: and this was the first time he had seen her, except now and then in the autumn of 1812, when she was hardly more than a child.[2]   Mr. Hogg records a brief interview " on the day of Lord Cochrane's trial " (this trial lasted two days, 8th and 9th June); and Mr. Peacock exhibits Shelley as helplessly in love with Mary before he had separated from Harriet.   " Nothing that I ever read in tale or history could present a more striking image of a sudden, violent, irresistible, uncontrollable passion." Shelley said on this occasion : " Every one who knows me must know that the partner of my life should be one who can feel poetry and understand philosophy ; Harriet is a noble animal, but she can do neither."

Mary, the only daughter of Godwin by his first wife the celebrated Mary Wollstonecraft, was born on the 30th of August 1797, and was consequently now in her seventeenth year.   She was rather short, remarkably fair and light-haired, with brownish-grey eyes,[3] a great forehead, striking features, and a noticeable

---

[1] The following is a copy of the certificate in the Register of St. George's Church: —" 164.   Percy Bysshe Shelley, and Harriet Shelley (formerly Harriet Westbrook, spinster, a minor), both of this Parish, were remarried in this Church by license (the parties having been already married to each other according to the rites and ceremonies of the Church of Scotland), in order to obviate all doubts that have arisen, or shall or may arise, touching or concerning the validity of the aforesaid marriage, by and with the consent of John Westbrook, the natural and lawful father of the said minor, this twenty-fourth day of March in the year 1814, by me, Edward Williams, Curate.   This marriage was solemnized between us—Percy Bysshe Shelley, Harriet Shelley, formerly Harriet Westbrook—in the presence of John Westbrook, John Stanley."—The phrase "according to the rites and ceremonies of the Church of Scotland" strongly confirms, to my mind, the allegation (see p. 45) that in 1813 Shelley and Harriet were remarried in Edinburgh ; for I do not find it anywhere suggested that their *first* marriage in Edinburgh, in 1811, had been conducted with any ecclesiastical form whatever.

[2] Mr. Peacock says it must have been between 18th April and 8th June that Shelley first saw Mary, and probably much nearer the later of the two dates than the earlier. If so, and if the *Stanzas, April* 1814 (vol. iii. p. 2) really indicate a clear purpose of separation between Shelley and Harriet, Mary cannot have been primarily responsible as the motive cause for that separation.

[3] Shelley ought to have known in 1818, when he wrote (see vol. iii. p. 227)

"O Mary dear, that you were here,
With your *brown* eyes bright and clear ! "

air of sedateness. Her earliest youth was by no means the period of her best looks—of which probably Mr. Thornton Hunt gives too exalted an idea when he compares her to the antique bust of Clytie. She was a little hot-tempered and peevish in youth (or, as Godwin wrote, " singularly bold, somewhat imperious, and active of mind "), and careless of dress and speech ; outspoken and tenacious of her opinions ; a faithful friend ; with " extraordinary powers of heart as well as head"; truthful and essentially simple, though somewhat anxious to make an impression in company. Shelley, in the last year of his life, said to Trelawny : " She can't bear solitude, nor I society—the quick coupled with the dead." The daughter of Mary Wollstonecraft and of Godwin could not be expected to set any great store by the marriage-tie, considered solely as such, and apart from the question of heartfelt love and voluntary constancy.

X.—THE SEPARATION FROM HARRIET.

Somewhere about the 17th of June—not later at any rate [1]— the married life of Shelley with Harriet came to a final close. She returned, with Ianthe, to the care of her father and sister, then living in retirement at Bath. Shelley (it has been said) gave her all the money he possessed,[2] stating to Mr. Westbrook that he was unable for the time to make her such an allowance as he could wish. He did however—at once or afterwards—make provision for her by a sum paid quarterly, which has been termed " sufficient." [3]

A great deal in this matter depends on the question of precise dates, which the materials at my command do not enable me to determine. It is certain (for I have it on the most unexceptionable authority) that letters from Harriet are or were in existence, written in moving terms, and marked by all the eloquence of truth, proving that Shelley at some time dis-

---

Yet Mr. Trelawny says "*grey* eyes." A portrait of Mary Shelley by Miss Curran, belonging to this gentleman, shows eyes that might be more fairly called grey than brown, but which have enough of a brownish tinge to account for Shelley's epithet. —" Rather short " (as in the text) appears to be accurate, notwithstanding a phrase, " this tall girl," used in a letter of Godwin, dated 21st February 1817 (see Mr. Paul's *William Godwin*, vol. ii. p. 246). From the context, the epithet appears to refer rather to womanly maturity than to actual height.

[1] Mr. Garnett has good grounds for saying this, as he knows that Shelley came to London on 18th June. Mr. Thornton Hunt speaks of the separation as taking place about the 24th of June.

[2] Middleton, vol. i. p. 268. The statement as to residence at Bath is taken from printed authorities, but I have some reason for doubting it.

[3] I find this stated in the article on Shelley in the *Penny Cyclopædia*. That article was, I believe, written by a distinguished man of letters who had at the time carefully investigated the facts of Shelley's life.

appeared from her cognizance, without making proper arrange-
ments, or giving any warning or explanation of his intentions.
Harriet had, for herself and her child, only fourteen shillings in
ready money at the moment. I have some grounds for inferring
that these letters date about the end of June. On the other
hand, it is no less certain that full forty days elapsed between
the separation of Shelley from Harriet, and his departure from
London with Mary Godwin; and that Harriet was in personal
communication with him fourteen days before the latter event.
On or about the 5th of July a letter of her own shows her to
have been then at Bath, and to have heard from Shelley about
the 1st of the same month. It is also plainly presumable that,
if Mr. Westbrook made an annual allowance of £200 to
Shelley and his family, that source of income would continue
accruing to the profit of Harriet when parted from Shelley; and
it is known that her husband wrote to her, soon after leaving
for the continent at the end of July, telling her "to take care
of her money"—thus manifestly implying that she had then
some money to take care of. After weighing all these counter-
acting and authentic details as well as I am able, I come to
the provisional conclusion that Shelley did at some time and
in a certain sense "abandon" Harriet—though, as likely as
not, without any intention, even at that moment, of leaving
his absence long unexplained; and that at any rate he came
to an explanation, and some sort of arrangement on her behalf,
before he left England.

Though I cannot regard Shelley as, in any correct sense of
the words, irresponsible for his actions, it is right to add here
that I am further informed, and again on excellent authority,
that about this period his sufferings from spasmodic attacks,
and consequent free use of laudanum, were so extreme that he
might have committed any wildness of action without surprising
those who were in the habit of seeing him. He would carry
the laudanum-bottle about in his hand, and gulp from it
repeatedly as his pangs assailed him. Indeed, in the early part
of July, he actually poisoned himself—not, I suppose, in the
least accidentally; and Mrs. Godwin had to implore Mrs.
Boinville to come over and nurse him, which was done with
the desired result, the cure being effected chiefly by walking
him incessantly about the room.

The parting from Harriet has been called a separation by
mutual consent. Harriet denied to Peacock that there was any
consent on her part. There is such a thing as reluctant but

unquerulous submission to the inevitable : unless one inter-
changes that term with the term consent, the materials as yet
published do nothing to invalidate Harriet's denial.[1]   Towards
the end of the year she gave birth to a child, Charles Bysshe,
who died in 1826.

On some day after 8th July, and therefore after the final
separation from Harriet, Shelley avowed to Mary the love
which he had, before that event, conceived for her.   I will
here borrow Lady Shelley's words, the first authentic published
record of the fact.   " To her, as they met one eventful day in
St. Pancras churchyard, by her mother's grave, Bysshe, in
burning words, poured forth the tale of his wild past—how he
had suffered, how he had been misled, and how, if supported
by her love, he hoped in future years to enroll his name with
the wise and good who had done battle for their fellow-men, and
been true through all adverse storms to the cause of humanity.
Unhesitatingly she placed her hand in his, and linked her
fortune with his own."   On the 28th of July they left England.
Before his departure with Mary, which had been notified to
Harriet, Shelley had ordered a settlement for the benefit of the
latter (whether this settlement took full effect is not specified) ;
towards November 1814 he informed her that there was money
at his banker's, "and she might draw as much as she liked " ;
he set money apart for her in 1815, as we shall see further on ;
he corresponded with her during his stay on the continent, and
after his return ; called upon her immediately after relanding
in England ; and, at least as late as December 1814, he gave
her good advice, and took trouble to advantage her.   Mary

---

[1] See, in the *Notes*, vol. ii. p. 415, an extract from what Mr. Garnett has very ably said
on the subject—with a view to the vindication of Shelley, but by no means to the depreciation of Harriet.   His main point is that, at some time between a day of June when
Shelley wrote a poem to Mary, and the 28th July when Shelley and Mary left England
together, the poet must have discovered that Harriet was not anxious to continue living
as his wife.   For my own part, I question whether the poem indicates that Shelley, being
in love with Mary, was then endeavouring to control his passion *out of regard to Harriet :*
it may not less plausibly be construed as an evidence of the mutual love of Shelley and
Mary, kept from the observation of outsiders through motives of prudence alone.   If this
latter view is adopted, the poem in question does not furnish a suggestion that any Indifference of Harriet to Shelley was discovered afterwards, or at all.   Distinct testimony
to that effect may exist, but has not yet been published.   I find, however, a very remarkable statement in Dr. Polidori's Diary (18th June), which I give for what it is worth :—
" He [Shelley] married ; and, a friend of his liking his wife, he tried all he could to induce
her to love him in turn."   This Catonian transaction, if true at all, must no doubt be
understood in the sense that Shelley, *after* he had discovered the mutual incompatibility
between himself and Harriet, found also that the happiness of a friend of his could be promoted by Harriet, and that he then furthered his suit with her.   At an earlier period of
his wedded life, he had shown himself by no means tolerant of Hogg's misconduct with
regard to Harriet.   Mr. Foster, in his *Life of Landor,* intimated that he was in possession of documents which throw light upon the entire affair of the separation. but to what
particular purpor* he did not disclose.

4 *

also continued on amicable terms with Harriet—at any rate no open hostility ensued. I am told that, at some time after the return of Shelley and Mary from the continent in this year 1814, he consulted a legal friend with a view to reintroducing Harriet into his household as a permanent inmate—it is to be presumed, as strictly and solely a friend of the connubial pair, Mary and himself: and it required some little cogency of demonstration on the part of the lawyer to convince the primæval intellect of Shelley that such an arrangement had its weak side.

Some points remain still to be revealed in this whole matter of the separation; but we are probably in a position to estimate already the main facts and their bearings. We shall never do justice to any one of the three parties concerned unless we consider these facts from *their* point of view, and not from that of persons whose opinions are fundamentally different.

Firstly, then, as regards Shelley, it appears to be certain that, after some two years or more of marriage, he found that Harriet did not suit him, partly through the limitations of her own mind and character, and partly through the baneful influence of her sister; that, having already reached this conclusion, he fell desperately in love with Mary Godwin; that this attachment (not then avowed nor confessedly reciprocated), combining with the previous motives, determined him to separate from Harriet; and that the separation, though at one moment a mere piece of abrupt *de facto* work on Shelley's part, was eventually carried out on a deliberate footing, and without decided neglect of her material interests. Shelley was an avowed opponent, on principle, to the formal and coercive tie of marriage : [1] therefore, in ceasing his marital connection with Harriet, and in assuming a similar but informal relation to Mary, he did nothing which he regarded as wrong—though (as far as anything yet published goes) it must distinctly be said that he consulted his own option rather than Harriet's.

Secondly, Harriet took no steps of her own accord to separate from Shelley, and had given no cause whatever for repudiation by breach or tangible neglect of wifely duty; but she did not offer a strenuous pertinacious resistance to the separation, nor exhibit a determined sense of wrong. Mr. Thornton

---

[1] See the strong expressions in the note to *Queen Mab*, pp. 223–25, written when Shelley was living in harmony with Harriet. Similar views are set forth in his correspondence, published and unpublished, close to the date of his eloping with and marrying her.

Hunt, indeed, thinks that she may rather have courted the separation at the moment, but only with the idea that it would cause a revulsion in Shelley's mind, inducing him submissively to solicit her return. If Shelley connected himself with Mary, Harriet, after the separation, connected herself with some other protector, and this probably, from the principles she had imbibed, with a conscience equally void of offence—at least at first.

Thirdly, there is no evidence at all that Mary did anything reprehensible with a view to supplanting Harriet, and securing Shelley for herself. When he, after leaving Harriet, sought her love, she freely and warmly gave it; and, in so doing, she again acted strictly within the scope of her own code of right.

Such, as far as my authorities go, are the clear facts of this case. They are simple and unambiguous enough; but no doubt liable to be judged with great severity by those who start from contrary premisses. We find three persons fashioning their lives according to their own convictions, and in opposition to the moral rules of their time and country. Two of them act spontaneously, and with a view to their own happiness; the third has her course predetermined by the others, or by one of them, and adapts herself to it with more or less acquiescence. For her it turns out very much amiss; and from her misfortunes or wrongs there will be a Nemesis to haunt the mutual peace of the others.

XI.—FIRST CONTINENTAL TRIP.

The household of Godwin consisted of his second wife, who had previously been married to a Mr. Clairmont; Mary, his daughter by his first wife; and William, his son by his second wife. Also Frances (or Fanny) Wollstonecraft, the daughter of Mary Wollstonecraft by Mr. Imlay, born before her marriage with Godwin, and always called Fanny Godwin; and two children of the second Mrs. Godwin by her former marriage—Jane (who adopted instead the name of Claire) Clairmont, and Charles Clairmont. Godwin, eminent as an author—admired for his powerful novel of *Caleb Williams*, and deeply reverenced by a knot of advanced thinkers as the philosopher of *Political Justice* and the *Enquirer*—carried on business as a bookseller at No. 41 Skinner Street. It is amusing to read of his displeasure if he was not addressed as " Esquire " on a letter-cover, and of Shelley's profound amazement at this displeasure.   Mary was treated in a domineering and unsympathetic spirit by her stepmother, and was consequently not happy at home.   Moreover, her connection with Shelley was not recognized but much resented by both stepmother and father.   Their going abroad together was effected by the lovers without concealment or hurry on their own account.   But Miss Clairmont was minded to accompany them, and this again was strongly objected to by Mrs. Godwin.   The consequence is that the three young people started in secret on the 28th July, a singularly sultry day, and crossed from Dover to Calais in a small boat, encountering a perilous squall and thunderstorm.   Mrs. Godwin, and a friend Mr. Marshall, pursued them to Calais, but without any avail.

Miss Clairmont was now sixteen years old, an Italian-looking brunette, "of great ability, strong feelings, lively temper, and, though not regularly handsome, of brilliant appearance."[1]   She shared Mary's independent opinions on questions such as that of marriage.   From this time onwards she became almost a permanent member of Shelley's household, whether abroad or in England.

Having reached Paris (where Shelley pawned his watch, and sent the money, I am informed, to Harriet), the travellers resolved to perform the remainder of their journey on foot, with occasional lifts, and an ass to carry their portmanteau.   The ass, however, proved to be "not strong enough for the place," and a mule was substituted when they quitted Charenton. Soon Shelley sprained his ankle ; walking became impossible for him, and an open voiture drawn by another mule replaced the former animal.   The route disclosed much horrible devastation perpetrated by the Cossacks and other invaders upon lately re-Bourbonized France.   The Alps came into view soon before the tourists reached Neufchâtel : "their immensity " (writes Mrs. Shelley, in her *History of a Six Weeks' Tour*, the authority for all these details) "staggers the imagination, and so far surpasses all conception that it requires an effort of the understanding to believe that they indeed form a part of the

---

[1] The name of Miss Clairmont occurs in the sequel of this Memoir seldomer perhaps than some readers might expect.   She is still living, and settled in Florence.   The statement that she was sixteen years old in 1814 is taken by me from a letter of her mother's which I have seen ; unless this was wilfully untrue, Mr. Kegan Paul (*William Godwin*, vol ii. p. 213) cannot be right in saying that she was " several years older than Fanny."

earth." A cottage by the Lake of Uri was the desired termination of the tour; but want of money now dictated a return to England, and from Brunen, a village by that lake, the travellers set their faces homewards with all despatch. They took the *Diligence par Eau* along the Reuss to Loffenberg. "After having landed for refreshment in the middle of the day, we found, on our return to the boat, that our former seats were occupied. We took others; when the original possessors angrily, and almost with violence, insisted upon our leaving them. Their brutal rudeness to us, who did not understand their language, provoked Shelley to knock one of the foremost down. He did not return the blow; but continued his vociferations until the boatmen interfered, and provided us with other seats." Shelley was a man of most eminent physical as well as moral courage; and this small anecdote deserves to be remembered accordingly. From Loffenberg a leaky canoe took the trio on to Mumph: "It was a sight of some dread to see our frail boat winding among the eddies of the rocks, which it was death to touch, and when the slightest inclination on one side would instantly have overset it." No doubt these experiences were utilised in *Alastor*. Returning by Basle, Mayence, and Cologne—finding some Germans "disgusting," and the Rhine a "paradise"—thence to Cleves, posting on to Rotterdam, and expending their last guinea at Marsluys—the travellers landed at Gravesend, after a rough passage, on the 13th of September.

The only literary result of this tour, on the part of Shelley, was the wild unfinished tale of *The Assassins*, which almost looks like a grave burlesque, but was no doubt written in all seriousness. He began it at Brunen, after reading aloud, on a rude pier on the lake, the account of the siege of Jerusalem in Tacitus.

XII.—DOMESTIC LIFE WITH MARY :—ALASTOR.

Soon after his return to London, and at the close of an interval of much pecuniary depression, a great improvement took place in Shelley's worldly position. His grandfather Sir Bysshe died on the 6th of January 1815; his father became Sir Timothy Shelley; Percy was the next heir to the baronetcy and the entailed estate. The result was a new arrangement whereby, in consideration of his giving up some expectations, a clear annual income of £1000 a year from his father was secured to

him, and he immediately set aside a portion for Harriet's use.[1]
He had been peculiarly solitary in these last few months. The
Godwins ignored him and Mary; some of his friends of the
preceding year had fallen away; and Hogg and Peacock were
perhaps his only habitual companions.

In the winter which began 1815 he walked a London hospital,
in order to acquire some knowledge of surgery which might enable
him to be of service to the poor. It has been said, indeed, that
he had now a sort of idea of studying medicine professionally;
feeling that it might be necessary for him to adopt some definite
calling in life, and having more inclination for this than for any
other. He had entertained the project as far back as the summer of 1811, prior to his marriage with Harriet, and had even
studied medicine then for a short while under a celebrated
surgeon. His own health, however, was very delicate in
1815; and in the spring an eminent physician pronounced
him to be in a rapid consumption. This passed away: his
lungs suddenly righted in 1818, but the other forms of
ill-health from which he suffered remained. A tour along the
south coast of Devonshire, and to Clifton, was made in the
summer.

He next rented a house at Bishopgate Heath, near Windsor
Forest; and passed here several months of comparative health
and tranquillity, spending whole days under the oaks of Windsor
Great Park. At the end of August, Shelley, with Mary (always
named Mrs. Shelley), Peacock, and Charles Clairmont, went in
a wherry towards the source of the Thames beyond Lechlade
in Gloucestershire. The beautiful *Lines in Lechlade Churchyard* were the result. Another possible result, in Mr. Peacock's
estimation, may have been the great taste for boating which
Shelley ever afterwards retained. This, however, is one of the
small points on which much difference of opinion has been expressed. An Eton schoolfellow, Mr. W. S. Halliday (quoted
by Hogg), affirms that Shelley never boated at Eton; whereas
Medwin says that Shelley not only spoke of boating as having
been his greatest delight at Eton, but had also, within the biographer's own knowledge, shown the same taste in still earlier
boyhood at the Brentford school, and Mr. Middleton speaks to
the same effect as regards Eton, naming Mr. Amos as Shelley's

---

[1] Shelley was not at once placed beyond embarrassment in consequence of his grandfather's death. Mr. Locker possesses an unpublished letter from the poet, dated 14th
April 1815, saying that he had "the most urgent necessity for the advance of such a sum"
as £500. The statement in the text as to Harriet may be relied upon, though not derived
from any printed source.

boating companion there. Hogg says nothing about boating by his friend as coming under his own observation at Oxford or afterwards; but relates as symptomatic a prank with washing-tubs played by the poet on a rill at Bracknell. Perhaps we should conclude that Shelley did a great deal of boating in boyhood, but little afterwards until this Lechlade trip revived the fancy. Mr. Peacock thinks that the excessive hobby which Shelley had for floating paper boats may also have been derived from his example: it was, however, according to Hogg,[1] a Shelleyan habit at Oxford. It has been said that on one occasion, having no other paper at hand, he launched a £50 bank post-bill on the pond in Kensington Gardens, and, with greater good luck than he deserved, succeeded in recovering it on the opposite bank. This Hogg denies; but Medwin will have it that such an incident did really occur with a £10 note on the Serpentine. Once, when Shelley was playing with paper boats, he jestingly said that he could wish to be shipwrecked in one of them—he would like death by drowning best. It is curious to note how many times, before the final catastrophe, something occurred to associate the idea of drowning with Shelley—now merely by way of joke, now by some passages in his writings, now by calamities in his family circle, now by premonitory danger to himself. One salient instance is pointed out by Lady Shelley, from an allusion made by the poet to an article in the *Quarterly Review* comparing him to Pharaoh in the Red Sea. " It describes the result of my battle with their Omnipotent God; his pulling me under the sea by the hair of my head, like Pharaoh; my . . . . entreating everybody to drown themselves; pretending not to be drowned myself, when I *am* drowned; and lastly *being* drowned."

Alastor, written in 1815 at some time after the Lechlade excursion, was published in the succeeding year in a small volume containing also the bulk of the short pieces classed in our edition as *Early Poems*. In *Alastor* we at last have the genuine, the immortal Shelley. It may indeed be said that the poem, though singularly lovely and full-charged with meaning, has a certain morbid vagueness of tone, a want of firm human body: and this is true enough. Nevertheless, *Alastor* is proportionately worthy of the author of *Prometheus Unbound* and *The Cenci*, the greatest Englishman of his age; which cannot fully be said even of *Queen Mab*, and must be peremptorily denied

---

[1] Hogg's *Life*, vol. i. pp. 83, 84. I *think* Hogg means (but his expressions are not very clear) that Shelley acquired the habit towards the end of 1810.

of any preceding attempts. It may well be supposed that the genial atmosphere of domestic love and intellectual sympathy in which Shelley was now living with Mary contributed to the kindly development of his poetic power.

XIII.—SECOND CONTINENTAL TRIP :—BYRON.

At the beginning of May 1816 Shelley and Mary, with her infant son William born on the 24th of January, and Miss Clairmont, again went abroad, reaching Paris on the 8th of the month. William was not strictly Mary's first-born; as a daughter had before come prematurely into the world, living only a few days. The practical reason for the trip was probably the obvious one—that they felt inclined for it: but Shelley somehow conceived that there was a more abstruse reason—viz., that his father and uncle (meaning, no doubt, Sir John Shelley-Sidney, not Captain Pilfold) were laying a trap for him with the view of locking him up, and that Mr. Williams, the agent of Mr. Madocks of Tanyrallt, had come down to Bishopgate, and given him warning of this plot, which the poet believed to be only one out of many that his father had schemed for the same purpose. That Shelley made such an allegation is certain from the testimony of Mr. Peacock; and that the allegation was untrue is convincingly represented on the same testimony. How this new delusion got into Shelley's head it is difficult to conceive—the objectlessness of inventing such a tale for Mr. Peacock's sole behoof being patent, not to speak of the lofty veracity of Shelley's character in essentials. We must remember that a poet is "of imagination all compact;" and, as no one had a better right than Shelley to the name of poet, none consequently had a readier store of imaginations which he propounded as realities. But even this was not the last mysterious transaction which beset his departing footsteps. The very night before his leaving London for the continent, a married lady of fashion, young, handsome, rich, and nobly connected, called upon him, and avowed that the author of *Queen Mab*, hitherto personally unknown to her, was her ideal of everything exalted in man, and that she had come to be the partner of his life. Shelley could but explain that he was no longer his own to dispose of; and, with much effusion and magnanimity on both sides, they parted. But the lady followed him to the continent, and many a time watched him, herself unseen, on the Lake of Geneva. The sequel of this story belongs to a later date. Such is the narrative which Shelley, not very long before his death, detailed to Medwin and Byron, and which the former has handed down to us with no lack of embellishing touches. Byron disbelieved the story, attributing all to "an overwrought imagination"; and everybody since seems to have agreed with him—Lady Shelley, for instance, saying that no sort of confirmatory evidence appears in the family papers. Medwin, however, is a believer.

The tourists reached Sécheron, near Geneva, on the 17th of May. On the 25th Lord Byron, with his travelling physician Dr. Polidori, arrived at the same hotel; and the two parties encountered on the 27th, if not before. Byron and Shelley had not previously met: they now found themselves in daily and intimate intercourse. Shelley expressed in 1818, in his introductory words to *Julian and Maddalo*, an estimate of Byron which he probably formed, in essential respects, soon after he first knew him in Switzerland. "He is a person of the most consummate genius, and capable, if he would direct his energies to such an end, of becoming the redeemer of his degraded country [*i.e.* according to the poem, not England but Venice. But it is his weakness to be proud: he derives, from a comparison of his own extraordinary mind with the dwarfish intellects which surround him, an intense apprehension of the nothingness of human life. . . . I say that Maddalo is proud, because I can find no other word to express the concentred and impatient feelings which consume him; but it is on his own hopes and affections only that he seems to trample, for in social life no human being can be more patient, gentle, and unassuming, than Maddalo. He is cheerful, frank, and witty." In fact, the feelings of Shelley for Byron were at all periods of a very mixed kind.[1] He admired intensely his poetic genius, and most intensely some of his performances—in especial *Cain* and certain sections of *Don Juan* (both of them works of a later date than 1816). He was totally destitute of uneasy personal vanity as a poet; and, so far from feeling any jealousy of Byron's splendid success both with cultivated judges and with ordinary readers, he very greatly undervalued *himself* in comparison, though on the other hand he was resolved not to be or appear in any way a literary satellite of the great luminary. At the present day we see all these things with very different eyes; and have to reason ourselves into believing that, while the author of *Childe Harold* and *Don Juan* was an intellectual power throughout Europe, and divided the laurel of poetry with

---

[1] For some reason which I do not find explained, Mrs. Shelley applied the name Albè to Byron.

Göthe, the author of *Prometheus Unbound* and *Epipsychidion*
was almost "nowhere," save only in the laudations of a few
partisans,[1] and in the foul mouths and hypocritical hysterics or
quarterly or other orthodox calumniators, heirs to all dearest
traditions of scribes and pharisees. *Queen Mab* and *The Cenci*
may have been partial exceptions. The former made some
faint sort of stir, in which its audacities of opinion count no
doubt for almost everything: *The Cenci* went through two
English editions in a short while.[2] But, as regards the other
poems, I presume it is no exaggeration to say that hardly one
of them sold, during Shelley's lifetime, to the extent of a hundred copies, in the open market of literature;[3] and perhaps
even ten copies would be a bold guess with respect to *Epipsychidion* and *Adonais*. Thus far as regards Shelley's literary relation to Byron. As to his personal relation, he found much to
fascinate him in the poet's company, and was always eagerly
susceptible to the finer points of his character; but he bitterly
censured his promiscuous and lowering immoralities, and
counted him, on more grounds and occasions than one, a
difficult man to keep friends with. "The canker of aristocracy
wants to be cut out" was one of his observations; and perhaps
nothing could be said in so small a space going equally close
to the substructure of all that was worst in Byron. The reader,
however, should turn to *Julian and Maddalo* itself, to refresh
at the fountain-head his recollection of what Shelley thought of
his brother-poet.

For his part, Byron had a most genuine regard for Shelley,
and a sincere relish for his society. He set great store by his
critical opinion, and admired his poetry very highly, though

[1] Some notices of Shelley in *Blackwood's Magazine* should be excepted, as neither
cliqueish nor abusive: see those of *Alastor, Rosalind and Helen*, and *Prometheus*, in
the volumes for 1819–20. They show—especially the first—sincere admiration and personal
kindliness of feeling, though there is more than enough about Shelley's portentous religious and other opinions. One of them, probably the critique of *Alastor*, was at the time
attributed by Shelley to Walter Scott. The review of *Prometheus* is certainly not un-
mixed praise: we read that "it is quite impossible that there should exist a more pesti-
ferous mixture of blasphemy, sedition, and sensuality." The later review of *Adonais* in
Blackwood is most outrageous—a tissue of scurrilous sneers and (as regards Keats) of low
callousness. The critic finds in the poem "two sentences of pure nonsense out of every
three: a more faithful calculation would bring us to ninety-nine out of every hundred."
[2] I follow other writers in mentioning *The Cenci* as a moderate success. Yet Shelley
had no reason to think it such up to 15th February 1821, at any rate, when he wrote to
Mr. Peacock (*Fraser's Magazine*, March 1860), "Nothing is more difficult and unwelcome than to write without a confidence of finding readers; and, if my play of *The Cenci*
found none or few, I despair of ever producing anything that shall merit them."
[3] "I hope Ollier has told you that Shelley's book sells more and more" is an expression
of Leigh Hunt in a letter dated 12th November 1818. This book must be the *Revolt of
Islam*, which *may* possibly have failed rather less manifestly than some other volumes:
yet Medwin says it "fell almost stillborn from the press." He uses a like phrase with
regard to *Prometheus Unbound*.

perhaps not with much of the insight of sympathy. On one occasion (so Mr. Trelawny informs me) he went so far as to say, " If people only appreciated Shelley, where should *I* be ? " Some of his own works, such as *Manfred* and the fourth canto of *Childe Harold,* are understood to owe something to the influence and suggestions of Shelley : others were shown to the latter day by day as written. A few of Byron's remarks upon his friend may here be not inappropriately cited. "You are all mistaken about Shelley. You don't know how mild, how tolerant, how good, he was in society, and as perfect a gentleman as ever crossed a drawing-room, when he liked and where liked."[1] " He is, to my knowledge, the least selfish and the mildest of men—a man who has made more sacrifices of his fortune and feelings for others than any I ever heard of." "You should have known Shelley to feel how much I must regret him. He was the most gentle, the most amiable and least worldly-minded person I ever met ; full of delicacy, disinterested beyond all other men, and possessing a degree of genius joined to simplicity as rare as it is admirable. He had formed to himself a *beau idéal* of all that is fine, high-minded, and noble, and he acted up to this ideal even to the very letter. He had a most brilliant imagination, but a total want of worldly wisdom. I have seen nothing like him, and never shall again, I am certain." Another statement made by Byron, very characteristic of himself, and placing Shelley in a light somewhat different from that in which one is wont to contemplate him, is that he was the only thoroughly companionable man under thirty years of age whom Byron knew. The following also deserves to be borne in mind ; though we must assuredly not interpret it so as to infer that there was the slightest taint of insincerity in Shelley's professions of extreme opinions or of personal friendship : Medwin understands it as referring more especially to Leigh Hunt's translations from Homer.[2] Byron is writing to Murray on the 25th October 1822, and Hunt is the main topic. " Alas, poor Shelley ! how he would have laughed had he lived ! and how we used to laugh now and then at various things which are grave in the suburbs ! " But perhaps the strongest of all evidences of the unique regard in which Lord Byron held Shelley, when we consider his lordship's habit of running down all his acquaintances from time to time, is that which I learn from Mr.

---

[1] So in Moore's *Life of Byron,* vol. ii. p. 622 ; not " where *he* liked," as I have mostly seen in quotations.
[2] Medwin's *Life,* vol. ii. p. 36.

Trelawny—that no word of detraction of Shelley ever issued from Byron's lips, within Trelawny's experience or belief. The assertion above quoted that Shelley had "a total want of worldly wisdom" must be understood with some qualification, as implying rather a contempt of self-seeking than any real inaptitude for the ordinary business of life. Byron himself clearly did not undervalue Shelley in this respect, having (besides other proof to the contrary) entrusted to him, along with Mr. Kinnaird, the negotiations for the publishing of the third canto of *Childe Harold*, the *Prisoner of Chillon*, and *Manfred ;* while Leigh Hunt states that Shelley had more capacity than himself for business (which is not indeed saying much), and Medwin speaks of him as very sagacious and rational in practical affairs, especially in the interest of his friends. Mr. Thornton Hunt also regards Shelley as having had very great ability to grapple with such affairs, though his own appreciation of his powers in that line was inadequate ; and Mr. Trelawny tells me that Shelley could do what few Englishmen can—hold his own perfectly well in personal bargaining with Italian tradesmen. In fact, while he would sacrifice anything for a principle, would fly in the face of all sorts of opinions and conventions, and would incur any amount of personal inconvenience to do a generous act, there is nothing, in Shelley's career as a grown man, to show that he was ill-fitted to cope with the world on its own terms. Not honesty alone, but highmindedness as well, is in one sense the best policy. There were no caprices, no pettinesses, no backslidings, to lower him in the eyes of such people as were capable of rightly estimating him. It is the tone of a hero, not a braggart, that we hear in those memorable words of his to Trelawny—" I always go on until I am stopped, and I never *am* stopped."

After passing a fortnight in the same hotel, the two travelling parties separated ; Byron and Polidori moving into the Villa Diodati, and Shelley, with Mary and Miss Clairmont, into a small house hard-by on the Mont Blanc side of the Lake. The Villa Diodati is very beautifully situated on the high banks, named Belle Rive, of the Lake near Coligny. Shelley's house was termed the Maison Chapuis or Campagne Mont Alègre : he and his would sometimes sleep at Byron's after sitting up talking till dawn. It was a remarkably wet summer ; which did not, however, prevent Shelley from being out on the lake at all hours of the day and night. On the 23rd of June he and Lord Byron, accompanied only by two boatmen and his lordship's servant, undertook a voyage round the Lake, lasting nine days; they visited Meillerie, Clarens, Chillon, Vevai, Lausanne.[1] On this occasion Shelley read for the first time the *Nouvelle Héloïse:* "an overflowing (as it now seems, surrounded by the scenes which it has so wonderfully peopled) of sublimest genius, and more than human sensibility." He would have liked to weep at the so-called Bosquet de Julie. In sailing near St. Gingoux (the scene of a similar incident in the *Nouvelle Héloïse*) the voyagers were overtaken by a tempest, and, through the mismanagement of one of the boatmen, were very nearly upset. Shelley, who somehow could never be taught to swim, considered himself in imminent danger of drowning. He refused assistance, sat on a locker, grasped the rings at both ends, and said he would go down. "I felt in this near prospect of death" (he wrote to Peacock on the 12th of July) "a mixture of sensations, among which terror entered, though but subordinately. My feelings would have been less painful had I been alone: but I knew that my companion would have attempted to save me, and I was overcome with humiliation when I thought that his life might have been risked to preserve mine."

This lake-trip with Byron was succeeded by a land-trip with Mary and Miss Clairmont. On the 20th of July the three started for Chamouni, Mont Blanc, the Source of the Arveiron, and the Glacier of Montanvert; he was nearly lost in a *mauvais pas* on the road to Montanvert. It would be no use to attempt here to give the details: the reader should consult the poem of *Mont Blanc*, composed on this occasion, and the letters which Shelley wrote at the time. I can only make room for a brief reference to the king of mountains. "Pinnacles of snow intolerably bright, part of the chain connected with Mont Blanc, shone through the clouds at intervals on high. I never knew— I never imagined—what mountains were before. The immensity of these aërial summits excited, when they suddenly burst upon the sight, a sentiment of ecstatic wonder not unallied to madness. And remember, this was all one scene: it all pressed home to our regard and our imagination. Though it embraced

---

[1] A letter from Shelley to Mr. Peacock, dated 17th July 1816, was in 1869 disposed of in the Dillon sale. The auctioneer's catalogue says that it " speaks of private affairs, choice of house in England, intended tour, philosophical remarks, acquaintance with Lord Byron, his character, long and descriptive account of a nine days' journey to Vevai and neighbourhood with Lord B. ; Rousseau's *Julie*, Castle of Chillon, &c. 'Lord Byron,' he says, 'is an exceedingly interesting person; and, as such, is it not to be regretted that he is a slave to the vilest and most vulgar prejudices, and as mad as the winds?'" This remarkable passage about Byron does not appear in any of the published letters.

a vast extent of space, the snowy pyramids which shot into the bright blue sky seemed to overhang our path : the ravine, clothed with gigantic pines, and black with its depth below, so deep that the very roaring of the untameable Arve, which rolled through it, could not be heard above—all was as much our own as if we had been the creators of such impressions, in the minds of others, as now occupied our own.   Nature was the poet whose harmony held our spirits more breathless than that of the divinest."   Shelley purchased near Mont Blanc "a large collection of all the seeds of rare Alpine plants, with their names written upon the outside of the papers that contain them. These I mean to colonize in my garden in England" [Mr. Peacock was at this time engaged in looking out a house for Shelley to reside in], "and to permit you [Peacock] to make what choice you please from them."

In the album kept for visitors at the Chartreuse at Montanvert Shelley found that his last predecessor had written some of the platitudes—well-meant platitudes they may be called when they are set down with any distinct meaning at all—about "Nature and Nature's God."   The author of *Queen Mab* took up the pen, and signed his name with the definition

είμι φιλάνθρωπος δημωκράτικός τ' άθεός τε.[1]

Some one added μωρός; and that was possibly the most sensible performance of the three.

Returning to his Genevese villa, Shelley resumed his habitual intercourse with Byron, and also with his old admiration Matthew Gregory Lewis, and had much spectral converse with both of them : he reasonably controverted the position which they advanced, that no one could consistently believe in ghosts without believing in a God.   Lewis, indeed, had already, at some earlier interview, been turning the thoughts of the visitors towards the supernatural ; and at his instance the whole party had undertaken to write tales of an unearthly or fantastic character.   In the long-run only two stories resulted from this suggestion ; the far-renowned *Frankenstein* of Mrs. Shelley, and *The Vampyre* by Dr. Polidori, embodying the nucleus of a tale sketched out by Byron.   Rather later, on the 18th of June, occurred an often-repeated incident, which is thus authentically jotted down in the physician's diary.   " After tea, 12 o'clock, really began to talk ghostly.   Lord Byron repeated some verses

---

[1] The spelling, at which Mr. Swinburne expresses the horror of a He lenist, is copied *literatim.*

of Coleridge's *Christabel,* of the witch's breast; when silence
ensued, and Shelley, suddenly shrieking, and putting his hands
to his head, ran out of the room with a candle. Threw water
in his face, and after gave him ether. He was looking at Mrs.
Shelley, and suddenly thought of a woman he had heard of who
had eyes instead of nipples; which, taking hold of his mind,
horrified him." Medwin says[1] that this story of the pectoral
eyes was to have been the subject-matter of the romance to be
written by Shelley, along with his wife's *Frankenstein;* which,
indeed, is possible enough, though it *may* only be a confusion
of incidents on the biographer's part. In illustration of the
vividness of Shelley's feelings in such matters it may be allow-
able to quote here another instance, though proper to an earlier
date, some time in 1815. He was then writing a *Catalogue of
the Phænomena of Dreams, as connecting Sleeping and Waking,*
forming part of *Speculations on Metaphysics;* and had come to
the mention of an ordinary country-view which he had seen
near Oxford, and which singularly corresponded to some dream
of his own in past time. Having written up to this point, Shelley finishes with—"Here I was obliged to leave off, overcome
by thrilling horror." And Mrs. Shelley adds:—"I remember
well his coming to me from writing it, pale and agitated, to
seek refuge in conversation from the fearful emotions it excited. No man, as these fragments prove, had such keen
sensations as Shelley. His nervous temperament was wound
up by the delicacy of his health to an intense degree of sensibility; and, while his active mind pondered for ever upon, and
drew conclusions from, his sensations, his reveries increased
their vivacity, till they mingled with and made one with
thought, and both became absorbing and tumultuous, even
to physical pain."

The Shelleys and Miss Clairmont left Geneva on the 29th of
August; and returned by Dijon and Hâvre, reaching London
about the 7th of September.

XIV.—HARRIET'S SUICIDE.

While the Shelleys were in Switzerland, Mr. Peacock had
settled at Great Marlow in Buckinghamshire: they paid him
a visit there in the earlier part of September, and selected a
house for themselves in the same town. Pending its being
fitted up, the poet stayed at Bath. Here he received news of

[1] *Conversations with Byron,* p. 150.

5

two suicides. The first was that of Fanny Godwin, who, having gone to Swansea, prior to paying a visit to her two maternal aunts in Ireland, suddenly poisoned herself with laudanum on the night of the 9th of October. No adequate motive could ever be assigned for this act: a hopeless passion for Shelley has sometimes been surmised, but this remains as a conjecture to which credence is advisedly refused by qualified inquirers. The second suicide touched the poet still more nearly. On the 9th of November Harriet Shelley drowned herself in the Serpentine, the body remaining unrecovered up to the 10th of December. Thus, in gloom, abasement, and despair, closed the young life which had been so bright and charming in the bridal days of 1811. The exact course of Harriet's life since June 1814 has never been accurately disclosed; and there is no lack of reason why, even if one had at command details as yet unpublished, one should hesitate to bring them forward. I shall confine myself to reproducing the most definite statement[1] as yet made on the subject—that of Mr. Thornton Hunt; omitting only one unpleasant expression which I have grounds (from two independent and unbiassed sources of information) to suppose overcharged. He unreservedly allows, with other biographers, that there was nothing to censure in Harriet's conjugal conduct before the separation; "but subsequently she forfeited her claim to a return, even in the eye of the law. If she left [Shelley],[2] it would appear that she herself was deserted in turn by a man in a very humble grade of life, and it was in consequence of this desertion that she killed herself." The same author says that, before this event, Mr. Westbrook's faculties had begun to fail; he had treated Harriet with harshness, "and she was driven from the paternal roof. This Shelley did not know at the time." Another writer[3] represents that Harriet —poor uncared-for young creature—suffered great privations, and sank to the lowest grade of misery. De Quincey says that she was stung by calumnies incidental to the position of a woman separated from her husband, and was oppressed by the

---

[1] The "most definite," save a statement, to the same effect as the omitted passage, made by some base calumniator in the *Literary Gazette*, in a review of *Queen Mab*, during Shelley's lifetime—and made in that instance as a charge against Shelley far more than against Harriet.

[2] I do not see the force of this expression. It is certain that in one sense Harriet did leave Shelley; and equally certain that (to say the very least) her leaving him was *less* of a voluntary act on her part than his leaving her was on his.

[3] C. R. S., in *Notes and Queries*, 2nd ser. vol. v. p. 373. His statement may perhaps be of no more authority on the point above cited than when he says that Mr. Westbrook died insolvent before Harriet's suicide, and that this took place " in the great basin of the Green Park."

loneliness of her abode—which seems to be rather a vague version of the facts. Mr. Kegan Paul affirms distinctly, "The immediate cause of her death was that her father's door was shut against her, though he had at first sheltered her and her children. This was done by order of her sister, who would not allow Harriet access to the bedside of her dying father." He can hardly, however, have been "dying" in November, 1816, as he took legal action against Shelley in 1817. In any case we will be very little disposed to cast stones at the forlorn woman who sought and found an early cleansing in the waters of death—a final refuge from all pangs of desertion, of repudiation, or of self-scorn.

I find nothing to suggest otherwise than that Shelley had lost sight of Harriet for several months preceding her suicide; though it might seem natural to suppose that he continued to keep up some sort of knowledge, if not of how *she* went on, at least of the state of his young children Ianthe and Charles. At all events, be he blameworthy or not in the original matter of the separation, or on the ground of recent obliviousness of Harriet or his children, it is an ascertained fact that her suicide was in no way immediately connected with any act or default of his —but with a train of circumstances for which the responsibility lay with Harriet herself, or had to be divided between her and the antecedent conditions of various kinds. It is moreover a fact clearly attested by Hogg that she had for years had a strange proclivity towards suicide — towards starting the topic, and even scheming the act. I know also, from a MS. letter of Shelley's written very soon after his elopement with Harriet, that, in the complaints of ill-treatment which she had made leading up to that event, a resolution of suicide was not pretermitted. "Early in our acquaintance," says Hogg [*i.e.*, in 1811], "the good Harriet asked me, 'What do you think of suicide?' She often discoursed of her purpose of killing herself some day or other, and at great length, in a calm resolute manner. She told me that at school, where she was very unhappy, as she said (but I could never discover *why* she was so, for she was treated with much kindness, and exceedingly well instructed), she had conceived and contrived sundry attempts and purposes of destroying herself. . . . She got up in the night, she said, sometimes, with a fixed determination of making away with herself. . . . She spoke of self-murder serenely before strangers; and at a dinner-party I have heard her describe her feelings, opinions, and intentions, with respect to

suicide, with prolix earnestness. . . . The poor girl's mono-
mania of self-destruction (which we long looked upon as a vain
fancy, a baseless delusion, an inconsequent hallucination of the
mind) amused us occasionally for some years : eventually it
proved a sad reality, and drew forth many bitter tears." Again,
about the middle of 1813, we find :—"She had not renounced
her eternal purpose of suicide ; and she still discoursed of some
scheme of self-destruction as coolly as another lady would ar-
range a visit to an exhibition or a theatre." All this requires to
be well pondered, as raising a strong presumption that Harriet
was a person likely enough to commit suicide, even without
being urged thereto by any great degree of unhappiness, or
other forcible motive. At the same time, it is true that there
may be a deal of talk about self-destruction, with very little
intention of it ; and Harriet *may* have caught the trick of such
talk from Shelley himself—who (as Mr. Hogg says) "frequently
discoursed poetically, pathetically, and with fervid melancholy
fancies, of suicide ; but I do not believe that he ever contemplated seriously and practically the perpetration of the crime."[1]
This last conclusion of Hogg's, however, will be considerably
modified in the minds of my readers who notice that Shelley
did really poison himself in the early and agitating days of his
passion for Mary Godwin; also of those who recollect how
Trelawny records that Shelley wrote on 18th June 1822, asking
that devoted friend to procure him, if possible, a small quantity
of the strongest prussic acid. "You remember we talked of it
the other night, and we both expressed a wish to possess it :
my wish was serious, and sprung from the desire of avoiding
needless suffering. I need not tell you I have no intention of
suicide at present ; but I confess it would be a comfort to me
to hold in my possession that golden key to the chamber of
perpetual rest."

Shelley, on receiving the news of his wife's suicide, hurried
up to London ; and now began his more special intimacy with
Leigh Hunt and his family. All authorities agree in testifying
to the painful severity with which the poet felt the shock, and
the permanence of the impression. Leigh Hunt says that Shelley
never forgot it ; it tore him to pieces for a time, and he felt re-

---

[1] Mr. Furnivall, son of the surgeon at Egham who attended the second Mrs. Shelley in
her confinement in 1817, and in whom (as Mr. Peacock reports) the poet had great confidence, tells me an amusing anecdote bearing on this point. The surgeon after attending
a *post mortem* examination, arrived at Shelley's house, and there found Leigh Hunt.
The two friends, especially Hunt, were talking rather big about the expediency and
attractions of suicide, when Mr. Furnivall proffered his case of surgical instruments for
immediate use—but without result.

morse at having brought Harriet, in the first instance, into an atmosphere of thought and life for which her strength of mind had not qualified her. Thornton Hunt speaks in the same strain : " I am well aware that he had suffered severely, and that he continued to be haunted by certain recollections, partly real and partly imaginative, which pursued him like an Orestes." Medwin says that the sorrow ever after threw a cloud over Shelley : indeed, he goes so far as to speak of its having brought on temporary derangement—which may probably be true in only a limited sense. Peacock says that " Harriet's untimely fate occasioned him deep agony of mind, which he felt the more because for a long time he kept the feeling to himself." Mr. Trelawny tells me that even at the late period when he knew Shelley—1822—the impression of extreme pain which the end of Harriet had caused to the poet was still vividly present and operative. Mr. Garnett adverts to a series of letters, not yet given to the world, written by Shelley about the middle of December, and therefore under the immediate pressure of his misfortune, which " afford the most unequivocal testimony of the grief and horror occasioned by the tragical incident. Yet self-reproach formed no element of his sorrow, in the midst of which he could proudly say '—— and ——' (mentioning two dry unbiassed men of business) ' every one does me full justice, bears testimony to the uprightness and liberality of my conduct to her.'" Mr. Garnett, indeed, concludes that, if Shelley, soon after the suicide of Harriet, appeared calm and unmoved to Peacock (as that writer affirms), this was presumably a symptom of his want of full expansive confidence in Peacock, rather than of his actual self-possession. I think, however, that such an argument may be pushed too far. The feelings of a strong but variously impressible character like Shelley's under such a conjuncture of circumstances are of a very mixed description : what is called " sentiment" does not cover the whole area. "Sentimentalism " is of course a very different thing from sentiment : but I may here take occasion to quote the noticeable statement of De Quincey, in allusion to a description he had heard of Shelley's personal appearance :—" This gave to the chance observer an impression that he was tainted, even in his external deportment, by some excess of sickly sentimentalism ; from which I believe that in all stages of his life he was remarkably free." For my part, I can imagine that he was not only, in a certain way, calm enough at times immediately after Harriet's death, whether to the eyes of Peacock or of other friends, but even that he could (as I am assured [1] he did some few months later) apply to her the emphatic term " a frantic idiot." He must no doubt have regarded her later career as one marked by great want of self-respect, and may have both felt and expressed himself strongly now and again, without derogating from the substantial rectitude and tenderness of his nature—qualities disputable only by creatures of the type of those Quarterly Reviewers who, at the same time that they represented Shelley's life as a compound of " low pride, cold selfishness, and unmanly cruelty," discerned also that " the predominating characteristic of his poetry was its frequent and total want of meaning," and that the *Prometheus* was " in sober sadness drivelling prose run mad," and " looked upon the question of Mr. Shelley's poetical merits as at an end." [2] And so indeed it was after the spawning of that opprobrium of the British and modern Muse, the *Prometheus Unbound.* " These be thy gods, O Israel !"

XV.—MARRIAGE AND MARRIED LIFE WITH MARY.

On the 30th of December 1816 Shelley married his dearly-loved Mary, at St. Mildred's Church in the City of London. Godwin made marriage an express condition of his continuing further intercourse with Shelley. Yet they had not all this while remained wholly estranged—some communication between them (very frigid at first) having recommenced as early at least as January 1815.

The Shelleys soon afterwards entered upon their residence at Marlow, Miss Clairmont and her brother Charles being along with them. Mr. Peacock was close by, and they saw something also of their next neighbour Mr. Maddocks (not the landlord and friend of the Tanyrallt days): of other mere neighbours they knew little or nothing. " I am not wretch enough to tolerate an acquaintance" was Shelley's phrase. The house was a large one situated away

---

[1] By Mr. Furnivall, who heard it repeatedly from his father.
[2] These expressions are accurately quoted from the *Quarterly Review* of April 1819 and October 1821; critiques of *Laon and Cythna*, the *Revolt of Islam*, and *Rosalind and Helen*, in the former article, and of *Prometheus Unbound* in the latter. Even these phrases fall short of what we find in the *Literary Gazette* of 1820, critiques of *The Cenci* and *Prometheus*. *The Cenci*, we are told, is the most abominable work of the time, and seems to be the production of some fiend : the reviewer hopes never again to see a book " so stamped with pollution, impiousness, and infamy." *Prometheus* is " little else but absolute raving: and, were we not assured to the contrary, we should take it for granted that the author was lunatic, as his principles are ludicrously wicked, and his poetry a *mélange* of nonsense, cockneyism, poverty, and pedantry." Further on we find the critic speak of "the stupid trash of this delirious dreamer," and "this tissue of insufferable buffoonery."

from the river, with extensive gardens and numerous rooms, well furnished by Shelley, and taken on a lease for twenty-one years. It is still standing, but partly converted into a beershop. Shelley lived here like a country-gentleman on a small scale, and probably (considering the lavish generosity he was continually exercising in other ways) beyond his means, though he was not either wasteful or unreckoning : friends were continually with him, and he almost kept open house. There were three servants, if not a fourth assistant, including a Swiss nursemaid for the infant William, named Elise. Shelley kept a well-sized boat for either sailing or rowing, but no horse or carriage. The boat had been named by him the *Vaga*, and so lettered : some humourist added the final syllable *bond*. It is said that he would frequently go to the woods of Bisham at midnight, and repeat his old process of conjuring the devil—who never came : but it seems more probable that he laughed bores to scorn by *saying* he had done this in his nocturnal rambles, than that he really did it. His daily routine of life at Marlow has been thus sketched by Leigh Hunt in a passage frequently quoted. "He rose early in the morning ; walked and read before breakfast ; took that meal sparingly ; wrote and studied the greater part of the morning ; walked and read again ; dined on vegetables (for he took neither meat nor wine) ; conversed with his friends, to whom his house was ever open ; again walked out ; and usually finished with reading to his wife till ten o'clock, when he went to bed. This was his daily existence. His book was generally Plato or Homer, or one of the Greek tragedians, or the Bible, in which last he took a great (though peculiar) and often admiring interest."[1] Shelley's charity at Marlow (as it had before been at Tanyrallt) was exemplary. He had a list of weekly pensioners, and exerted himself in all sorts of ways, equally with purse and person, to relieve the distress of the lacemakers and others in his neighbourhood. In attending some of the poor in their cottages, reckless of infection, he caught a bad attack of ophthalmia. This not only troubled him at the time ; but he had a relapse of the malady at the end of the same year, 1817, severe enough to prevent his reading, and again as late as January 1821.

About March 1817, at Hunt's house in Hampstead, Shelley met Keats, and also the brothers James and Horatio Smith,

---

[1] Mr. Trelawny tells me that such was Shelley's interest in the Bible—the *Old* Testament in especial—that he said on one occasion that, if he could save only one book from a general catastrophe of letters, he would select the Bible. What he particularly valued was its historic and poetic antiquity.

wealthy city-men, and authors of the *Rejected Addresses* and various other witty writings. He became intimate with Horatio, whom he esteemed very highly, and who, when Shelley was at a later date in Italy, transacted many money-matters for him, whether of business or liberality. " Keats did not take to Shelley as kindly as Shelley did to him : being a little too sensitive on the score of his origin, he felt inclined to see in every man of birth a sort of natural enemy ; " [1] and, in his after period of failing health, a certain irritable suspiciousness got possession of him. It seems clear, too, that he set a very mediocre value upon Shelley's poetic performances ; indeed, he regarded him apparently as a mere effervescent tyro, to whom a word or two of good advice, but hardly of encouragement, would be appropriate. On his receiving a copy of *The Cenci*, the only remark he made, having the character of direct criticism, in his letter of acknowledgment, was—" You, I am sure, will forgive me for sincerely remarking that you might curb your magnanimity, and be more of an artist, and load every rift of your subject with ore." And then further on : " I am in expectation of *Prometheus* every day. Could I have but my own wish effected, you would have it still in manuscript, or be but now putting an end to the second act." [2] These phrases may have been strictly sincere, and therefore so far proper for Keats to write : but they were certainly grudging, from the still younger author of so imperfect a production (however glorious in poetic potentialities) as *Endymion* to the author of such a monument of varied power as *The Cenci :* even *Alastor* must, in point of maturity, be placed a good deal ahead of *Endymion.* When we weigh all the habitual jealousies between rival poets, along with the something very like patronizing depreciation vouchsafed by Keats, we shall watch with a warmer glow of sympathy the flood of shining generosity and impetuous loving admiration which the celestial soul of Shelley poured through *Adonais.* His detailed critical opinion of Keats will be more appositely introduced when we come to speak of that poem.

XVI.—THE CHANCERY SUIT.

Meanwhile a Chancery suit had been commenced to determine whether Mr. Percy Bysshe Shelley or Mr. John Westbrook was the more proper person to elicit any intellectual and moral

---

[1] Leigh Hunt's *Autobiography*, pp. 266-7.   [2] *Shelley Memorials*, p. 143.

faculties with which the ruling power of the universe might have gifted the poet's first two children.   In the eyes of a bandaged Justice the retired hotel-keeper proved to be clearly better fitted for this function than the author *in esse* of *Alastor*, and *in posse* of the *Triumph of Life.*

Mr. Westbrook refused to give up, at Shelley's request, the two children to his keeping—and every considerate person will respect the motives and feelings of the father of the unfortunate Harriet in this matter ; and in their name he filed a petition in Chancery, alleging that Shelley had deserted his wife, was in opinion an atheist, and intended to bring up the children in accordance with his own views.   *Queen Mab* was cited in proof of the author's condemnable speculations concerning religion and the relation of the sexes.   The petition also stated that Mr. Westbrook had lately invested £2000 four per cents in the names of trustees, to be handed over eventually to the children, and the dividends applied meantime to their maintenance and education.   Shelley's legal adviser in this suit was Mr. Longdill, and Brougham is stated to have been employed as counsel —on which side I do not find recorded.   It would appear that Shelley drew up his own replication to the petition, for he speaks of "my Chancery-paper" as "a cold, forced, unimpassioned, insignificant piece of cramped and cautious argument."[1]

The judgment of Lord Chancellor Eldon was delivered on or about the 23rd of August.[2]   The most essential passages run as follows :—" I have carefully looked through the answer of the defendant, to see whether it affects the representation, made in the affidavits filed in support of the petition, and in the exhibits referred to, of the principles and conduct in life of the father in this case.   I do not perceive that the answer does affect the representation, and no affidavits are filed against the petition. . . There is nothing in evidence before me sufficient to authorize me in thinking that this gentleman has changed, before he has arrived at twenty-five, the principles he avowed at nineteen ; and I think there is ample evidence, in the papers and in conduct, that no such change has taken place. . . . This is a case in which, as the matter appears to me, the father's principles cannot be misunderstood ; in which his conduct, which I cannot but consider as highly immoral, has been established in

---

[1] See p. 421.
[2] According to Medwin, 17th March ; and this date reappears in other publications. But a letter from Mr. Longdill, dated 5th August 1817, cited in the *Shelley Memorials*, p. 75, proves the earlier date to be incorrect.

proof, and established as the effect of those principles—conduct
nevertheless which he represents to himself and to others, not
as conduct to be considered as immoral, but to be recommended
and observed in practice, and as worthy of approbation. I consider this, therefore, as a case in which the father has demonstrated that he must and does deem it to be a matter of duty
which his principles impose on him to recommend, to those
whose opinions and habits he may take upon himself to form,
that conduct, in some of the most important relations of life, as
moral and virtuous, which the law calls upon me to consider as
immoral and vicious—conduct which the law animadverts upon
as inconsistent with the duties of persons in such relations of
life, and which it considers as injuriously affecting both the
interests of such persons and those of the community. I cannot therefore think that I shall be justified in delivering over
these children, for their education, exclusively to what is called
the 'care' to which Mr. Shelley wishes it to be entrusted." [1]
It is stated that the poet had intended to place the children
with a lady thoroughly qualified for such a post, Mrs. Longdill.
The order of the Court of Chancery proceeded to restrain the
father or his agents from taking possession of the infants, or
intermeddling with them till further orders. The case could
have been carried by appeal into the House of Lords ; but probably Shelley felt that he should obtain no redress there, and
he dropped further proceedings. He did not, however, lose
sight of practical contingencies which might affect the case ;
for we find him, as late as 26th January 1819, and all the way
from Naples, writing to Mr. Peacock : "We have reports here
of a change in the English ministry. To what does it amount?
for, besides my national interest in it, I am on the watch to
vindicate my most sacred rights, invaded by the Chancery
Court."

The result was that the children were handed over to the
guardianship of Mr. and Miss Westbrook, and more immediately to that of a clergyman of the Church of England, Dr.
Hume.[2] Shelley, who never saw them again, had to set apart,

---

[1] The judgment of Lord Eldon, it will be observed, says nothing of "desertion" of
Harriet by Shelley. It has been stated to me that his lordship said during the proceedings something to the effect that "Shelley had left the children to starve, and the grandfather had taken them up, and had a right to keep them." But, as the written judgment
is silent on this point, I should presume that Lord Eldon either spoke loosely or was reported unprecisely.
[2] I find this name in a letter from Horatio Smith, dated 13th April 1821, given in the
Shelley Memorials, p. 168. From the same book, p. 75, it appears that a Mr. Kendall
was recommended as a guardian during the suit : whether he actually obtained the
appointment in the first instance I cannot say.

out of his income of £1000 a year, £200 for the children, which sum was regularly deducted by Sir Timothy.[1] At one time, in 1821, some complication ensued; and Shelley, then in Italy, found himself suddenly without a penny of incomings. The matter, however, was pretty soon set right through the intervention of Horatio Smith, and apparently without Sir Timothy's having been privy to the harsh and unneeded stoppage.

Of all the blows brought down upon Shelley by his conscientious adherence, in word and deed, to sincere convictions, this appears to have been the one which he felt most profoundly. He was at this time almost domesticated with the family of Leigh Hunt, then residing in Lisson Grove; and that affectionate and warmly loved and trusted friend attests that the bereaved father could never afterwards venture so much as to mention the children to him. He had some fears moreover that the son of his second nuptials, William, would also be taken away, and he contemplated leaving England in consequence; but nothing came of this. His indignation winged more than one quivering shaft of verse against Lord Eldon. About the same time he was made answerable for some of Harriet's liabilities, incurred without any knowledge on his part, and was in some danger of arrest: this also passed over.

Mary meanwhile continued to reside at Marlow. Here her third child, Clara, was born on the 3rd of September. Shelley was with her at the time; and would walk, or perhaps row, down to Egham, a distance of about sixteen miles, to see the surgeon, Mr. Furnivall, and, on arriving, would take no refreshment beyond a bowl of milk. His exceeding good-nature impressed this gentleman, who considered indeed that Mary was somewhat too free and exacting in ordering her husband about, which he submitted to with the docility of a child. One is more inclined to smile over Shelley's *étourderie* than to attribute to him anything wilfully amiss, when one learns that the larger part of the obstetrical bill remained unpaid at the time of the family's departure from Marlow to Italy, and for ever afterwards.[2]

The fewest words should here be hazarded or wasted regarding the rights or wrongs of the Lord Chancellor's decision. I

---

[1] These are the sums named in the *Shelley Memorials*, p. 75. Yet it would seem afterwards, p. 168, that the sum for Shelley's own use was £880, and for the children only £120 per annum.
[2] I am indebted to Mr. Furnivall's son for these minor but characteristic details.

understand that its legal validity has never been overruled, but that probably it would not now be allowed to count as a precedent. Previous writers have, with befitting fairness, pointed out that it proceeds on the grounds not solely nor strictly of speculative opinion, but of conduct framed according to opinion unrecanted. Without over-refining upon this point, we may say that logical minds which accept as a principle "saving faith," with practice not disjoined therefrom, are entitled, in the ratio of their logicality, to accept Lord Eldon's judgment as righteous; logical minds which affirm this to be unrighteous will, in the like ratio, demur to the theory of the saving faith. It is a very spacious arena for discussion; and he who denounces the judgment or the judge in this English "Mortara case," without going several steps further, is presumably at least as much of a partisan as of a reasoner.

XVII.—THE REVOLT OF ISLAM.

His reverses did not depress Shelley, but nerved him to greater exertions. While the Lord Chancellor was about to brand him as less fit for the most rudimentary duties of social life than any other man in England, he was preparing to prove himself one of the few men then living in the world predestined to immortality. *Laon and Cythna*, now known as *The Revolt of Islam*, was written in the summer and early autumn of 1817. It was composed chiefly as the poet was seated on a high promontory of Bisham Wood, or was drifting in his boat. The principal particulars regarding the genesis of the poem are to be found in its preface, dedication, and notes; to these therefore I refer the reader.

Some copies of *Laon and Cythna* were ready for delivery by Christmas 1817; but, after a very few had been issued—(it is generally said, only three, but one finds reason to believe there were rather more than this)—the publisher, Mr. Ollier, became alarmed at the audacities of the poem, especially its main incident of conjugal love between a brother and sister; and, under strong pressure from him, Shelley reluctantly consented to make some modifications. It has been said that he was at last "convinced of the propriety"[1] of so doing : at any rate, he did it. The changes are not numerous, affecting only fifty-five lines besides the title-page and some sentences in the preface. Captain Medwin—so he informs us—was told by Shelley

---

[1] *Shelley Memorials*, p. 83.

that this poem, and the *Endymion* of Keats, were written in
friendly rivalry; and that the compact was to produce both
works within six months, which Shelley at all events very
nearly managed.

It was a great effort, and a near approach to a great poem;
clearly, in more senses than one, greater than *Alastor*, though
its vast scale and unmeasured ambition place it still more obviously in the category of imperfect achievements. Gorgeous
ideality, humanitarian enthusiasm, and a passionate rush of invention, more especially of the horrible, go hand in hand in the
Revolt of Islam. It affects the mind something like an en-
chanted palace of the *Arabian Nights.* One is wonderstruck
both at the total creation, and at every shifting aspect of it; but
one does not expect to find in it any detail of the absolute
artistic perfection of a Greek gem, nor any inmate of consummate interest to the heart. Its flashing and sounding chambers
are full of everything save what one most loves at last, repose
and companionship.

With these few wretchedly inadequate—not to say presump-
tuous—remarks, I must leave the *Revolt of Islam;* only further
observing that, whatever its imperfections of plan and execution, it is not alone a marvellous well-head of poetry, but, in
conception and tone, and in its womanly ideal embodied in
Cythna, a remarkably original work: it was greatly unlike any
poem that had preceded (so far as I know), and even the
demon of imitation has left it solitary.

XVIII.—SHELLEY QUITS ENGLAND FOR ITALY :—ROSALIND AND HELEN.

Another pulmonary attack towards the end of the autumn of
1817 made Shelley think gravely of what it would behove him
to do ; and he eventually resolved to go to Italy (he and Hogg
had studied the Italian language in 1813), with no definite idea
of when he would find it practicable to return. He never did
return : the prophet who, in the spring of 1818, quitted England, a grudging and unwitting stepmother, was never again to
encounter in person dishonour from his own country and his
own people.

Health was the motive put forward by Shelley for his departure ; perhaps the state of his finances also had something to
do with it, and more particularly the involvements which he was
perpetually incurring through his unbounded munificence to
others, and in especial he had to consign the infant Allegra to

the care of her father, Byron, at his requisition. It is a remark of Mr. Thornton Hunt, and I have no doubt a true and suggestive one, that a fixed characteristic of Shelley was this—that if he had one sufficient cause for any action, he would specify that, and ignore all minor motives ; and that he was thus, without any real foundation, sometimes regarded as uncandid or reserved. This would explain how he may, with entire personal truth and self-consistency, have simply alleged health as his reason for leaving England ; although, had the motive of health been absent, other causes also would have sufficed.

To give some idea of Shelley in one of the most prominent of his personal traits, I will here cite, regardless of the sequence of date, a few out of the many acts of generosity recorded of him. Some others have been mentioned already, and how many more remain unrecorded ! The reader will bear in mind that the income of Shelley and his family was, from 1812 to 1814, something like £400 a year; from 1815 to the middle of 1817, £1000 ; and from the latter date onwards, after the deduction made under the order in Chancery, about £800.

" He was able, by restricting himself to a diet more simple than the fare of the most austere anchorite, and by refusing himself horses, and the other gratifications that appear properly to belong to his station (and of which he was in truth very fond), to bestow upon men of letters, whose merits were of too high an order to be rightly estimated by their own generation, donations large indeed if we consider from how narrow a source they flowed :"[1] he was besides most delicate in the manner of conferring such obligations. He repeatedly gave away all his money before reaching a coach-office, and was consequently obliged to walk to town ; and he once entered the grounds of his close neighbour at Marlow, Mr. Maddocks, without shoes, having bestowed his on a poor woman. Almost immediately after his expulsion from Oxford, he offered through his father's solicitor to accept, in lieu of his claim to the entailed estate of £6000 per annum (perhaps he had not then a clear idea of the amount), an annuity of £200, leaving all the residue for his sisters—an act of almost unjustifiably self-oblivious good-nature. He proposed at one time to raise money on a *post obit*, to settle it on a lady whom Medwin was desirous of marrying ; but this his cousin, with all right feeling, declined. During his stay at Marlow, having written a pamphlet named *A Proposal for*

---

[1] Hogg, vol. i. p. 245. I suppose the case more particularly, though not alone, here referred to, is that of Mr. Peacock, already mentioned in our pages.

putting Reform to the Vote throughout the Country,[1] he proffered £100, a full tenth of his income for a year, to further the
project. In the last four or five years of his life he frequently
assisted Leigh Hunt; and in one instance (perhaps towards the
end of 1818)[2] presented him with £1400, which he had raised
by an effort with a view to relieving his friend from debt. He
produced large sums—I believe about £6000 in all—to pay
off Godwin's debts. The following singular jotting occurs in
Dr. Polidori's diary: "When starving, a friend to whom he had
given £2000, though he knew it, would not come near him."
That Shelley was ever "starving" is no doubt not true, though
it is highly consistent with probability that he sometimes could
not count upon daily money to meet daily necessities; the
"£2000" may be mythical in a like *degree* with the starvation,
rather than absolutely so. His personal disinterestedness,
apart from liberality to others, was equally marked. Leigh
Hunt says, "He had only to become a yea-and-nay man in the
House of Commons, to be one of the richest men in Sussex.
He declined it, and lived upon a comparative pittance. Even
the fortune that he would ultimately have inherited, as secured
to his person, was petty in comparison." I presume that there
is substantial truth in this ; save that the incident referred to is
probably the same which I have already traced elsewhere with
a different colouring—the offer of a large fortune on condition
that he would entail it on his eldest son. Upon Percy's refusal,
the money, it is stated, went to his brother John.[3] Medwin says
also that he refused, at a time of pecuniary straits, an offer
of £3000 from Sir John Shelley-Sidney to resign his contingent
interest in the Penshurst estates. This is given as an instance
of the romantic value he attached to his indirect connection
with the descent from Sir Philip Sidney, and may be a
figment.

[1] There was also a second pamphlet written at Marlow, relative to some recent political
executions—"We pity the Plumage, but forget the Dying Bird. An Address to the
People on the Death of the Princess Charlotte. By the Hermit of Marlow." [Privately
printed, and also reprinted of late years.]

[2] I found this surmise on an expression in a letter from Hunt, 9th March 1819, "You
know the difficulties which I foolishly suffered to remain upon me when Shelley did that
noble action." (*Hunt's Correspondence*, vol. i. p. 126.) Medwin, however, puts the
affair later, at the time when Hunt was about leaving England, or towards the autumn of
1821. He also introduces into this matter "Horace Smith, who not only advanced the
passage-money, but a very considerable sum for the payment of his debts—as much, I
think Shelley told me, as £1400." (*Life of Shelley*, vol. ii. p. 137.) Of course we are to
understand that, though Smith *advanced* the money, the *donor* of it was still Shelley.

[3] *Biographie des Contemporains*, 1834. There are many incorrectnesses in this article
about Shelley, and in others in French books. I should therefore regard the statement in
the text as merely a rumour requiring verification, were it not that indisputable MS.
authority exists for the facts as narrated by me on p. 32.

I have mentioned above a pamphlet on the subject of Parliamentary Reform. Shelley (as we have seen) did not give his name on the title-page, but figured as " The Hermit of Marlow." The whirligig of time has brought-in many revenges to Shelley, and this among others—that the Tories found it their interest and necessity to pass in 1867 almost the very scheme of Reform which the poet and " dreamer," the atheist and democrat, had suggested in 1817; for it makes little difference whether we speak of a payment of money in " direct taxes " or in " rating." " He disavowed any wish to establish universal suffrage at once, or to do away with monarchy and aristocracy, while so large a proportion of the people remained disqualified by ignorance for sharing in the government of the country, though he looked forward to a time when the world would be enabled to ' disregard the symbols of its childhood; ' and he suggested that the qualificationfor the suffrage should be *the registry of the voter's name as one who paid a certain small sum in direct taxes.*" [1]

After staying in London towards the beginning of 1818 to settle some business, Shelley, with his wife and Miss Clairmont, left for Italy on the 11th of March, and proceeded straight to Milan. The infants followed on from England in due course. The party spent about a month in Milan, visiting thence the Lake of Como, where they thought of passing the summer; but this proved unfeasible, and early in May they went on to Pisa.[2] Here, on this first visit, they found little satisfaction, and shifted after three or four days to Leghorn; where, in the Via Grande, they stayed till the 5th of June, and made acquaintance with Mr. and Mrs. Gisborne. This lady had been intimate with Mary Wollstonecraft, and was a friend of Godwin, who indeed had wished to marry her after Mary's death. She was highly amiable and accomplished, and " completely unprejudiced; " and Shelley, though he spoke of her in one instance as " the antipodes of enthusiasm," found much pleasure and satisfaction in her society both now and afterwards. Mr. Gisborne also was a man of extensive scholarship and of liberal views, which the poet supposed to be the reflex of those of his wife. Shelley thought him dull—an opinion from which Mr. Peacock afterwards saw reason to differ, and which

---

[1] *Shelley Memorials*, pp. 87–8. Condensed from the final paragraph of the pamphlet.
[2] Many interesting details as to the sojourn and localities in Italy will be found in Mrs Shelley's notes in these volumes. I therefore touch upon them the more lightly.

does not seem to have affected the pleasantness of Shelley's own intercourse with him.

From Leghorn the Shelleys and Miss Clairmont went to the Bagni di Lucca. Here he finished *Rosalind and Helen*, a poem which he had begun at Marlow, and laid aside, setting on it only a mediocre value. His wife now prevailed on him to complete it. Shelley has evidently put a good deal of *himself* into this poem—the character and broken health of Lionel, his connexion with Helen, and the legal complication whereby Rosalind is bereft of her children; and, if we were to assess the merits of a poem by the number of beautiful lines and exquisite images it comprises, we should have to accord a very honourable place to *Rosalind and Helen*. On the whole, however, it may be pronounced a comparative failure, being a somewhat *washy* performance. We read it because it is Shelley's, and are repaid for the enterprise by its lovely and thick-coming fancies; but, under other circumstances, we should not read it, nor consider its individual charms a sufficient inducement. Shelley published the poem in 1819, but still cared little about it. In July, feeling for the nonce incapable of original composition, he took up the *Symposium* of Plato, and made in ten mornings' work his beautiful but abridged and not rigidly correct version of it. He also began, but never finished, a prefatory essay to the *Symposium, On the Literature, the Arts, and the Manners, of the Athenians*, intended to exhibit the diversities between antique and modern life and modes of thought.

XIX.—JULIAN AND MADDALO.

On the 17th of August 1818 Shelley went to Venice, where Byron was staying: Mrs. Shelley wrote that he had started " on important business." He arrived at midnight of the 22nd, in a storm of wind, rain, and lightning, and saw Byron on the ensuing day: they rode along the Lido, and repeated this exercise almost every evening. Byron offered Shelley and his family the use of his villa, I Capuccini, near Este, not far off; and they spent a few weeks here, varied by visits to Venice itself. They quitted Este on the 7th of November, going southwards.

During the stay here, Shelley lost the youngest of his four surviving children. Little Clara, who bore a resemblance to her father, suffered from heat and teething; the parents hurried

6

from Este to Venice for advice—so hastily that they had forgotten to bring their passports, and so impetuously that they made way nevertheless; but to no purpose—Clara died on reaching the city.

The visit to Venice produced one imperishable result—the poem of *Julian and Maddalo*, which was written, wholly or chiefly, in the villa at Este. Beautiful as is *Alastor*, and splendid the *Revolt of Islam*—impossible as it would have been for any but a very great poet in his early prime to produce either of these works—it cannot be said that the one or other is, on its own sole showing, the sufficient basis for such a renown as that of Shelley now is, and will be till the extinction of the English language. Each of them is an *expanding* of power —each a progression towards a goal; each would be a divine suggestion had no perfect development ensued afterwards, but still a suggestion, and not absolutely a monument. Time, to whom the ruin of an empire is child's-play, and who had lately had his will with that of a Napoleon, might have addressed himself to the rather tougher task of extinguishing the *Revolt of Islam*, and might possibly have succeeded, had that poem not been followed up by others greater, and in especial more ripe and rounded, than itself. But *Julian and Maddalo* was the abolition of the anarch's power over Shelley : as he set the finishing hand to that work, he ceased to be a subject of Time, and became a citizen of Eternity.

I shall not here attempt any analysis of the beauties of *Julian and Maddalo*, and still less any discussion of such blemishes as criticism can detect in it. But I must point to its position amid the astonishing series of masterpieces which its still very youthful author (twenty-six years of age) now found himself inspired to produce. Along with *Prometheus Unbound* and *The Cenci*, *Julian and Maddalo* appears to me to complete the supreme trine of Shelley's genius.[1] *Prometheus* (with which one might associate the *Witch of Atlas* as hardly if at all less perfect, *Epipsychidion*, and, had it been completed, no doubt the *Triumph of Life*) represents ideality ; *The Cenci*, tragedy ; *Julian and Maddalo*, a poet's perception of the familiar. The *Letter to Maria Gisborne* illustrates that same faculty, under

---

[1] *I. e.*, confining the question to works of considerable length. If I might venture to express an opinion on the point, I should say that the very finest piece of work—creation and fashioning combined—which he ever produced is the *Ode to the West Wind* (vol.iii. p. 48) : but that is short. The *Stanzas written in Dejection near Naples, Ode to Liberty, Hymn of Apollo, Skylark,* and *Lines written on hearing the News of the Death of Napoleon,* are brothers *very* near the throne—not to speak of others

more simple conditions : no other poem of Shelley's can be cited in this connection. It would be a great mistake to regard *Julian and Maddalo* as simply a familiar poem, such as, from differing points of view, are many of Wordsworth's or (in our own days) the *Dora* of Tennyson : neither is it an express idealization of the familiar. Were it intended as either of these, it must be called a patchy piece of execution. It is rather (as I have endeavoured above to express the thing) a poet's perception of the familiar : and the deepest property of it is the perfect limpidity of mind and word—I take no count here of mere difficulties of diction—whereby the poet makes the thing perceptible from his own poetic point of view to others also who are not poets. There is no apparent *theory* of how to produce such a result, but a concrete production of it. I am not sure that the same thing had ever been exactly attempted before, or has been thoroughly attained since, at least in English. One cannot cite any writing of Shakespeare as a precedent; for, though he is of course quite as familiar and quite as poetic in motive, and even more so in numerous details, there are in him other prominent elements of perception—as the romantic and humorous—which take the result into a different class. The same, *mutatis mutandis*, may be said of Byron's *Don Juan*—which was begun just about the time that *Julian and Maddalo* was written, but Shelley, I believe, heard nothing of it then.

The fact is that the range and variety of Shelley's powers have been very much undervalued, and even mis-stated. You talk of Shelley to an ordinary poetic reader, and find that the only common ground of criticism regarding him is his ideality —his flights of speculation, imagination, and imagery, which are regarded (and justly in many particular instances) as merging into the fanciful and dreamlike. You cite *The Cenci :* it is then unhesitatingly admitted that Shelley demonstrated a tragic power of the first class in recent centuries, but even this does not sink deep into the conviction. In sober truth, Shelley showed his mastery in six several and very diverse lines of poetic faculty; and was in some of them unprecedented or unparagoned, and in none other than original. I have already specified three phases of his poetry—1, the ideal (*Prometheus, Witch of Atlas, Triumph of Life, Epipsychidion, Adonais,* and others); 2, the tragic (*The Cenci*); 3, the poetic-familiar (*Julian and Maddalo*). To these must be added—4, the lyric (choruses of *Prometheus* and *Hellas,* and a multitude of minor poems);

6 *

5, the grotesque (*Peter Bell the Third*, and, as a less perfect but still noticeable example, *Swellfoot the Tyrant*); 6, poetic translation, in which, for uniform and exalted success in varying lines of work, I presume him to be unrivalled among Englishmen—and this may be said without advancing the untenable proposition that he is always absolutely side by side with his original in either spirit or detail. Shelley was decidedly adverse to the general run and mode of translations from the poets; and no wonder he was so, when we consider his own thrilling susceptibility to poetry, and capacity for rendering it into another tongue. It would be only fair to add, as a 7th phase of attainment, the didactic-declamatory, exemplified in *Queen Mab;* for in that department (as already remarked) this poem, however juvenile and imperfect, and however unsatisfactory the class of work may itself be, stands uncommonly high. I perceive only one sort of thing which Shelley attempted with indifferent success—sustained narrative. That is the main practical ingredient, though not the intellectual motive power, of the three early works, *Alastor*, the *Revolt of Islam*, and *Rosalind and Helen*. In each of these instances, or at any rate the first two, he succeeded well in allying narrative to idealism, but in all three there is a peccant element of unrealism, a slippery hold upon the human, which makes the result approach to the conditions of failure. He is a Jacob wrestling with angels after professedly accepting the challenges of earthly athletes. When we consider that the highly varied and transcendently beautiful poetic result above referred to was all the doing of a young man under thirty, we recognize an intellect only less versatile than sublime; and the mind is overweighted in surmising what he might have found it possible to achieve had an ordinary span of life, of from fifty to seventy years, been allotted to him. It remains no doubt none the less true that in Shelley the predominant quality of all is the ideal; and that this tinges most of his work, and at times even blemishes it. He was himself particularly attached to the metaphysical element in his poetry, which is of course one great constituent of its idealism. But to lose sight of the other qualities is to shut our eyes to salient facts and indisputable triumphs. When anybody can point, in English literature, to a better modern tragedy than *The Cenci*, a predecessor of *Julian and Maddalo* in the same class of the poetic-familiar, a much choicer bit of intellectual grotesque than *Peter Bell the Third*, or translations superior to those from Homer, Euripides, and Göthe, let him do so; and then, not before, let him parrot the old cry that the ideal, whether in the way of invention and imagery, or of lyrical or rhetorical work (though even this would not be so very narrow a field), is the sum and substance of Shelley.

The poet sent *Julian and Maddalo* to Hunt on the 15th of August 1819, to be published anonymously; but no such publication took place during his lifetime—for what reason I do not find explained. Mr. Ollier appears to have suggested that it should come out in the same volume with the *Prometheus*, to which Shelley objected on account of the essential difference of style. The non-appearance of *Julian and Maddalo*, with the poet's name to it, is to be regretted; as its general tone, and especially the interest which must have attached to it as introducing Byron, would probably have promoted Shelley's repute among ordinary readers beyond what could be hoped for from any of his other works save only *The Cenci*.

XX.—ROME AND NAPLES.

Shelley, with his wife and Miss Clairmont, reached Rome on the 20th of November. "Since I last wrote to you" (he says to Peacock in a letter of the 22nd of December) "I have seen the ruins of Rome, the Vatican, St. Peter's, and all the miracles of ancient and modern art contained in that majestic city. The impression of it exceeds anything I ever experienced in my travels. We stayed there only a week, intending to return at the end of February, and devote two or three months to its mines of inexhaustible contemplation. . . . The Forum is a plain in the midst of Rome, a kind of desert full of heaps of stones and pits; and, though so near the habitations of men, is the most desolate place you can conceive. The ruins of temples stand in and around it; shattered columns; and ranges of others complete, supporting cornices of exquisite workmanship; and vast vaults of shattered domes distinct with regular compartments, once filled with sculptures of ivory or brass. The temples of Jupiter, and Concord, and Peace, and the Sun, and the Moon, and Vesta, are all within a short distance of this spot. Behold the wrecks of what a great nation once dedicated to the abstractions of the mind! Rome is a city, as it were, of the dead—or rather of those who cannot die, and who survive the puny generations which inhabit and pass over the spot which they have made sacred to eternity. . . . The English burying-place is a green slope near the walls, under the pyramidal tomb of Cestius, and is, I think, the most beautiful and solemn cemetery I ever beheld. To see the sun shining on its bright grass—fresh, when we first visited it, with the autumnal dews—and hear the whispering of the wind among the leaves of the trees which have overgrown the tomb of Cestius, and the soil which is stirring in the sun-warm earth, and to mark the tombs, mostly of women and young people who were buried there, one might, if one were to die, desire the sleep they seem to sleep. Such is the human mind: and so it peoples with its wishes vacancy and oblivion."

From Rome the travellers went on to Naples—Shelley preceding the ladies by three days, and arriving on the 1st of December. He saw an assassination just as he entered the city[1]—a young man, pursued by a man and woman out of a shop, being stabbed to death by the former at a blow. The horror which Shelley felt and expressed at this crime met with no response from a Calabrian priest, his fellow-traveller. " External nature in these delightful regions," he remarks, " contrasts with and compensates for the deformity and degradation of humanity." This is only one of many passages in which Shelley intimates a low opinion, sometimes even a positive loathing, of the Italians. The earliest such passage naturally occurs in a letter from Milan (20th April 1818) at the opening of his Italian experiences, which, so far as scenery, climate, and general associations, were concerned, charmed him from the first. "The people here, though inoffensive enough, seem, both in body and soul, a miserable race. The men are hardly men: they look like a tribe of stupid and shrivelled slaves, and I do not think that I have seen a gleam of intelligence in the countenance of man since I passed the Alps. The women in enslaved countries are always better than the men ; but they have tight-laced figures, and figures and mien which express (oh, how unlike the French !) a mixture of the coquette and prude, which reminds me of the worst characteristics of the English." To the above remarks Mrs. Shelley[2] appends a note :— "These impressions of Shelley with regard to the Italians, formed in ignorance and with precipitation, became altogether altered after a longer stay in Italy. He quickly discovered the extraordinary intelligence and genius of this wonderful people, amidst the ignorance in which they are carefully kept by their rulers, and the vices fostered by a religious

---

[1] So in Shelley's own letter, 22nd December 1818 (*Essays and Letters*, vol. ii. p. 139). Mrs. Shelley, in a letter dated in the same month (*Shelley Memorials*, p. 108), says "between Capua and Naples."

[2] *Essays and Letters*, vol. ii. p. 96.

system which these same rulers have used as their most successful engine." One must accept (and I should be the last to wish
attenuated) this testimony of Mrs. Shelley's : yet I confess that
the published letters of her husband hardly bear it out. The
following passages may be noted. "The modern Italians seem
a miserable people—without sensibility, or imagination, or understanding. Their outside is polished : and an intercourse
with them seems to proceed with much facility, though it ends
in nothing, and produces nothing. The women are particularly
empty, and, though possessed of the same sort of superficial
grace, are devoid of every cultivation and refinement." (Bagni
di Lucca, 25th July 1818.) " I had no conception of the excess
to which avarice, cowardice, superstition, ignorance, passionless
lust, and all the inexpressible brutalities which degrade human
nature, could be carried, until I had passed a few days at
Venice." (Venice, 8th October 1818.) "The common Italians
are so sullen and stupid it's impossible to get information from
them: at Rome . . . . the people seem superior to any in Italy."
(Naples, 26th January 1819.) The next extract does certainly
show some progression. "We see something of Italian society.
The Romans please me much, especially the women ; who,
though totally devoid of every kind of information, or culture
of the imagination or affections or understanding, and in this
respect a kind of gentle savages, yet contrive to be interesting.
Their extreme innocence and naïveté, the freedom and gentleness of their manners, the total absence of affectation, make an
intercourse with them very like an intercourse with uncorrupted
children, whom they resemble in loveliness as well as simplicity.
I have seen two women in society here of the highest beauty :
their brows and lips, and the moulding of the face, modelled
with sculptural exactness, and the dark luxuriance of their hair
floating over their fine complexions ; and the lips—you must
hear the commonplaces which escape from them, before they
cease to be dangerous. The only inferior part are the eyes ;
which, though good and gentle, want the mazy depth of colour
behind colour with which the intellectual women of England
and Germany entangle the heart in soul-inwoven labyrinths."
(Rome, 6th April 1819.) But in the next almost contemporary
extract we again relapse—"The Italian character does not improve upon us " (Rome, 26th April 1819): and this identical
expression is used in a letter of the same date written by Mrs.
Shelley to Mrs. Gisborne. All these remarks, it is true, belong
to the first thirteen months of Shelley's sojourn in Italy : yet,

even as late as 15th February 1821, he could term Emilia Viviani "the only Italian for whom I ever felt any interest."

Mrs. Shelley considered that the removal to and sojourn in Italy were advantageous to her husband in almost all respects; and this was probably his own predominant feeling as well. We find, however, in some of his letters, the expressions that he would some day return to England through pure weakness of heart; that he would like to be back there but for his restricted means, and would wish to dwell near London; and that England is the most free and refined of countries. Yet the climate, had there been no other objection, would have been a very serious one. In the first letter (April 1818) which Shelley wrote to Peacock from Milan, he had said—"In the chilling fogs and rains of our own country, I can scarcely be said to live"; and an entry in Mrs. Shelley's diary of 14th May 1824 (months after her husband's death) says, speaking of England: "Mine own Shelley! what a horror you had of returning to this miserable country!"

In Naples the Shelleys lodged near the Royal Gardens, facing the Bay: they were very solitary, the poet's health was bad, and he was often gloomy. Still, he had days of great enjoyment from the scenery, which he naturally enough thought the most beautiful to be found within the bounds of civilization, and from visits to Pompeii and Vesuvius; the latter he regarded as, "after the glaciers, the most impressive exhibition of the energies of Nature I ever saw." The family returned to Rome in March, intending to go back to Naples for the second half of the year 1819, but this purpose remained unfulfilled.

According to the account which Shelley gave to Byron and Medwin, he re-encountered in Naples the married lady who had proffered him her love in 1816. She had arrived in that city on the same day as himself; and, when they met, she informed him of the persistent though hopeless affection with which she had tracked his footsteps. Here also she now died; and Shelley said that he had left Naples the earlier on that account. Unless Medwin has indulged his invention in a very unjustifiable way in this matter, or unless Shelley himself did the like, we have before us this alternative; either that the poet narrated a strange tissue of delusions, or that the allegations were substantially true. I have no wish to uphold the latter (contrary to the conviction of better-informed persons) as the only admissible solution: but I think that a few symptoms of collateral evidence deserve careful attention. That Shelley became unusually

melancholy at Naples is an acknowledged fact; and that ill-
health was not the sole cause of this is also recognized. In his
Stanzas Written in Dejection near Naples we find a remarkable
expression :

> " Alas ! I have nor hope nor health,
>   Nor peace within nor calm around ;
>
>   .   .   .   .   .
>
>   Nor fame nor power *nor love* nor leisure."

Considering the deep mutual attachment which undoubtedly
subsisted between Shelley and his wife, it is difficult to infer
that he intended this statement to reflect upon her, or upon
himself as related to her. It is also clear that he did not make
Mary the confidante of any unhappiness which may just now
have affected him, of deeper import than his ill-health. Her
own statement[1] is conclusive on this point. "Though he preserved the appearance of cheerfulness, . . . yet many hours were
passed when his thoughts, shadowed by illness, became gloomy,
—and then he escaped to solitude, and in verses, *which he hid
from fear of wounding me,* poured forth morbid but too natural
bursts of discontent and sadness. One looks back with unspeakable regret and gnawing remorse to such periods ; fancying
that, *had one been more alive to the nature of his feelings*, and
more attentive to soothe them, such would not have existed.
And yet, enjoying as he appeared to do every sight or influence
of earth or sky, it was difficult to imagine that any melancholy
he showed was aught but the effect of the constant pain to
which he was a martyr." Some while afterwards (May 1820)
Shelley wrote to Peacock that Italy had done much good to his
health, and "but for certain moral causes" would probably
have cured it. The "moral causes" thus reticently referred to
are neither defined nor distinctly apparent. It may also deserve
noting that Shelley, speaking of *Julian and Maddalo* in a letter
of 15th December 1819, expressed his intention "to write three
other poems, the scenes of which will be laid at Rome, Florence,
and Naples, but the subjects of which will be all drawn from
dreadful or beautiful realities, as that of this was." If the
Naples romance was a figment, of course no affinity can be surmised between it and this statement ; but the latter might not
unnaturally suggest that something of moment had come under
Shelley's observation at Naples, and, if his story was true, one
might conjecture that this was the destined theme of his poem.
Finally, I may call attention to Medwin's intimation (not very

---

[1] Vol. iii. p. 39.

precisely expressed) that the verses entitled *Misery* were written in connection with the same events: he says that the poet gave him to understand as much. But this, I am assured on good authority, is not correct.

The reader will have noticed above Mrs. Shelley's strong expressions regarding herself, "unspeakable regret and gnawing remorse." Still more emphatic and explicit are the terms in her poem *The Choice*, written shortly after her husband's death.[1]

> " First let me call on thee. Lost as thou art,
> Thy name aye fills my sense, thy love my heart.
> O gentle spirit, thou hast often sung
> How, fallen on evil days, thy heart was wrung:
> Now fierce remorse and unreplying death
> Waken a chord within my heart, whose breath,
> Thrilling and keen, in accents audible
> A tale of unrequited love doth tell.
> It was not anger : while thy earthly dress
> Encompassed still thy soul's rare loveliness,
> All anger was atoned by many a kind
> Caress or tear that spoke the softened mind.
> It speaks of cold neglect, averted eyes,
> That blindly crushed thy soul's fond sacrifice.
> My heart was all thine own ; but yet a shell
> Closed in its core, which seemed impenetrable,
> Till sharp-toothed misery tore the husk in twain,
> Which gaping lies, nor may unite again.
> Forgive me ! let thy love descend in dew
> Of soft repentance and regret more true.
> In a strange guise thou dost descend, or how
> Could love soothe fell remorse, as it does now ?
> By this remorse and love, and by the years
> Through which we shared our common hopes and fears,
> By all our best companionship, I dare
> Call on thy sacred name without a fear."

These lines confirm into clear conviction the impression which one may have previously formed from various sparse indications, that the conjugal happiness of Shelley and Mary was not an absolutely still and glassy stream—there were ripples in it. For instance, the poem *To Edward Williams* (vol. iii. p. 100) can hardly, I think, be understood in any other sense, whatever may be its further purport. This is dated 1821: so is *Ginevra*, wherein marriage is characterized as

> " life's great cheat—a thing
> Bitter to taste, sweet in imagining."

This, however, relates rather to the *woman's* lot in married life. Trelawny's *Recollections* offer some suggestions to the like

---

[1] Lately published in Mr. Forman's handsome and minutely and reverently laborious edition of Shelley.

general effect; and Mr. Thornton Hunt says that perhaps Mary troubled Shelley by "little habits of temper, and possibly of a refined and exacting coquettishness." Still, the utmost that can be deduced of this sort from published records leaves unaltered the main result—that Shelley and Mary were happy in each other, and well matched.

XXI.—DEATH OF WILLIAM SHELLEY, AND BIRTH OF PERCY.

Another sorrow, and one which he felt deeply, befell Shelley soon after his return to Rome. His son William died on the 7th of June,[1] aged three years and a half, after only a few days' illness. He was a beautiful and engaging child, and obviously the favourite of his father, who watched his deathbed for sixty hours, without closing his eyes. Several references to the boy are to be found among the poems, more especially after his death. Shelley, the father of five children, was now practically a childless man. The two whom Harriet had brought him were confiscated by an almost unexampled stretch of law; those whom he must have loved yet more affectionately, if only for the sake of their mother Mary—

> ("And from thy side two gentle babes are born
> To fill our home with smiles ")[2]—

were now all gathered away into the quiet fold of the great shepherd Death. William was buried in the protestant cemetery at Rome. This Shelley had described (as we have seen) only half a year before to his friend Peacock in terms of tenderness and beauty that now, in retrospection, might almost seem charged with presentiment, and will seem triply so charged before the end of the fourth succeeding year. Over the fresh-closed grave, and in all the sadness of loss, Shelley could yet say: "I envy death the body far less than the oppressors the minds of those whom they have torn from me. The one can only kill the body : the other crushes the affections." An inscribed gravestone was placed in the cemetery for William during Shelley's lifetime (not under his personal direction, but seemingly under that of Miss Curran, the friend at Rome who painted the often-engraved portrait of the poet)—and, as it turned out, was wrongly placed : for, when soon afterwards that grave was opened with a view to removing the child's corpse to

---

[1] So inscribed on the tombstone, and so in a letter of Shelley's to Peacock, written the following day. Mrs. Shelley says "6th June" (*Essays and Letters*, vol. ii. p. 178). Perhaps the death occurred in the night-hours, 6 to 7 June.
[2] *Revolt of Islam*, Dedication.

lie close beside his father's ashes, the bones beneath were found to be those of an adult. William's actual burial-place is not now precisely known.

But Nature had some compensation early in store for the bereaved parents. On the 12th of November 1819, at Florence, Mary gave birth to another son, her last child, Percy Florence, the present Baronet. Her sorrow for William had been most poignant; and no doubt the advent of the new baby was a great relief to Shelley, for her sake as well as his own. Percy was a somewhat delicate infant; and we read more than once of projected removals which the parents, both of them enthusiastic travellers, would otherwise have been inclined for, set aside in the interest of his health. ·

Between the dates of William's death and Percy's birth the Shelleys had been staying at the Villa Valsovano, between Leghorn and Monte Nero. Here Shelley again saw a great deal of Mrs. Gisborne and her husband; and was initiated by her into the reading of Spanish, especially Calderon's plays. Mr. Charles Clairmont, who, having been a year or more in Spain, visited Shelley at this time *en route* to Vienna, where he settled down for life, was also of use to the · poet's Spanish studies. We owe to these his fine translation from the *Magico Prodigioso.* He regarded Calderon as next to Shakespeare among mediæval dramatists, and far superior to the Elizabethans, such as Beaumont and Fletcher. Another and less manifestly congenial matter engaged Shelley much at this period. He started a scheme for a steamer to ply between Marseilles and Leghorn, for the pecuniary benefit of the Gisbornes, and of Mr. Henry Reveley, a son of Mrs. Gisborne by a previous marriage : he was an engineer, and engaged in the building of the steamer, which would have been the first to navigate the Gulf of Lyons. The project, however, after a great deal of interest taken in it by Shelley, and of money supplied by him, broke down—the Gisbornes and Mr. Reveley having found it necessary to return to England : they were afterwards in Italy again for a while.

The Shelleys, still with Miss Clairmont in their company, went on to Florence early in October. The climate of this city was very inimical to Shelley, the keen winds from the Apennines being overmuch for his nerves. Probably also the water, which is here impregnated with lime, disagreed with him. It would be sure to do so if, as Medwin says, he suffered from nephritis; and we find it recorded in Shelley's letters that the bad water at Ravenna tortured him at a later date. and that the not needing to distil water at Pisa was one serious motive in favour of that city as a residence.[1]

During his stay in Florence he was wont to pass several hours daily in the galleries, and made a study of art, more especially sculpture, going a good deal beyond anything he had previously attempted or felt impelled towards. This study so grew upon him that afterwards, in Pisa, he regarded it as a great loss of happiness to be, in comparison with the opportunities of Rome and Florence, cut off from works of art.

XXII.—SHELLEY ON THE FINE ARTS.

I will here collect, though in a very summary and imperfect manner, some details of Shelley's feeling concerning the fine arts, not including poetry. He has left, both in letters and in separate memoranda, various observations on the subject, which the student of his opinions should consult for information, and very generally for force and beauty of expression.

In his early youth Shelley was indifferent to the fine arts of form, including architecture; afterwards he took a deeply admiring interest in sculpture, and at a later date in painting as well. From boyhood, however, he had a habit of sketching or scrawling on books or loose paper—as for instance pines and cedars, in memory of those at Field Place; or afterwards reminiscences of objects of Nature at Lymouth, mountains, spectres, or any form, graceful or fantastic, that flitted across his inner eye. I have seen some of these scribblings, proper to 1812 and to his closing years, and discern in them a certain readiness of touch which seems to speak to early training, of the milder " drawing-master " kind, neither wholly lost nor much improved upon by after practice. Here it is a tree, in the style of what the drawing-master terms "foliage;" there a church-steeple, with two devils on the balustrade, one of them smoking a pipe; or again a man straddling with supreme disregard of his vertebral column.

At the period of which we are now speaking, Shelley's sojourn in Italy, he turned his attention seriously to questions of art; going so far as to say that one of his chief objects in that country was to observe, " in statuary and painting, the degree in which, and the rules according to which, that ideal beauty of which we have so intense yet so obscure an apprehension is realized in external forms." His chief admiration was naturally

---

[1] *Essays and Letters*, vol. ii. pp. 259, 261.

given to Grecian art : in sculpture as in other manifestations of intellect he found the Greeks to be " the gods whom we should worship." In painting he placed Raphael highest, and next him . . . whom? Guido and Salvator Rosa ! The works of these three painters, indeed, he regarded [1] as " the only things that sustain the comparison " with the antique. We trace here the docility of mind with which a sympathetic observer who is no expert can be talked into fancying that he sees in particular works the qualities which they are credited with, and which he knows, from his own elevated perceptions, would be the highest of qualities if only they were actually there. All Europe was bedribbled, in Shelley's time, with nonsense about the ideal beauty of Guido, and the titanic sublime of Salvator : and Shelley, who knew the true and incommensurable value of the sublime and ideal, was teachable enough to suppose that he really saw them in works wherein their too frequent substitutes are upturned whites of eyes, posing limbs, and zigzag lightning amid tattered pines. This at least is the explanation I offer to myself of the result—intense admiration of Guido and Salvator—arising from these *data;* Shelley, who really knew what idealism, beauty, and sublimity, are,—and Guido and Salvator, who professed to embody them upon canvas. And this may be said without denying to those painters such measure of genius and attainment as they assuredly did possess and show forth. But even Shelley " drew the line somewhere : " he drew it above the Caracci and Domenichino, spite of the stertorous applause with which the performances of these artists have always, and especially about his time, been greeted. He also rejected the allurements of the Roman arabesque style.

To Michelangelo Shelley did no justice—unless perhaps quite towards the last. Here again his opinions were those of a beginner—a sincere beginner at any rate, as, instead of chiming-in with the real or supposititious connoisseurs, he boldly stood by his own impressions (which are in fact almost universally the veritable impressions on this subject of people who have not largely studied and compared fine art), and avowed himself revolted with the physical grandeur, the colossal externalism, of the Florentine demigod. " He has not only no temperance, no modesty, no feeling for the just boundaries of art (and in these respects an admirable genius may err), but he has no sense of beauty, and to want this is to want the sense

---

[1] Letter of 23d March 1819.

of the creative power of mind. . . . But hell and death are his real sphere." If, with respect to Michelàngelo, Shelley had thoroughly laid to heart his own valuable theory "that the canons of taste, if known, are irrefragable, and that these are to be sought in the most admirable works of art,"[1] he would sooner or later have come to a different or greatly modified conclusion. In fact, he appears finally to have enlarged his perception, for we find in his admirable *Defence of Poetry*, written in 1821, the following passage: " It exceeds all imagination to conceive what would have been the moral condition of the world if neither Dante, Petrarch, Boccaccio, Chaucer, Shakespeare, Calderon, Lord Bacon, nor Milton, had ever existed; if Raphael *and Michelangelo* had never been born; if the Hebrew poetry had never been translated; if a revival of the study of Greek literature had never taken place; if no monuments of ancient sculpture had been handed down to us; and if the poetry of the religion of the ancient world had been extinguished together with its belief." The passage in *Marenghi* relative to the greatness of Florentine sculpture must also be held to include—and even principally to apply to— Michelangelo. This poem was written before Shelley had studied the works of that mighty genius with any amplitude.

His visit to Pompeii was very impressive and delightful to Shelley, partly from the beauty of individual works, and especially from the free play allowed to natural influences. " I now understand why the Greeks were such great poets; and above all I can account, it seems to me, for the harmony, the unity, the perfection, the uniform excellence, of all their works of art. They lived in a perpetual commerce with external nature, and nourished themselves upon the spirit of its forms. Their theatres were all open to the mountains and the sky : . . . the odour and the freshness of the country penetrated the cities." In another connection, after visiting Ravenna, he observes : " It seems to have been one of the first effects of the christian religion to destroy the power of producing beauty in art."

With respect to architecture, Shelley was greatly struck, besides various antique buildings, with the splendour of Milan Cathedral, more especially its outside. He was no admirer of St. Peter's ; and one can see, on more occasions than one, how much less impressed he was by the architectural than by

---

[1] These terms are not Shelley's own, but Mrs. Shelley's, as a summing-up of her husband's views (Preface to the *Essays and Letters*, p. xvii).

the natural beauties of the scenes he visited—as, for instance, Palestrina and the Baths of Caracalla.

As a boy he loved music : " he could not bear any turns or twists in music, but liked a tune played quite simply." This art, indeed, affected him deeply ; and, though there is nothing to show that he had any practical knowledge of it, he could go to the small extent of playing a tune on the piano with one hand (if not possibly somewhat further than this). Yet he had not, properly speaking, "an ear for music," nor was he at all in the habit of singing or humming tunes. To decidedly ugly sounds he was painfully sensitive ; as, for example, the voice of a Scotch servant-girl at his Edinburgh lodgings, recorded by Hogg. Yet I think we are scarcely bound to believe that " *whenever* she entered the room, or even came to the door, he rushed wildly into a corner, and covered his ears with his hands." When asked what she had had for dinner, the damsel invariably replied, "Sengit heed and bonnocks ; " and this produced from Shelley, seemingly with the like constancy, the appeal—"Send her away, Harriet ! oh, send her away ! for God's sake, send her away ! " Shortly before his leaving England in 1818, he became an assiduous frequenter of the Italian opera, luxuriating much in Mozart ; and was singularly delighted with one ballet, as danced by Madlle. Milanie. Of ordinary theatres he saw very little : in fact, as far as comedy was concerned, he entertained a strong feeling of moral aversion. " *There* is comedy in its perfection," he said in one instance. "Society grinds down poor wretches into the dust of abject poverty, till they are scarcely recognizable as human beings ; and then—instead of being treated as what they really are, subjects of the deepest pity—they are brought forward as grotesque monstrosities to be laughed at."

XXIII.—PROMETHEUS AND THE CENCI.

We have now come to Shelley's zenith. Like a Dante passing from heaven to heaven under the escort of Beatrice, the poet of *Julian and Maddalo* stepped at once into another demesne of poetry, and yet into another : in each he plucked and now wears its own peculiar, long-delaying, unperishing laurel.

There is, I suppose, no poem comparable, in the fair sense of that word, to *Prometheus Unbound*. The immense scale and boundless scope of the conception ; the marble majesty and extra-mundane passions of the personages ; the sublimity of ethical aspiration; the radiance of ideal and poetic beauty which saturates every phase of the subject, and almost (as it were) wraps it from sight at times, and transforms it out of sense into spirit; the rolling river of great sound and lyrical rapture; form a combination not to be matched elsewhere, and scarcely to encounter competition. There is another source of greatness in this poem neither to be foolishly lauded nor (still less) undervalued. It is this :—that *Prometheus Unbound*, however remote the foundation of its subject-matter, and unactual its executive treatment, does in reality express the most modern of conceptions—the utmost reach of speculation of a mind which burst up all crusts of custom and prescription like a volcano, and imaged forth a future wherein man should be indeed the autocrat and renovated renovator of his planet. This it is, I apprehend, which places *Prometheus* clearly, instead of disputably, at the summit of all latter poetry :[1] the fact that it embodies, in forms of truly ecstatic beauty, the dominant passion of the dominant intellects of the age, and especially of one of the extremest and highest among them all, the author himself. It is the ideal poem of perpetual and triumphant progression—the Atlantis of Man Emancipated.

This supreme work was not yet completed when another only less great (many excellent judges think it the higher of the two) was also produced. I have already referred to *The Cenci* as the noblest English tragedy of modern times—a position which has been very generally and unreservedly accorded to it. The question of comparative merit is one to be determined according to sympathy rather than direct competition; and those minds — for the most part the soundest and finest — which embrace human character in powerful conflict and interaction as the one unrivalled subject of poetry are fully justified in preferring *The Cenci* to *Prometheus*. I have stated above the ultimate ground for my own contrary estimate : the *Prometheus* is a typical work in a quite other sense than *The Cenci*, and, being typical not only of the highest things but most emphatically of the inventor's mind, it is, I think, his one unparalleled masterpiece. *The Cenci* is moreover, if I am not mistaken, a more chequered achievement; the characters of Count Cenci

---

[1] I confine my view solely to *English* poetry; one or two very great foreign names must occur to the reader's mind, and abash mine from so much as taking them into account. I may add that nothing is said in the text about the flaws perceptible in *Prometheus Unbound*—occasional supersubtleties of thought, defects of execution, &c. &c. : not that I dispute their being there, but that my immediate purpose does not demand their indication

and Beatrice, and all the portion of the play in which they figure, being throughout a weft very superior to the warp which constitutes the residue. With these mere generalities, and referring the reader to the drama itself, and Shelley's preface and his wife's notes, for further elucidation, I leave this splendid performance. In my own notes will likewise be found, as regards both *The Cenci* and *Prometheus*, many particulars as to the views and aims of Shelley in relation to them, especially as to his wish to get the former acted on the stage.

Prometheus Unbound was begun while the poet was staying at Byron's villa at Este in or about September 1818, and was continued, to the end of the third act, up to the early days of April 1819: the fourth lyrical act was an afterthought, only completed late in December of the same year, at Florence. The estimation in which the poem was held by enlightened contemporaries is enshrined in the anecdote that Campbell, the now rapidly evanescent artificer of *Pleasures of Hope* and *Gertrude of Wyoming*,[1] said to Medwin: "*Prometheus Unbound* —it is well named: who would *bind* it?"

The Cenci was written chiefly in the Villa Valsovano, being begun on the 14th of May, and finished towards the middle of August 1819.[2] Shelley said to Trelawny: "I don't think much of it: it gave me less trouble than anything I have written of the same length." To Peacock he wrote that the composition had been "a fine antidote to nervous medicines, and kept up, I think, the pain in my side, as sticks do a fire."

The Cenci and *Prometheus* were respectively published in England in or about March and August 1820.

XXIV.—POEMS ON SUBJECTS OF THE DAY.

It may be convenient to group together here at once a few

---

[1] These operose performances will no doubt be long survived by some of the national lyrics of the same author, which are indeed very fine. As Medwin affirms (*Life of Shelley*, vol. i. p. 334, and vol. ii. p. 196) that Campbell used the expression above quoted in talking to Medwin himself, we are bound to credit that he did so. However, it was not Campbell's own joke, but Theodore Hook's, in the *John Bull*. The *Literary Gazette* also got hold of it; for the review of *Prometheus* in that paper says—"We turn to *Prometheus Unbound*, humbly conceiving that this punning title-page is the soothest in the book, as no one can ever think him worth binding." I believe Campbell was not a contributor to the *Literary Gazette*, and should not therefore be branded, even by surmise, as the vile and loathsome ruffian who wrote that critique—or rather that libel. The vomit of creation who wrote another libel, in the form of a review of *Queen Mab*, in the same paper (see p. 114), was apparently a different person; for he admitted some poetic ability in *Queen Mab* and in Shelley, whereas the reviewer of *Prometheus* acknowledged absolutely none,—and the like, to all intents and purposes, may be said of the reviewer of *The Cenci*, probably the same individual.

[2] Shelley, in a letter to Leigh Hunt dated 15th August 1819, says he is "on the eve of completing" this tragedy. Lady Shelley therefore antedates it a little in stating (*Shelley Memorials*, p. 114) that it was finished "a month or two after" the day given to its dedication, 29th May.

poems of Shelley's inspired by incidents, fertile of indignation or of laughter, then going on in England.

The most valuable of these is *Peter Bell the Third*, which indeed has always appeared to me a *chef d'œuvre* of its kind, indicating possibilities of power in Shelley which it would certainly have been as contrary to his wishes as to his habits to work to any great extent, but which would have qualified him to descend into the arena of partisan satire, and to sear many doggish foreheads and readily-turned backs with the indelible brand of his scorn.[1] Nor is this the only poem in which a similar faculty is conspicuous. *Peter Bell the Third* is no doubt, and from its subject and tone must be, a much slighter as well as less finished performance than Byron's *Vision of Judgment;* but I think it is only inferior, and not very greatly so either, to that burst of Olympic cachinnation, that ever-pointing finger of obloquy. Shelley's squib—(for it is and professes to be no more, only that the squib which a Uriel can fire off differs considerably from that of a Guy-Fawkes boy)—was concocted during or immediately after his stay at the Villa Valsovano.

His other satirical work, *Swellfoot the Tyrant,* was begun a year later, August 1820. Shelley appears a little out of his groove here : one might compare him to a good public speaker in the pathetic style, who, taking up the humorous style at a moment's notice, finds himself well capable of working it, but unelastic in gesture and play of countenance. Still, *Swellfoot* also is a choice performance, with a spice of Aristophanic and another of Rabelaisian grotesque, none the less genuinely Shelleyan, and therefore truly imaginative. The drama was printed and just published anonymously ("London, published for the Author by J. Johnston, 98 Cheapside, and sold by all Booksellers, 1820")[2] when a menace from the Society for the Suppression of Vice caused its immediate withdrawal. The intelligent reader will no doubt not believe that it was written in a fit of entire Carolinian enthusiasm. If he does, he will be undeceived by the following extract from a letter which Shelley addressed to Mr. Peacock on the 12th of July 1820. "Nothing, I think, shows the generous gullibility of the English nation more than their having adopted her sacred Majesty as the

---

[1] The poet was not unconscious of his capacities in this line. One of his letters, dated 25th January 1822, says, "I began once a satire upon satire, which I meant to be very severe : it was full of small knives, in the use of which practice would have soon made me very expert." Of this satire I find no trace nor even mention elsewhere.

[2] Mr. Trelawny possesses a copy of this effusion in its original form.

7 *

heroine of the day, in spite of all their prejudices and bigotry. I, for my part, of course wish no harm to happen to her, even if she has, as I firmly believe, amused herself in a manner rather indecorous with any courier or baron. But I cannot help adverting to it as one of the absurdities of royalty that a vulgar woman, with all those low tastes which prejudice considers as vices, and a person whose habits and manners every one would shun in private life, without any redeeming virtues, should be turned into a heroine because she is a queen, or, as a collateral reason, because her husband is a king, and he, no less than his ministers, is so odious that everything, however disgusting, which is opposed to them, is admirable."

About the same time as *Peter Bell the Third*, Shelley wrote the *Masque of Anarchy*, the record of his fiery and righteous zeal against the authors of that "Manchester Massacre" which was then crimsoning the soil and the cheeks of Englishmen—a slaughter, by the mounted yeomanry, of several men and women who were attending an open-air Reform meeting at Peterloo. This poem was sent in November 1819 to Hunt for publication in the *Examiner;* but was withheld for prudential reasons, and never saw the light until separately printed in 1832. With great elevation of soul, and many splendid and unforgettable stanzas, *The Masque of Anarchy* is not, I think, exactly a masterpiece. One perceives that in it Shelley is writing something other than his own style ; and the further he deviates from that, or the nearer he comes to the conditions he has chosen to prescribe for himself, so much the more faltering is his pace. There is a half-dozen of shorter poems, belonging to the same year, also denunciatory of the then political condition of England. These again, and on similar grounds, are among Shelley's less successful compositions : though the sonnet, *England in 1819*, and the *Similes for Two Political Characters*, have great energy of virus. He had a strong impression about this time that the misgovernment of his native country would bring on bankruptcy and actual revolution.

XXV.—PISA TO RAVENNA :—EPIPSYCHIDION.

On the 26th of January 1820 the Shelleys removed to Pisa : [1] and in or about May, for the sake of the infant Percy's health,

---

[1] Miss Clairmont now remained behind at Florence, and was not again domesticated with the Shelleys—may indeed never have seen Shelley more. She appears, however, from a letter of the poet's dated 28th April 1822 (*Essays and Letters*, vol. ii. p. 280), to have been then with Mrs. Shelley at Spezia, close by Lerici. Captain Medwin met Miss Clairmont living *en pension* in Florence in 1820.

to the Bagni di Pisa (or di San Giuliano), four miles off. Shelley's own health also benefited here. At Pisa he had seen a good deal of the celebrated physician Vaccà, who recommended him to leave his ailments to nature, without medicine, which he mainly did henceforward. The acquaintance with this distinguished man was the more pleasant to Shelley, as their liberal political views were in sympathy. Some portion of the spring and summer was spent likewise at the house recently occupied by the Gisbornes at Leghorn. In August the Shelleys were back at the Bagni di Pisa.

Somewhere about this time, Shelley (we are told) having called at the Pisa Post-Office, an English officer in the Portuguese service apostrophized him with the exclamation, "What ! are you that damned atheist Shelley ?" and, without more ado, struck him to the ground with a stick, stunning him at the moment. He was a tall and powerful man. Shelley looked-up his acquaintance Mr. Tighe (a son of the authoress of the poem of *Psyche*), "who lost no time in taking measures to obtain satisfaction."[1] The proficient in theism and blackguardism was traced to the hotel of the Tre Donzelle, and thence to Genoa, whither Mr. Tighe (and it is said Shelley also) followed him : but he was never run down. This is another of the singular stories told by Shelley, and discredited by most of his hearers or biographers : the inclination of my own mind would be to accept it, were it not that I find Mr. Trelawny a decided disbeliever. Another authority informs me that some adventure of some kind or other did undeniably occur to Shelley at *a* Post-Office—but this was the Post-Office of Rome, and the date 6th May 1819. Possibly the narrator, Medwin, is more abroad in the auxiliary than in the leading circumstances of the case.

This gentleman[2]—"Captain Medwin, of the 24th Light Dragoons "—Shelley's second cousin and old schoolfellow, was now in Italy on his return from Bombay, and the poet invited him to his house at the Bagni di Pisa. It may have been towards the end of October that he arrived. A few days afterwards the Serchio river and a connecting canal overflowed their banks, flooded the neighbouring houses, including the Shelleys', and

[1] This is the expression used by Medwin (*Shelley Papers*, p. 59). It is obviously rather a loose one, considering that the assailant was never brought to book, and I am not sure whether or not we ought to understand it as implying that Shelley meant to fight a duel. Probably it does : though the poet " had some scruples about duelling," as appears *inter alia* from an anecdote, of trivial consequence, as to his receiving a sort of pettish challenge from Dr. Polidori in 1816, on account of some dispute in boating. This Shelley laughed off, but Byron resented it a little more seriously.
[2] He died at an advanced age in the summer of 1869.

dictated a rapid retreat.   They and Medwin returned accordingly to Pisa, which, of all the cities visited by the poet, was on
the whole the one that suited his health best   He lived on the
south side of the Arno, next door to the marble palace which
stands inscribed "Alla Giornata." Medwin had a severe attack
of illness here, and Shelley tended him for six weeks with unremitting and minute carefulness.

It was soon afterwards that Shelley became acquainted with
the beautiful Contessina Emilia Viviani, with whom he had a
long-memorable *affaire de cœur*—as it may perhaps be most
appropriately termed.   He knew a certain Professor or ex-Pro-
fessor P., an ecclesiastic, and confessor in the family of the
Conte Viviani.   The "Professore" is amusingly sketched by
Medwin, and seems to have been a scamp of the impurest water
—at any rate a very talented, accomplished, and learned scamp,
and a first-rate talker. [1]   He spoke to Shelley of the two
daughters of the Conte, who, in consequence of the dislike of a
young stepmother, had been shut up in convents—the elder,
Emilia, in the Convent of St. Anne, in the suburbs of Pisa : and
he proposed to introduce Shelley to her.   I do not find the
exact date given, but presume it to have been late in the autumn
of 1820.   Shelley visited Emilia, and was enraptured with her :
her dreary seclusion, under which she pined miserably, the
beauty equally of her mind and person, excited his tenderest
sympathies.   He made unsuccessful efforts to obtain her libera-
tion from the convent, and exchanged locks of hair with her.
Many of her letters to Shelley are still extant.   Mostly she addresses him as " Caro Fratello," but in at least one instance she
uses the startling term "Adorato Sposo." [2]   "Emilia," says
Medwin, " was indeed lovely and interesting. Her profuse black
hair, tied in the most simple knot, after the manner of a Greek
Muse in the Florence Gallery, displayed to its full height her
brow, fair as that of the marble of which I speak.   She was also
of about the same height as the antique. Her features possessed
a rare faultlessness and almost Grecian contour, the nose and
forehead making a straight line.   Her eyes had the sleepy volup-
tuousness, if not the colour, of Beatrice Cenci's.   They had

---

[1] The *bon-mot* which is said to have cost him his professorial chair is too neat to be
omitted.   He was out at night in the streets of Pisa in company not strictly ecclesiastical
or academic ; and, being challenged by the patrol, replied—"Son un uomo pubblico, in
una strada pubblica, con una donna pubblica."

[2] The passage, I am informed, is much to the following effect. Emilia is comparing
herself to flowers at dawn-time, which have all the freshness of the dew upon them, and
whose honey has been robbed as yet by no bee: "You alone have been my bee, *O
adorato sposo.*"

indeed no definite colour; changing with the changing feelings to dark or light, as the soul animated them. Her cheek was pale too, as of marble—owing to her confinement and want of air, or perhaps 'to thought.'" Emilia Viviani was soon after visited by Mrs. Shelley, as well as her husband, and in the carnival was allowed to pay them visits in return. Some further particulars concerning her will be found in my notes to *Epipsychidion.*

The one thing which it is important to know about her now is that she inspired that subtle and astonishing poem. I am not aware that even

> " A scandal-monger beyond all belief "

has ever said or insinuated that Shelley's love for Emilia (for love, in a certain sense, it may clearly be called) was other than " Platonic : " if anybody *has* said so, the statement is presumably as unworthy of attention as it is incapable of mathematical disproof. The reader who observes that *Epipsychidion* is the only one of Shelley's long poems to which his widow appended no word of comment may perhaps infer that the Platonization was not absolutely to her mind : but that is neither here nor there. The poem—to take it on its own showing—reveals a state of feeling which most people have never experienced ; and this moreover it describes in terms which they cannot understand. As a pure outpouring of poetry, a brimming and bubbling fountain of freshness and music, magical with its own spray-rainbows, *Epipsychidion* is beyond praise, and beyond description. It is indeed (to the best of my knowledge) the most glowing and splendid idealization of the passion of love —or poem of ideal love, to put the same thing in inverted terms—ever produced in any language. I may confess, however, to doubting whether it is quite justifiable to complicate so abstract a poetic conception with so many obscurities or sublimations of personal allusion left unravelled. In *Epipsychidion* the very mood of mind tends towards the intangible ; while the framework of imagery or symbol remains to this day an enigma to students of the poetry and the life of Shelley —and this *as* a framework, not to speak of difficulties of detail or diction : and in such cases the reader who is puzzled is also palled. But Shelley, like Zeus, was a cloud-compeller ; and, of *his* clouds, even the most vaporous refuses to disperse.

The poem was written [1] towards the beginning of 1821, and was sent in February to London, and there published, semi-published, or nominally published, without Shelley's name. There was a small edition to be had for the buying, and no buyer applied. Shortly after this, Shelley wrote his noble *Defence of Poetry*, in reply to an article by Peacock in Ollier's *Literary Miscellany*. The *Defence* is an incomplete treatise; two other parts were to have been written.

Early in 1821 (probably before the end of January) Medwin brought Shelley acquainted with Edward Ellerker Williams, formerly a lieutenant in the 8th Dragoons, and his wife Jane. Lieutenant Williams had at first been in the navy, and then some years in India: he was about a year younger than Shelley, with something of a consumptive tendency lately come upon him. [2] Medwin says that he was a lineal descendant of a daughter of Cromwell. The Williamses were in the enjoyment of fairly competent means, and had two children. This acquaintance, which soon ripened into friendship, proved eminently pleasing to all concerned. Williams was gentle, generous, and fearless, fond of the water and manly exercises, with some faculty for drawing, and capable of writing correct verse. Of Mrs. Williams, whose musical proficiency and taste were a great delight to Shelley, we know from himself that she realized his antecedent conception of the Lady in *The Sensitive Plant:* could any more be said? The warmth of Shelley's feelings for Mrs. Williams, as disclosed in the various exquisite poems he addressed to her [3]—which all passed through her husband's hands—may indeed be said to hover on the confine between friendship and love; a love as refined and delicate as it was tender, and such as the true husband of Mary and genuinely attached friend of Williams could without blame both entertain and avow. Such a sentiment is one of the purest as well as most beautiful known to man.

These were years of revolution: and indeed what years, since the great disintegration of 1789–93, have not been so? and how many more are we not destined to see until the work of those mighty days shall be in some approximate degree openly ac-

---

[1] Mr. Trelawny assures me very positively that Shelley first wrote *Epipsychidion* in Italian verse, and presented it to Emilia, and afterwards turned the Italian into English. This is a very startling assertion, and I hardly know how to take it.
[2] Medwin mentions this, with confirmatory details. I found Mr. Trelawny both unaware and sceptical of the alleged fact.
[3] See the poems, *Remembrance* (vol. iii. p. 100) &c., and my notes upon them.

cepted and firmly constituted? Spain and Naples had risen in 1820, and had been welcomed by the noble enthusiasm and the not less noble strains of Shelley: now, in 1821, it was the turn of Greece. On the 1st of April Prince Alexander Mavrocordato, whose acquaintance the poet had made at Pisa, called upon him, produced a proclamation issued by his cousin Prince Ypsilanti, and declared that Greece—the Holy Land of Shelley's heart and intellect—would once again be free. The result was the drama of *Hellas*, of which more anon.

The Shelleys were now no longer leading the secluded—sometimes solitary—life which had mostly been their lot in Italy, and which (as the reader may have already noted) was likely to be little to the taste of Mary, nor entirely so to her husband's, though it must be regarded as reasonably congenial, in the long run, to his real and deeper requirements. At present Medwin was in their house, and had been studying Arabic with the poet: Mavrocordato was the most constant visitor, and used to play at chess with Shelley, who was not a good hand at the game: the Williamses were on terms of increasing intimacy;—and he already saw something in private of Sgricci, the famous improvvisatore, whose faculty filled Shelley with admiring wonder.[1] Towards the end of this year, the circle of his acquaintances in Pisa enlarged greatly. Shelley and Williams did a good deal of boating together on the Arno, the Serchio, and its canal; recorded in the beautiful fragment *The Boat on the Serchio*, and in the note of Mrs. Shelley (which the reader should consult for details) to the poems of 1821. By July she and her husband were again at the Bagni di Pisa.

Hence Shelley went to pay Byron a visit at Ravenna, which he reached on the evening of the 6th of August. "One would think" (he wrote to his wife on that day, while at Bologna *en route*) "that I were the spaniel of Destiny; for, the more she knocks me about, the more I fawn on her. I had an overturn about daybreak; the old horse stumbled, and threw me and the fat vetturino into a slope of meadow, over the hedge. My angular figure stuck where it was pitched; but my vetturino's spherical form rolled fairly to the bottom of the hill, and that with so few symptoms of reluctance in the life that animated it that my

---

[1] The MS. book by Shelley which has passed through my hands contains a longish criticism by the English poet, written in Italian, of the improvisation of the tragedy of *Ettore* by Sgricci. It appears to have been done for publication in some review. Sgricci was born near Arezzo in 1788, and died in 1836.

ridicule (for it was the drollest sight in the world) was suppressed by my fear that the poor devil had been hurt. But he was very well."

XXVI.—THE WITCH OF ATLAS, ADONAIS, HELLAS.

For convenience sake, I link here these three poems, the last compositions of some length (excluding *Epipsychidion*, already mentioned, and *Charles the First* and the *Triumph of Life*, both unfinished) which the thaumaturgic hand of Shelley was destined to indite. In strictness, however, we have already overpassed the date of the *Witch of Atlas*, and not quite reached that of *Hellas*.

The former was written in August 1820, in three days following a pedestrian excursion which Shelley had made alone up the Monte San Pellegrino, starting from the Bagni di Pisa. He sent it off to Mr. Ollier on the 20th of January 1821, but it was not published till after the poet's death. Neither Shelley nor any one else tells us who or what the Witch of Atlas is; and I am surprised not to find the subject so much as debated in any book of biography or elucidation.[1] It appears to me that, if we understand the Witch to be the Spirit (or *a* Spirit) of Beauty, in the most unrestricted sense of that word, we shall find significant many passages in the poem which otherwise read as mere brilliant fantasies : not that I perceive this clue to lead into *every* intricate recess and twilight cranny of the maze. If it fails in delicate hands, we may perhaps assume that, along with the symbolism or intention of the poem, Shelley mixed up some elements of what may be called a "fairy tale," equally enchanting, imperishable, and arbitrary. However this may be, he never, or scarcely at all, did anything more splendid than the *Witch of Atlas :* from first to last, it is consummate in imagination and workmanship. To some extent it pairs with *Epipsychidion ;* and I think it is even the more finely artistic product of the two.

Keats died on the 23rd of February 1821, at Rome : Shelley (who had some months before invited his brother-poet to stay with him in Italy, but without any direct result) did not know of his death immediately, but, having learned it, he wrote *Adonais* in or about May as "the image of his regret and honour for poor Keats," and considered it "perhaps better, in point of execution, than anything he had written." The beauty and energy of its treatment are assuredly very great ; and it will always

---

[1] This was written in 1869. Since then, in 1875, Mr. Swinburne (*Essays and Studies*) has offered some observations on the point. He professes to dissent from my suggestion, but to me he seems to coincide with it pretty closely.

possess an exceptional interest, as the tribute of love and admiration which one great poet eagerly paid to another, and as the record of his scorn against the literary bats who, by instinct and preference combined, had been flying for years past with leathern wings in the face of the light. If we distinguish between the execution and interest of the work on one side, and its poetical invention on the other, it may be doubted whether *Adonais* will eventually take, in the latter respect, a first-class position among Shelley's poems. To conceive such a subject from a truly original point of view is supremely difficult, and I question whether even Shelley can be said to have entirely attained to that. But, while one is reading *Adonais*, all such demur is waived in delight at the wonderful flow of poetry.

Any argument to prove the genuineness of Shelley's enthusiasm for Keats would be an impertinence; and still more impertinent any attempt to show that his enthusiasm was so beset with qualifications as not to be genuine at all. But it will be perfectly legitimate to exhibit, from Shelley's own writings, what was the precise balance of his mind on this subject. The first thing to be observed is that he admired *Hyperion* incomparably more than any other composition of its author; and the next, that, in the residue, he found much more to indicate genius than to justify the particular shapes in which that had developed itself. I shall here set down the principal observations; after which *Adonais* (with its preface) will have to speak for itself, as embodying what Shelley found it really essential to tell the world about Keats, when the work of the latter was accomplished, and its total value roughly ascertainable. "I have read Keats's poem [*Endymion*]: much praise is due to me for having read it, the author's intention appearing to be that no person should possibly get to the end of it. Yet it is full of some of the highest and the finest gleams of poetry; indeed, everything seems to be viewed by the mind of a poet which is described in it. I think, if he had printed about fifty pages of fragments from it, I should have been led to admire Keats as a poet more than I ought, of which there is now no danger." (6th September 1819.) "I have lately read your *Endymion* again, and even with a new sense of the treasures of poetry it contains, though treasures poured forth with indistinct profusion. This people in general will not endure; and that is the cause of the comparatively few copies which have been sold. I feel persuaded that you are capable of the greatest things, so you but will." ('To Keats, 27th July 1820.)[1] "Keats's new volume has arrived to us, and the fragment called *Hyperion* promises for him that he is destined to become one of the first writers of the age. His other things are imperfect enough, and, what is worse, written in the bad sort of style which is becoming fashionable among those who fancy that they are imitating Hunt and Wordsworth.[2] . . . . Where is Keats now? I am anxiously expecting him in Italy, when I shall take care to bestow every possible attention on him. I consider his a most valuable life, and I am deeply interested in his safety. I intend to be the physician both of his body and his soul; and to keep the one warm, and to teach the other Greek and Spanish. I am aware, indeed, in part, that I am nourishing a rival who will far surpass me : and this is an additional motive, and will be an added pleasure." (11th November 1820.) "Among the modern things which have reached me is a volume of poems by Keats; in other respects insignificant enough, but containing the fragment of a poem called *Hyperion*. . . . It is certainly an astonishing piece of writing, and gives me a conception of Keats which I confess I had not before." (15th November 1820.) " Among your anathemas of the modern attempts in poetry, do you include Keats's *Hyperion?* I think it very fine. His other poems are worth little :[3] but, if the *Hyperion* be not grand poetry, none has been produced by our contemporaries." (To Peacock, 15th February 1821.) " I am willing to confess that the *Endymion* is a poem considerably defective, and that perhaps it deserved as much censure as the pages of your Review record against it : but, not to mention that there is a certain contemptuousness of phraseology (from which it is difficult for a critic to abstain) in the review of *Endymion,* I do not think that the writer has given it its due praise. Surely the poem, with all its faults, is a very remarkable production for a man of Keats's age ; and the promise of ultimate excellence is such as has rarely been afforded even by such as have afterwards attained high literary eminence. Look at book ii. line 833, &c.,

---

[1] This very interesting letter, then in the possession of Mr. Lewes, was published in an article by that gentleman on Shelley in the *Westminster Review* for April 1841: it is not printed elsewhere, I think. Shelley hereby conveys to Keats the invitation (mentioned in our next extract) to stay with him in Pisa.

[2] Here follow some very severe observations on some poem or other, represented only by a —— in print. The poem indicated is not one of Keats's.

[3] Such a strong expression as this must not be taken too literally or thoroughly. Medwin says, and one can fully believe it is correct, that Shelley "often spoke with great admiration" not only of *Hyperion*, but also of *Isabella* and the *Eve of St. Agnes.*

and book iii. line 113 to 120: read down that page, and then again from line 193. I could cite many other passages to convince you that it deserved milder usage. . . . . There was no danger that it should become a model to the age of that false taste with which I confess that it is replenished. . . . . Allow me to solicit your especial attention to the fragment of a poem entitled *Hyperion*, the composition of which was checked by the review in question. The great proportion of this piece is surely in the very highest style of poetry. I speak impartially, for the canons of taste to which Keats has conformed in his other compositions are the very reverse of my own." (To the Editor of the *Quarterly Review*, 1820, but not eventually sent.)

Hellas was written in the autumn of 1821, finished about the end of October, and published early in the following spring. It must no doubt have been very rapid work, for Shelley himself terms it "a mere improvise." Based as it is in general scheme on the *Persæ* of Æschylus, and inartificially constructed out of the veering news of the day, this poem is still a solid and beautiful piece of work; and contains, especially in its lyrical choruses, many passages than which neither Shelley nor the English language has anything much better to show. It was fitting that the last complete work of some considerable length written by the glorious poet should be the expression of his deep-seated love for Greece, at a moment when to worship the land of Homer, Miltiades, Sophocles, and Plato, was also to hail the downfall of a crushing despotism, and the reawakening of a self-devoted people. The poet, the scholar, and the zealot of liberty, speak with one trumpet-tone in *Hellas*.

XXVII.—CRITIQUES AND SELF-CRITIQUES.

Here, unfortunately for ourselves and posterity, we have come to very nearly the close of Shelley's literary career. It may therefore now be not inappropriate to collect some of his utterances regarding his own position as a poet, and his attitude towards criticism from without, very generally abusive. Some of his most important expressions on these subjects are to be found in the prefaces &c. to his poems, to which the reader should refer. I will here extract only one of these, too important to be passed over. It occurs in a letter to Godwin, consequent upon that friend's strictures upon the *Revolt of Islam*, and is given in Mrs. Shelley's note to the poem (p. 421). "In this have I long believed that my power consists; in sympathy, and that part of the imagination which relates to sentiment and contemplation.

I am formed, if for anything .not in common with the herd of
mankind, to apprehend minute and remote distinctions of feeling, whether relative to external nature or the living beings
which surround us, and to communicate the conceptions which
result from considering either the moral or the material universe
as a whole. Of course, I believe these faculties, which perhaps
comprehend all that is sublime in man, to exist very imperfectly
in my own mind. . . . . I cannot but be conscious, in much of
what I write, of an absence of that tranquillity which is the attribute and accompaniment of power."

Other important observations are as follows (I give the first
merely as being the earliest definite expression[1] that we have
from Shelley on the point):—" You must know that I either am
or fancy myself something of a poet." (To Godwin, 24th February 1812.) " My poems[2] will, I fear, little stand the criticism,
even of friendship. Some of the later ones have the merit of
conveying a meaning in every word, and all are faithful pictures
of my feelings at the time of writing them ; but they are in a
great measure abrupt and obscure. One fault they are indis-
putably exempt from—that of being a volume of fashionable
literature." (January 1813.) "In poetry I have sought to avoid
system and mannerism : I wish those who excel me in genius
would pursue the same plan." (To Keats, 27th July 1820.)
"My thoughts aspire to a production of a far higher character
[than *Charles the First*]; but the execution of it will require
some years.[3] I write what I write chiefly to inquire, by the
reception which my writings meets with, how far I am fit for so
great a task or not." (22nd February 1821.) " If I understand
myself, I have written neither for profit nor for fame. I have
employed my poetical compositions and publications simply as
the instruments of that sympathy between myself and others
which the ardent and unbounded love I cherished for my kind
incited me to acquire." (1821.) " The poet and the man are
two different natures : though they exist together, they may be
unconscious of each other, and incapable of deciding on each
other's powers and efforts by any reflex act. The decision of

---

[1] Except one printed for the first time in my notes, vol. iii. p. 441.
[2] The poems here referred to, spoken of as "a volume of Minor Poems," have never
been published : unless we suppose some of those relegated to our Appendix to have been
included among them. The letter from which our extract comes was written, it will be
observed, about the time when *Queen Mab* was finished.
[3] Is this the *Triumph of Life?* One might suppose so, because, in a previous letter
(16th February 1821), Shelley had said : "I *am employed* in high and new designs in
verse : but they are the labours of years perhaps."

the cause, whether or no I am a poet, is removed from the present time to the hour when our posterity shall assemble : but the court is a very severe one, and I fear that the verdict will be *Guilty—Death.*" (19th July 1821.) " I despair of rivalling Lord Byron, as well I may; and there is no other with whom it is worth contending." (9th August 1821.) " How do I stand with regard to these two great objects of human pursuit [fame and money]? I once sought something nobler and better than either ; but I might as well have reached at the moon, and now, finding that I have grasped the air, I should not be sorry to know what substantial sum, especially of the former, is in your hands on my account. The gods have made the reviewers the almoners of this worldly dross ; and I think I must write an ode to flatter them to give me some, if I would not that they put me off with a bill on posterity, which when my ghost shall present, the answer will be 'no effects.'" (To Mr. Ollier, 25th September 1821.) "Lord Byron has read me one or two letters of Moore to him, in which Moore speaks with great kindness of me ; and of course I cannot but feel flattered by the approbation of a man my inferiority to whom (!) I am proud to acknowledge." (11th April 1822.) "I do not write : I have lived too long near Lord Byron, and the sun has extinguished the glow-worm—for I cannot hope (with St. John) that 'the light came into the world, and the world knew it not.'" (May 1822.)

The preceding extracts relate mainly to the poet's own estimate of his works : those which succeed have to do with his critics. " As to the Reviews, I suppose there is nothing but abuse; and this is not hearty or sincere enough to amuse me." (6th April 1819.) " Of course it gives me a certain degree of pleasure to know that any one likes my writings; but it is objection and enmity alone that rouses my *curiosity.*" (6th September 1819.) "If any of the Reviews abuse me, cut them out and send them : if they praise, you need not trouble yourself. I feel ashamed if I could believe that I should deserve the latter : the former, I flatter myself, is no more than a just tribute. If Hunt praises me, send it, because that is of another character of thing." (6th March 1820.) "I am, speaking literarily, infirm of purpose. I have great designs, and feeble hopes of accomplishing them. I read books, and though I am ignorant enough, they seem to teach me nothing. To be sure, the reception the public have given me might go far to damp any man's enthusiasm. They teach me, it may be said, only what is true : very true, I doubt not, and the more true the less agreeable. I can compare my experience in this respect to nothing but a series of wet blankets." (15th November 1820.) "The reviews of my *Cenci* (though some of them, and especially that marked ' John Scott,' are written with great malignity) on the whole give me as much encouragement as a person of my habits of thinking is capable of receiving from such a source—which is inasmuch as they coincide with and confirm my own decisions. My next attempt (if I should write more) will be a drama, in the composition of which I shall attend to the advice of my critics, to a certain degree. But I doubt whether I *shall* write more. I could be content either with the hell or the paradise of poetry : but the torments of its purgatory vex me, without exciting my powers sufficiently to put an end to the vexation." (20th January 1821.)[1] "I hear that the abuse against me exceeds all bounds. Pray, if you see any one article particularly outrageous, send it me. As yet, I have laughed : but woe to these scoundrels if they should once make me lose my temper. I have discovered that my calumniator in the *Quarterly Review* was the Reverend Mr. Milman.[2] Priests have their privilege." (11th June 1821.) "I write nothing, and probably shall write no more. It offends me to see my name classed among those who have no name. If I cannot be something better, I had rather be nothing. My motive was never the infirm desire of fame ; and, if I should continue an author, I feel that I *should* desire it. This cup is justly given to one only of an age—indeed, participation would make it worthless : and unfortunate they who seek it and find it not." (10th August 1821.) "Do not let my frankness with you, nor my belief that you deserve it more than Lord Byron,[3] have the effect of deterring you from assuming a station in modern literature which the universal voice of my contemporaries forbids *me* either to stoop or to aspire to. I am, and I desire to be, nothing." (To Leigh Hunt, with regard to the proposal of *The Liberal*, 26th August 1821.) "The man must be enviably happy whom Reviews can make miserable. I have neither

---

[1] This letter is misdated "1820" in the *Shelley Memorials*, p. 135. It alludes to the *Witch of Atlas*, which was written in August 1820,—not to speak of other conclusive indications.

[2] See the note to *Adonais* (vol. ii. p. 453). The statement in our text applies to the critique of *Laon and Cythna* in 1819—not to that of *Prometheus*, which latter review was only printed in October 1821.

[3] According to the full context, the thing which Hunt "deserves more than Lord Byron " is not "station in modern literature " (which would have been a grotesque flattery on Shelley's part), but Shelley's "frankness " in explaining his own relation to the scheme proposed

curiosity, interest, pain, nor pleasure, in anything, good or evil, they can say of me. I feel only a slight disgust, and a sort of wonder that they presume to write my name." (25th January 1822.)

These extracts—which could easily be supplemented by the statements of biographers, were it worth while—speak for themselves. They indicate that Shelley was absolutely above the level of criticism, and was, as a poet, his own sufficient law to himself; but that, at the same time, his comparative languor of production in the last year or so of his life was partly due to the perception that, however much he might exert his poetic powers, their results met with no adequate sympathy or recognition. He would have done nothing to curry favour: being received with disfavour time after time, he was the less inclined to re-encounter it once more. Though sometimes despondent, he was by no means unconscious (as how *could* he be?) of his own powers both of reason and of imagination, of the calibre of his poems, and of their right to appeal to posterity if not to contemporaries. At one time, indeed, he had considered the poetic faculty in himself to be hardly equal to the logical and metaphysical, and perhaps he never definitely reversed this estimate: but he resolved, at an early stage of his career, to use poetry as his means of self-expression, and he directed his studies accordingly.

XXVIII.—RAVENNA TO LERICI.

Shelley, as we have seen, arrived on the 6th of August 1821 on a visit to Byron at Ravenna. The latter was now domesticated with the Countess Guiccioli, whose judicial separation from her husband had been effected, but she was just at present staying at Florence. Shelley considered Byron immensely improved by this connexion: " he is becoming what he should be —a virtuous man." Yet he soon found that the change of conduct was not exactly the result of a change in ideas,—that the quasi-husband of La Guiccioli was still essentially much the same man as the miscellaneous debauchee of Venice: and he concluded that the lady, a truly loving and loveable person, would hereafter "have plenty of leisure and opportunity to repent her rashness." Byron had at Ravenna " two monkeys,[1] five cats, eight dogs, and ten horses; all of whom (except the horses) walk about the house like the masters of it. Tita the

---

[1] *Three* monkeys, along with "an eagle, a crow, and a falcon," are mentioned in another of Shelley's letters.

Venetian [late a gondolier, afterwards with Byron in Greece up to his death, and finally a messenger in the India House in London] is here, and operates as my valet; a fine fellow with a prodigious black beard, and who has stabbed two or three people, and is one of the most goodnatured-looking fellows I ever saw."

Among the first things that Shelley heard from Byron was a calumny affecting Shelley himself, in which Mr. and Mrs. Hoppner, whom he had known in Venice, were mixed up. Mr. Hoppner was Consul-General there, his wife was a native of Switzerland; and the impression which Shelley had received of them in the former instance was peculiarly favourable and sympathetic. He now wrote to Mary, asking her to refute the calumny, which he regarded as a most vile and disgraceful one. "Imagine my despair of good, imagine how is it possible that one of so weak and sensitive a nature as mine can run further the gauntlet through this hellish society of men." Mary felt as indignant as her husband, and wrote a letter in reply, which Byron engaged to forward to the Hoppners with his own comments. What this calumny was has never yet been distinctly stated. Mrs. Shelley's reply refers to "C.'s illness at Naples," and to the last letter of Elise—who, as we have seen, had been a nursemaid in Shelley's family since the time when they were sojourning near Geneva.[1] A sentence from his answer to Mary is worth extracting. "I do not wonder, my dearest friend, that you should have been moved. I was at first; but speedily regained the indifference which the opinion of anything and anybody, except our own consciences, amply merits, and day by day shall more receive from me." The strong expressions used in these letters should not be understood as truly misanthropic: Shelley was to the last thoroughly free from misanthropy, properly so called.

There was a question at this time whether Switzerland or some other place should be selected for the residence of Byron and the Countess Guiccioli. At his friend's request, Shelley

---

[1] The following is a passage in Shelley's letter. "The calumny . . . is evidently the source of the violent denunciations of the *Literary Gazette*—in themselves contemptible enough, and only to be regarded as effects, which show us their cause." We turn to the *Literary Gazette* for 19th May 1821, critique of *Queen Mab;* and find Shelley (by implication) termed an "incestuous wretch"—and then farther on: "To such [a man] it would be a matter of perfect indifference to rob a confiding father of his daughters, and incestuously to live with all the branches of a family whose morals were ruined by the damned sophistry of the seducer."

wrote to the lady, dissuading her and her family from choosing Switzerland; and she in reply begged Shelley not to leave Ravenna without bringing Byron along with him. Shelley regarded such a request from a lady as a law; and determined therefore not to lose sight of Lord Byron for any time until he should have brought him to Pisa, which his lordship was now minded to select for his sojourn.[1]

At Ravenna was started, apparently by Byron,[2] the project of a quarterly review or magazine, to be the organ for the author of *Cain* and *Don Juan*, and his immediate friends, to express their not invariably well-received sentiments. Shelley conveyed the proposal to Leigh Hunt on the 26th of August, saying that Byron's suggestion was for the three to publish in this magazine all their future original compositions, and to share the profits. Shelley at first opposed Byron's scheme; and, in writing to Hunt, he expressed in confidence his resolute determination not to accept either any part of the profits, or any lustre that might be reflected on himself, in popular eyes, by so close an association with Byron. Moreover he was afraid of both shackling himself and injuring the other writers by such a joint plan. He did, however, furnish some writings for the magazine, which commenced soon after his death under the name of *The Liberal* (the title first suggested was *The Hesperides*); but, even had he survived, he would have had no pecuniary interest in it.

The routine of life at Ravenna is thus described by Shelley. "Lord Byron gets up at two. I get up, quite contrary to my usual custom (but one must sleep or die, like Southey's sea-snake in *Kehama*), at twelve. After breakfast we sit talking till six. From six till eight we gallop through the pine-forests which divide Ravenna from the sea; then come home and dine; and sit up gossiping till six in the morning. I do not think this will kill me in a week or fortnight, but I shall not try it longer."

The Autumn and winter of 1821–2 were spent in Pisa by both Byron and Shelley. The former inhabited the Casa Lanfranchi: Shelley and his wife were in the Tre Palazzi on the opposite

---

[1] A very brief record of the opinion which La Guiccioli formed of Shelley may here be preserved. James Smith records of her conversation, not long after the death of Byron, "Bysshe Shelley she denominates a good man."

[2] Medwin, however, says that the first suggestion was made by Shelley, with a view to benefiting Leigh Hunt. This is quite conceivable; though the project, as schemed out for taking practical shape. is ascribed to Byron.

side of the Lungarno.¹ As we have already noted, they had now
plenty of society—in fact, more than enough for the poet.
Daily meetings with Byron, riding, pistol-practice—at which
both the poets were more than fairly good, Shelley's hand being
particularly steady—cheered or diverted many hours. Shelley
was not a graceful horseman, though he had had considerable
practice. The Williamses were now living in their own apartments in the same house with the Shelleys. The poet had
about this time a singular plan of life in his head : he wished to
obtain political employment at the court of a native Indian
prince, and consulted his friend Peacock, who had for some
three years held an appointment in the India House, as to the
feasibility of the plan. The reply was that such a post was
open to none save servants of the East India Company.

About the beginning of 1822 another friend was added to
this Pisan circle, and one who soon established a position of
great prominence and intimacy—Mr. (commonly called Captain) Edward John Trelawny. We owe to this gentleman one of
the best books extant regarding the poet, whom he understood
and loved at once. The genuine worshiper of Shelley will always entertain a respectful affection for Trelawny, still happily
among us; not to speak of the singular interest attaching to
his own career in Greece, and previously in a wandering sea-
life shadowed forth with more or less accuracy in that fascina-
ting book, *The Adventures of a Younger Son.* The first meeting
with Shelley must be told in Trelawny's own words. "The
Williamses received me in their earnest cordial manner. We
had a great deal to communicate to each other, and were in
loud and animated conversation, when I was rather put out by
observing in the passage near the open door, opposite to where
I sat, a pair of glittering eyes steadily fixed on mine : it was
too dark to make out whom they belonged to. With the acute-
ness of a woman, Mrs. Williams's eyes followed the direction
of mine, and, going to the doorway, she laughingly said:
'Come in, Shelley; it's only our friend Tre just arrived.'
Swiftly gliding in, blushing like a girl, a tall thin stripling held
out both his hands : and, although I could hardly believe—as I
looked at his flushed, feminine, and artless face—that it could
be the poet, I returned his warm pressure. After the ordinary
greetings and courtesies, he sat down and listened. I was

¹ They had been in the Casa Frassi, Lungarno, in 1820—as appears from a letter, of
the 7th March in that year, addressed by Mrs. Shelley to Miss Sophia Stacey, now Mrs.
Catty.

silent from astonishment. Was it possible this mild-looking beardless boy could be the veritable monster at war with all the world?—excommunicated by the Fathers of the Church, deprived of his civil rights by the fiat of a grim Lord Chancellor, discarded by every member of his family, and denounced by the rival sages of our literature as the founder of a Satanic school ? I could not believe it: it must be a hoax. He was habited like a boy, in a black jacket and trowsers which he seemed to have outgrown—or his tailor, as is the custom, had most shamefully stinted him in his ' sizings.' [The jacket was an object of some scorn to Mrs. Shelley.] Mrs. Williams saw my embarrassment, and, to relieve me, asked Shelley what book he had in his hand. —' Calderon's *Magico Prodigioso:* I am translating some passages in it.'—' Oh, read it to us ! ' Shoved off from the shore of commonplace incidents that could not interest him, and fairly launched on a theme that did, he instantly became oblivious of everything but the book in his hand. The masterly manner in which he analysed the genius of the author, his lucid interpretation of the story, and the ease with which he translated into our language the most subtle and imaginative passages of the Spanish poet, were marvellous, as was his command of the two languages. After this touch of his quality I no longer doubted his identity. A dead silence ensued. Looking up, I asked ' Where is he?'—Mrs. Williams said : ' Who? Shelley? Oh, he comes and goes like a spirit, no one knows when or where.' Presently he reappeared with Mrs. Shelley."

The translation which he was now making from Calderon was almost contemporaneous with that, still finer and more difficult, from Göthe's *Faust;* a work which he read about this time " over and over again, and always with sensations which no other composition excites: it deepens the gloom and augments the rapidity of ideas." Shelley had, however, been familiar with *Faust* for years past. Mr. Peacock says that Brockden " Brown's four novels [*Wieland, Ormond, Edgar Huntly,* and *Arthur Mervyn*], Schiller's *Robbers*, and Göthe's *Faust* [which last he began reading in 1815], were, of all the works with which he was familiar, those that took the deepest root in his mind, and had the strongest influence in the formation of his character." The translation from *Faust* appeared in the first number of the *Liberal;* both this and the Calderon translation had been done to serve as the basis of a paper which Shelley meant to write. Göthe became acquainted with the former, and expressed his hearty approbation of it.

The poet thought Trelawny noble and generous; and Mrs. Shelley soon—too soon—had reason to regard him as the only quite disinterested friend she had at hand.   He it was who, at a very early date of the acquaintanceship, suggested the idea of the boat which was to prove so ill-omened.   On the 15th of January he offered the model of an American schooner; but this design was overruled by Williams, who proposed another that he had brought from England, done by a naval friend, the reverse of perfectly safe.   This Trelawny got an intimate acquaintance at Genoa, Captain Daniel Roberts, R.N.,[1] to undertake.   The boat was named the *Don Juan*, and was to be the property of Shelley and Williams jointly.   Captain Roberts remonstrated against the design, but could not dissuade Williams from it.

Two singular incidents, which threatened serious consequences but came to little, marked the close of Shelley's stay in Pisa.

In December he learned that a man had been condemned to be burned to death at Lucca for an act of sacrilege—the scattering of the eucharistic wafers off an altar.   One less inimical than Shelley to intolerance and the modes of " Iberian priests " might well have felt some measure of indignant horror at such a sentence.   He forthwith proposed to Byron and Medwin that they and himself should arm, rescue the man at all costs on his coming forth for execution, and carry him off to the Tuscan frontier.   He also communicated with Lord Guilford, the English minister at Florence, and was preparing to promote a general memorial to the Grand Duke.   It soon turned out, however, that the judicial atrocity was not to be perpetrated: the prisoner had had his sentence commuted to labour at the galleys.

On the 24th of March occurred a *fracas* much talked of in books relating to Lord Byron, but which must here be dismissed with brevity.   Byron, Shelley, Count Pietro Gamba (brother of La Guiccioli), Captain Hay, Trelawny, and Mr. Taafe, an Irish gentleman, were riding near the gate termed Le Piagge, with the ladies following in a carriage, when a serjeant-major of hussars, named Masi, dashed through them, disconcerting Mr. Taafe, who was not a good rider.   He appealed to Byron, who, along with Shelley, rode after the serjeant-major.   A disturbance ensued; Masi slashed about

---

[1] This gentleman survived till 1873.

with his sword, and made some show of ordering out the guard
at the gate, to arrest the party; Byron and Gamba spurred on
towards the Casa Lanfranchi. The serjeant-major now as-
saulted Trelawny; when Shelley interposed his body, and
received a smart blow with the hilt of the sword, which knocked
him off his horse, and was sufficiently severe to turn him sick.
Some further incidents led up to the crowning feat—which was
a stab with a pitchfork administered to the hussar by a servant
of Byron or of the Gambas. The wound was of some gravity,
but not mortal. Shelley spoke of the whole affair as " a trifling
piece of business enough." It sufficed, however, along with
some other quarrels and deeper-lying political causes, to make
the government send out of Tuscany Count Pietro Gamba and
his father, and hence also to abridge the stay in Pisa of Lord
Byron, who moved off to Leghorn, and soon afterwards to
Genoa.

XXIX.—SHELLEY AT LERICI.

On the 26th of April the Shelleys and Williamses left Pisa
for the Casa Magni, a house situated on the very edge of the
sea-shore, between the villages of Lerici and San Terenzo, in
the Genoese territory. The poet had made a casual visit to
this coast in the preceding summer, and had ever since pondered its attractions of land and sea for a residence during the
hot season. The house, a white building with arches, had once
been a Jesuit convent, and was perfectly lonely; the scenery
was soft and sublime; the natives were semi-savages; provi-
sions had to be fetched from Sarzana, at a distance of three
miles and a half, and the general means of comfort were scanty,
like the victuals. A dining-room and four bed-rooms composed the establishment, which the wives did not greatly relish,
but made extremely pleasant with music, conversation, and
tender domesticities. Shelley's constant habits of benevolence
did not abate in this wild and half-inhabited region : wherever
there was sickness in a house within his range, there would he
be found, nursing and advising.[1]

The small schooner, the *Don Juan*, arrived on the 12th of
May. Shelley and Williams retained a sailor-boy, named
Charles Vivian, who was expert at managing her; and her
first performances filled them with satisfaction. Of course they
were now continually out on the sea, and the milder pleasures

---

[1] I give this interesting fact from the statement of a friend, Mr. Franklin Leifchild,
who stayed a little while on the spot some years ago, and there met an old man who
recollected Shelley and his ways - and this one among them.

of inland navigation sank into insignificance.   Shelley, according to the skilled evidence of Trelawny, was extremely awkward
at sea, besides having his mind continually elsewhere; Williams
was not unpromising, but inexperienced.   Both were far more
confident than cautious, and disinclined to submit to the warn-
ings addressed to them by Trelawny as to the great difference
between the chances well out at sea and those of the land-
locked bay close to their residence.   It was a season of sultry
heat and long drought: but this was, to Shelley, small objection
or none, for he revelled in heat, and would court any amount
of scorching, whether from the sun of summer abroad, or from
the winter fire within-doors.   There was something portentous,
a kind of ominous and trance-like splendour, in the scene and
the season.   We hear its echoes in the *Triumph of Life;* a
poem whose long processional suspense, and full-charged
visionary mysticism, might seem to derive from days muttering
with low thunder, and heavy with unrelaxed glare or gathering
densities of cloud.   In his boat or in some sea-cave, in oppression of sunlight or tremulous softness of moonlight, Shelley
continued this astonishing poem.   He had begun it at Pisa,
after throwing aside the drama of *Charles the First*—an under-
taking which he mentions now and again with a strong feeling
of its lofty requirements, but no great personal relish for the
work.   Probably, among friends and acquaintances at Pisa, and
with more than enough to fritter away his time, he found it
difficult to concentrate his mind and hand for so grave and
unaccustomed an effort.   "A devil of a nut it is to crack," he
said in a letter to Mr. Peacock, dated in January 1822.

Nor were portents wanting of another kind than those of sea,
sky, and climate.   Here are three curious stories, pertaining to
the last couple of months of Shelley's life, and of which the
reader may make what he pleases.

On the 6th of May Shelley and Williams were walking on the
terrace of the house in a moonlight evening, when the poet
grasped his companion's arm violently, and stared hard at the
surf, exclaiming, "There it is again—there!"   He ultimately
"declared that he saw, as plainly as he then saw me [Williams],
a naked child rise from the sea, and clap its hands as in joy,
smiling at him."   This child was Byron's natural daughter
Allegra, who had died of fever in the Convent of Bagnacavallo
on the 19th of April.[1]

On the 23rd of June he was heard screaming at midnight in

---

[1] So in a copy of the register.   Byron had "20 April" inscribed on a tablet.

the saloon. The Williamses ran in, and found him staring on vacancy. He had had a vision of a cloaked figure which came to his bedside, and beckoned him to follow. He did so ; and, when they had reached the sitting-room, the figure lifted the hood of his cloak, disclosed Shelley's own features, and, saying "Siete soddisfatto?" vanished. This vision is accounted for on the ground that Shelley had been reading a drama attributed to Calderon, named *El Embozado, ó El Encapotado*, in which a mysterious personage, who has been haunting and thwarting the hero all his life, and is at last about to give him satisfaction in a duel, finally unmasks, and proves to be the hero's own wraith. He also asks "Art thou satisfied?"—and the haunted man dies of horror.

On the 29th of June some friends distinctly saw Shelley walk into a little wood near Lerici, when in fact he was in a wholly different direction. This was related by Byron to Mr. Cowell.

Shelley had received news on the 20th that Leigh Hunt and his family had reached Genoa. Hunt, after some deliberation, and extraordinary delays in the transit, was come to Italy to join in the project of *The Liberal*. Shelley had by this time resolved that he could not even so much as act as the link between Lord Byron and Hunt: but he at once prepared to start in the *Don Juan* to Leghorn, whither the new-comer was proceeding to meet his lordship. After his two months at Lerici, perhaps the happiest he had ever known, and marked by an interval of unusually good health, he went off to Leghorn on the 1st of July, with Williams. He was in high spirits ; Mary, who, having recently had a miscarriage, was unable to accompany her husband, felt uncommonly depressed, and beset by melancholy forebodings. High spirits were themselves ominous of evil to Shelley; who "had recently remarked that the only warning he had found infallible was that, whenever he felt peculiarly joyous, he was certain that some disaster was about to ensue." A wind in the north-west, we are told, no less than extreme heat, was wont to exhilarate him. The last verses which Shelley wrote, and which have not come down to us, consisted of a welcome to Leigh Hunt.

A voyage of seven hours and a half took Shelley to Leghorn, where he greeted Hunt with fervid impetuosity. He rushed into his arms, exclaiming that he was "so inexpressibly delighted—you cannot think how inexpressibly happy it makes me !" He then went on with Hunt to Pisa, where both himself and Byron retained their residences ; and he saw his friends settled in their apartments in the Casa Lanfranchi, which Byron, after some friendly debates between himself and Shelley, had fitted up for the family.[1] Shelley accompanied Hunt about Pisa, still in high spirits, though his friend thought him less hopeful than of old.

A considerable change for the better had, however, taken place in Shelley's exterior during his residence in Italy. He had grown larger and more manly; his chest was perhaps three or four inches fuller in girth; his voice was stronger, his manner more confident and less changeful. His hair, still youthful in abundance and growth, had at a very early age (I presume as soon as 1817, or even sooner) begun to turn grey, and this had continued, though not to a very serious extent; but his visage remained unwrinkled, and his general aspect almost boyish (as we have just seen in Trelawny's account). This, however, was very much a matter of varying expression: no face was a live-lier mirror of the subtle change and play of emotion than Shelley's—and, as the feeling shifted, he might have been taken at this period for nineteen years of age, and immediately after-wards for forty. His countenance took every expression—earnest, joyful, touchingly sorrowful, listlessly weary; but the predominant aspect was one of promptitude and decision. In describing Shelley's appearance at the threshold of manhood, I said that his features " were in some sort feminine." Trelawny has employed the same epithet; and I am told that, on one occasion while out walking with a friend in Italy, Shelley was taken for a woman in man's clothes. But this feminine aspect is liable to be understood in too positive a sense, especially by persons who accept the portraits in good faith. Mr. Thornton Hunt says that the poet was not, properly speaking, feminine-looking; his shoulders, though not broad, were too square for that, and " the outline of the features and face possessed a firm-ness and *hardness* entirely inconsistent with a feminine charac-ter : the outline was sharp and firm,"—the beard not strong, but clearly marked.[2] The general look was delicate, but " the

---

[1] Some accounts say that Shelley was the paymaster: but I suppose his own statement (*Relics of Shelley*, p. 187) in a letter to Hunt must be taken as conclusive : " Lord B. had kindly insisted upon paying the upholsterer's bill."

[2] Some approach to a pair of moustachios, Trelawny infoms me, had about this time been made by Shelley—but they were very little of a pair. As regards his general appear-ance, I may perhaps as well give here the notes which I roughly jotted down concerning the portrait by Miss Curran (daughter of the Irish statesman) when I saw it in 1868 in the Exhibition of National Portraits at South Kensington, to which it had been contri-buted by Sir Percy Shelley. My notes were made at a time when the detailed statements left by biographers as to Shelley's appearance were by no means present to my memory : and, by their entire consonance with those statements so far as apparent age and com-

points" (as a grazier has it) showed far more than common masculine vigour. And this was in Shelley's character, as well as his face. With all his tremulous sensibility and superficial shyness, he possessed not only a great power of fascination, but uncommon force of will—to which, indeed, the tenour of his life bears amplest testimony. All who approached him tended to yield to his dictate: "his earnestness was apt to take a tone of command so generous, so free, so simple, as to be utterly devoid of offence, and yet to constitute him a sort of tyrant over all who came within his reach."

Whatever may have been his mood of the moment, whether "in high spirits" or "less hopeful than of old," Shelley took anything but a cheerful view of the prospects of Leigh Hunt in connexion with Lord Byron; and some effort was needed to control his own indignation at the shiftiness of his lordship. The latter had determined to leave Tuscany in consequence of the exile of the Gambas, and showed little disposition to fashion his plans according to the necessities or conveniences of Hunt with regard to the proposed magazine: moreover Mrs. Hunt, long in bad health, was pronounced by Vaccà to be hopelessly consumptive (although in fact she survived to an advanced age).

Two letters dated the 4th of July, one to Mrs. Shelley and the other to Mrs. Williams, are the last lines of writing extant from the hand of Shelley, and prove how acutely he felt for the distresses and uncertainties of his newly arrived friends. The reply of Mrs. Williams, written on the 6th, is also extant, and has been shown to me by Trelawny. It contains a farther singular foreboding: a reference—playful at the moment, but immediately turned into tragic—to Shelley's being about to join Plato in another world. In the poet's own letter to his wife the final words are "I have found the translation of the *Symposium;*" which, we may suppose, he was looking up for insertion in the *Liberal.* He himself was indeed bidden to another symposium —one which endures through eternity, at which Socrates is a

plexion are concerned, may tend to confirm the accuracy of the portrait, with regard to these points at least. The work was painted in 1819 (begun on 7th May, the day after the affair at the Roman Post-Office), when Shelley's real age was twenty-seven. "Small life-size. Age about nineteen. Plain green background. Waved hair, dark or darkening brown. Complexion fair, but as if a good deal exposed to air, giving rather a coppery-red hue. Eyes quite a dark blue. Mouth *entrouvert*, with a kind of curl of aspiration and apprehending. Open shirt, blue coat. Quill in hand; left not seen. Gives a decided impression of a poet, and the bad qualities of the picture are not of an offensive kind. Flat broad painting, very slight but not thin."—I am told that the late distinguished painter Mulready knew Shelley well, and said it was simply impossible to paint his portrait—he was "too beautiful."

guest once more, with Plato, Dante, Shakespeare, Bacon, and how many others beloved by Shelley, none more exalted than he, none crowned with a purer or more perennial garland.

XXX.—DEATH AND OBSEQUIES.

Shelley left Pisa on the night of the 4th of July for Leghorn, where he chiefly remained the next three days, though he was in Pisa again on the 6th and 7th. On this latter day, the last whose evening he was to witness, he said to Mrs. Leigh Hunt: " If I die to-morrow, I have lived to be older than my father ; I am ninety years of age." Williams at Leghorn was homesick, short as his absence had been ; Shelley troubled, and anxious to return in consequence of a desponding letter he had received from his wife. He brought from his banker's a canvas bag full of Tuscan crown-pieces. On Monday the 8th, about 3 P.M., they set sail from Leghorn for Lerici, taking leave of Trelawny, who was in charge of Byron's yacht the *Bolivar*, and who by a fatality was prevented from accompanying them owing to the want of a port-clearance, and the consequent prospect of the full term of quarantine. Captain Roberts watched with his glass, from the top of Leghorn light house, the progress of Shelley and Williams along the waves.

The day was terribly hot, with a dull dense calmness ; clouds were gathering from the south-west, black and ragged. The Genoese mate of the *Bolivar* remarked too truly to Trelawny that " the devil was brewing mischief." A sea-fog came up, and wrapped the boat from sight.

"I went down into the cabin," says Trelawny, "and sank into a slumber. I was roused up by a noise overhead, and went on deck. . . . It was almost dark, though only half-past six o'clock. The sea was of the colour, and looked as solid and smooth as a sheet of lead, and covered with an oily scum. Gusts of wind swept over without ruffling it ; and big drops of rain fell on its surface, rebounding as if they could not penetrate it. There was a commotion in the air, made up of many threatening sounds coming upon us from the sea. Fishing-craft and coasting vessels under bare poles rushed by us in shoals, running foul of the ships in the harbour. As yet the din and hubbub was that made by men ; but their shrill pipings were suddenly silenced by the crashing voice of a thunder-squall that burst right over our heads. For some time no other sounds were to be heard than the thunder, wind, and rain. When the fury of the storm, which did not last for more than twenty minutes, had abated, and the horizon was in some degree cleared, I looked to seaward anxiously, in the hope of descrying Shelley's boat among the many small craft scattered about." No trace of her was to be seen : she had made Via Reggio by the time the storm burst.[1]

Days ensued of horrible suspense to the wives—alas ! the widows—of Shelley and Williams, and of harrowing search and unremitting exertion to Trelawny. These need not now be dwelt upon. On the 22nd of July two corpses were found washed ashore ; that of Shelley near Via Reggio on the Tuscan coast—that of Williams near the tower of Migliarino, at the Bocca Lericcio, a distance of three miles. This corpse was in a piteous state : of Shelley's " the face and hands, and parts of the body not protected by the dress, were fleshless." A volume of Æschylus [2] was in one pocket : Keats's last book, lent to him by Hunt, and doubled back at the *Eve of St. Agnes*, was in the other, as if hastily thrust away when Shelley, absorbed in reading, was suddenly disturbed. Williams had seemingly attempted to swim : Shelley, being unable to do this, had more than once declared that, in any such contingency, he would be no trouble to anybody, but go down at once. It was only a few months before that the poet, inspirited by witnessing Trelawny's ease in swimming, had made a disastrous attempt for himself, and would then have drowned but for his companion's succour : he took it with the utmost coolness, saying—" It's a great temptation ; if old women's tales are true, in another minute I might have been in another planet." Three weeks later than Shelley and Williams, the sailor-boy, Charles Vivian, then a mere skeleton, was also thrown ashore, about four miles off. In September the schooner likewise was found : she had not capsized, but had sunk in ten to fifteen fathom water, and was considerably injured,[3] especially by a hole in the stern.

On the 8th of July, the day of Shelley's death, two Italian feluccas or fishing-boats had started, along with his schooner, in the same direction ; so Trelawny has recently stated in print. On the same evening or the following morning an English-made

---

[1] Medwin considered that he had seen the *Don Juan* at the moment of her disappearance. He says that on the afternoon of 8th July, being on a merchant-vessel five or six miles from the Bay of Spezia, he saw to leeward a schooner which he regarded as an English pleasure-boat. The squall burst, and concealed the schooner from view : when it lulled, no trace of her was visible. (*Life of Shelley*, vol. ii. p. 278.)

[2] Some authorities say " Sophocles," but it is a mistake.

[3] " Uninjured," says Mrs. Shelley, (vol. iii. p. 122). But the precise details given by Lady Shelley, from the examination made by Captain Roberts, show this to be a mistake (*Shelley Memorials*, p. 201)—not to speak of other testimony.

oar, believed to have come out of the schooner, which the Italian sailors however strenuously denied, was noticed in an Italian boat at Leghorn, one of those that had gone out and returned on the same occasion. Captain Roberts, who examined the schooner carefully after her recovery, came to the conclusion at first that she had been swamped in a heavy sea, but afterwards that she had been run down by one of the feluccas in the squall; and in this the Genoese dockyard authorities, and other competent persons generally, agreed. Some suspicions of foul play arose: it was surmised (as recorded by Leigh Hunt and his son) that a native boat had attempted to board the *Don Juan* piratically, tempted by the sum of money that she carried. Any suspicion of this kind, however, remaining unconfirmed, died out; and for years and years past nobody had disputed the conclusion that the schooner had been either swamped by the sea or accidentally run down. It is only of late, 1875, that the old suspicion of a shameful and detestable crime has again been publicly raised, and with added circumstance and cogency. It was said [1] that an old sailor had recently died at Spezia, confessing to the priest that he was one of the crew that ran-down Shelley and Williams, and he begged the priest to publish the confession. The crime, he said, was committed under the impression that Lord Byron was on board, with a large sum of money. They did not intend to sink the boat, but to board her and murder Byron: she sank as soon as struck. Trelawny considers this alleged confession to be highly consistent with the internal evidence of the case, and he still believes it to be true. The story was somewhat closely investigated at the time by persons on the spot; and it appears to be established that in 1863—not so recently as had at first been inferred—a boatman died near Sarzana, making (or at any rate alleged on reasonable authority to have made) a confession of his having taken part in the murder, as above stated, of Shelley and Williams. [2] Beyond this, the roots of the question have not yet been reached. What

---

[1] Miss Trelawny wrote this from Rome on 22nd November 1875 to her father, the friend of Shelley.

[2] Sir Vincent Eyre, writing to the *Times* on 28th December 1875, says that the account is this: "A boatman, dying near Sarzana, confessed about twelve years ago that he was one of the five who, seeing the English boat in great danger, ran her down, thinking Milord Inglese was on board, and they should find gold." This account reaches us by the following stages: (1) Sir V. Eyre was, in May 1875, informed as above by (2) a lady, an old friend of the Shelley family, living in a villa overlooking the Bay of Spezia, who had been so informed by (3) an Italian noble once residing in the vicinity, but now dead, who had been so informed by (4) the priest to whom the confession was made—and who (as Sir Vincent implies) did not violate the secret of the confessional because he left the boatman unnamed. Sir Vincent mentioned the matter to a friend of the Trelawny family and thus it came round to Miss Trelawny in November 1875.

we really want to know is, not whether some such confession was in fact rumoured in 1863, and again in 1875, but whether it was actually made, and was demonstrably or probably true. This has not yet been settled in the affirmative; and one would be fain to credit the negative as long as one can.

The corpses of Shelley and Williams were in the first instance buried in the sand, and quick-lime was thrown in. But such a process, as a final means of disposing of them, would have been contrary to the Tuscan law, which required any object thus cast ashore to be burned,[1] as a precaution against plague; and Trelawny, seconded by Mr. Dawkins, the English Consul at Florence, obtained permission to superintend the burning, and carry it out in a manner consonant to the feelings of the survivors. This process was executed with the body of Williams on the 15th of August—on the 16th with Shelley's. A furnace was provided, of iron bars and strong sheet-iron, with fuel, and frankincense, wine, salt, and oil, the accompaniments of a Grecian cremation: the volume of Keats was burned along with the body.[2] Byron and Leigh Hunt, with the Health-Officer and a guard of soldiers, attended the poet's obsequies. It was a glorious day, and a splendid prospect—the cruel and calm sea before, the Apennines behind. A curlew wheeled close to the pyre, screaming, and would not be driven away; the flame arose golden and towering. The corpse had now turned a dark indigo-colour. "The only portions that were not consumed," says Trelawny, "were some fragments of bones, the jaw, and the skull; but what surprised us all was that the heart remained entire. In snatching this relic from the fiery furnace, my hand was severely burnt." The ashes were coffered, and soon afterwards buried in the Protestant Cemetery in Rome. This was done at first under the direction of Consul Freeborn, and with the usual rites, for the authorities were urgent for immediate

---

[1] This is distinctly stated both by Mrs. Shelley and by Lady Shelley. Yet Trelawny shows quite as clearly that the burning of the bodies was only allowed after some solicitation, and was "an unprecedented proceeding." We are to understand that summary burning, as for instance in a lime-kiln, would have been the ordinary Italian plan: and that the "unprecedented" thing was the removal of the once hastily interred bodies, the ceremonial cremation after the classic pattern, and the delivery of the ashes to the surviving relatives.

[2] Captain Trelawny has no recollection of this detail: and he of course is *the* authority for all matters connected with the cremation. Still, it seems difficult to disregard the statement in the *Shelley Memorials* (p. 200), probably derived from Leigh Hunt: "The copy of Keats was lent by Leigh Hunt, who told Shelley to keep it till he could give it to him again with his own hands. As the lender would receive it from no one else, it was burnt with the body." The like statement is made in Leigh Hunt's *Autobiography*; and a letter from Mr. Browning (Hunt's *Correspondence*, vol. ii. p. 266) also makes it plain that Hunt continued to give this account of the matter.—I have lately (May 1877) been informed on good authority that the volume of Keats was buried in the sand along with Shelley's corpse; and that, when the corpse was taken up, the volume was found to have entirely perished, save only its binding. The latter may or may not have been burned.

action ; but Trelawny, shortly visiting the spot, found that Shelley's grave lay amid many others,—so he exhumed the ashes, and redeposited them, with no further consultation of the authorities, in a spot of ground selected and purchased by himself.   He planted six young cypresses and four laurels by Shelley's grave, and had his own dug close beside, with a stone which remains (and long may it remain) uninscribed. He added the quotation from Shakespeare to the inscription upon Shelley's grave, which runs exactly as follows :—

PERCY   BYSSHE   SHELLEY

COR   CORDIUM

NATUS IV AUG. MDCCXCII

OBIIT VIII JUL. MDCCCXXII.

" Nothing of him that doth fade
But doth suffer a sea-change
Into something rich and strange."

Though buried in the Protestant Cemetery, Shelley is not strictly in the same enclosed ground with his son William and Keats, but in a space immediately adjoining.   He is in the *new* cemetery, they are in the *old* one.   Further burials in the old cemetery were discontinued about this period, because the College of Fine Arts in Rome objected (and reasonably) that the frequent planting of cypresses and other trees in that en-closure would obscure the view of the pyramid of Caius Cestius.

I will here only add that Mary Shelley returned to England (whither she had been preceded by Mrs. Williams) in the autumn of 1823, died in February 1851, and is interred at Bournemouth.   Not far off, at Christchurch, her son has erected a sumptuous monument to her and his illustrious father's memory.   His own seat, Boscombe, is in the same vicinity.   This son, Percy Florence, succeeded to the baronetcy on the death of Sir Timothy in April 1844.   Godwin had died in 1836.

XXXI.—ANECDOTES AND EXCERPTS.

I find myself little inclined or qualified to dilate at this point upon Shelley's character and genius, or upon the loss which the world and English literature suffered in his death.   If his writings do not speak for themselves to the reader's intellect and heart, and if the record of so lofty, beautiful, and pure a life—one so steeped in every noblest enthusiasm, and develop-ing into every noblest performance—is not sufficient, the biographer may well despair of supplementing these.   I at any rate feel an oppressive sense of incompetence, of the meagreness and futility of verbal estimate, as I stand within the mighty shadow, and reflect what terms might be wanted to express it. Reverence and love, and a passionate tribute of admiration, may best beseem the biographer : and these are not the feelings which find their most apt expression in analytic words—rather in silence and absorption of spirit.

As regards the poems, the only observation I wish to add here is that their astonishing beauty of musical sound—admitted on all hands as one of their quite exceptional excellences—is combined with, perhaps partly dependent on, an indifference, uncommon in degree among finished poetical writers, to mere *correctness* of rhyming structure. The precise attention I had to bestow on this point brought the fact very forcibly before me—revealed a looseness of rhyming very much greater than I had before observed in my less technical readings of Shelley. Now, as Shelley himself opined, "the canons of taste are to be sought in the most admirable works of art;" and the combination, in his poems, of inexactitude of rhyming with almost unrivalled music of sound, suggests strongly whether this may not after all be the *right way* to attain the highest forms of verbal harmony in poetry—of course, given the true and great master. I will not enlarge upon the point, but simply append a list of loose rhymes to be found upon five pages[1] taken absolutely at random ; a list selected with a purpose would exhibit a still stronger case :—"Lot, thought—alone, shone—afar, war—stood, flood—evil, revel—strong, among—none, groan—drove, love—sinecure, fewer—count, front, account—require, Oliver—off, enough—down, one—promotion, motion—amid, pyramid—floors, alligators—river, ever, wheresoever—thee, thee (twice over)—low, how—fail (rhymeless)—despair, dear—accept not, reject not." Try yet two other pages at random :—"Good, solitude, flood—lot, thought—alone, on—firmament, lament—despair, here—withdrawn, gone, moan—burning, morning—die, me—fell, befell."

It will, I think, be more to the purpose of a true presentation of Shelley's character if, instead of perorating upon it, I cite here a few out of the many illustrative anecdotes; and these I shall cull with the sole object of such illustration, and in the words (mostly condensed) of the narrators—careless whether the impression produced by them be grave or mirthful. I will

[1] Of my edition of 1870.

also add two estimates of Shelley's genius given by pre-eminent living poets, and of enduring value when the mere exercitations of critics shall have vanished from record.   Shelley's personality was especially self-consistent—a solid rock of native genuineness, giving forth varied but not inharmonious manifestations. No one ought to be surprised at singularities, oddities, or semi-absurdities, in these phases of character; and anybody whose sympathy is with *men*, and not with such substitutes as "humanity," the "poet-soul," or the like cheap abstractions, will feel the greatness in Shelley even more conceivable, instead of less so, when he has thoroughly explored the by-ways of his nature.   The little that Mrs. Shelley has written concerning her husband shows a love and admiration of his personal character of which only a small part should be set down to the score of conjugal affection; and the unconventional nature of Trelawny, oscillating between violence and romance, seems to have entered into Shelley's more sympathetically than that of any other biographer.   To Hogg and Peacock, valuable as were their acumen and opportunities, Mr. Thornton Hunt demurs as writers of Shelley's life in àny complete sense; and his remark on his father in the same capacity appears to me particularly right.   Leigh Hunt "was scarcely suited to comprehend the strong instincts, indomitable will, and complete unity of idea, which distinguished Shelley: accordingly we have from my father a very doubtful portrait, seldom advancing beyond details which are at once exaggerated and explained away by qualifications."—I now proceed to the anecdotes, to which I append the names of the several narrators, and the date, actual or approximate, to which the circumstances pertain. The flavour of an anecdote is very volatile, and seldom uninjured by transfer into a different vehicle of words.

Shelley in boyhood "had a wish to educate some child, and often talked seriously of purchasing a little girl for that purpose. A tumbler who came to the back door to display her wonderful feats attracted him, and he thought she would be a good subject for the purpose : but all these wild fancies came to nought. He did not consider that board and lodging would be indispensable." (Miss Shelley, *circa* 1807.)

"If mercy to beasts be a criterion of a good man, numerous instances of extreme tenderness would demonstrate his worth. We were walking one afternoon in Bagley Wood : on turning a corner, we suddenly came upon a boy who was driving an ass. It was very young and very weak, and was staggering beneath

a most disproportionate load of faggots; and he was belabour-
ing its lean ribs angrily and violently with a short, thick, heavy
cudgel.   At the sight of cruelty Shelley was instantly trans-
ported far beyond the usual measure of excitement : he sprang
forward, and was about to interpose with energetic and indignant vehemence.   I caught him by the arm, and to his present
annoyance held him back, and with much difficulty persuaded
him to allow me to be the advocate of the dumb animal.   [En-
sues a dialogue between Hogg and the boy, in which the latter
is put to shame.]   Shelley was satisfied with the result of our
conversation.   Although he reluctantly admitted that the acri-
mony of humanity might often aggravate the sufferings of the
oppressed by provoking the oppressor, I always observed that
the impulse of generous indignation, on witnessing the infliction
of pain, was too vivid to allow him to pause."   (Hogg, *circa*
1810.)—"I wish you to look out for a home for me and Mary
and William, and the kitten who is now *en pension*."   (Shelley,
from Mont Alègre, to Peacock in England, 1816.)—"The
Grotta del Cane we saw, because other people see it; but
would not allow the dog to be exhibited in torture, for our
curiosity.   The poor little animals stood moving their tails in
a slow and dismal manner, as if perfectly resigned to their
condition—a cur-like emblem of voluntary servitude.   The
effect of the vapour, which extinguishes a torch, is to cause
suffocation at last."   (Shelley, 1819.)

   "It now seems an incredible thing, and altogether incon-
ceivable, when I consider the gravity of Shelley, and his invin-
cible repugnance to the comic, that the monkey-tricks of the
schoolboy could have still lingered; but it is certain that some
slight vestiges still remained.   The metaphysician of eighteen
actually attempted once or twice to electrify the son of his
scout—a boy like a sheep, by name James; who roared aloud
with ludicrous and stupid terror whenever Shelley affected to
bring by stealth any part of his philosophical apparatus near to
him."   (Hogg, *circa* 1810.)—"It may be imagined that Shelley
was of a melancholy cast of mind.   On the contrary, he was
naturally full of playfulness, and remarkable for the *fineness* of
his ideas ; and I have never met any one in whom the brilliance
of wit and humour was more conspicuous.   In this respect he
fell little short of Byron ; and perhaps it was one of the great
reasons why Byron found such a peculiar charm in his conversation."   (Medwin, *circa* 1821.)—"Shelley, like other students,
would, when the spell that bound his faculties was broken, shut

his books, and indulge in the wildest flights of mirth and folly
We talked and laughed, and shrieked and shouted, as we
emerged from under the shadows of the melancholy pines.
The old man I had met in the morning gathering pine-cones
passed hurriedly by with his donkey, giving Shelley a wide
berth, and evidently thinking that the melancholy Englishman
had now become a raving maniac." (Trelawny, 1822.)

"With how unconquerable an aversion do I shrink from political articles in newspapers and reviews! I have heard people
talk politics by the hour, and how I hated it and them! I went
with my father several times to the House of Commons, and
what creatures did I see there! What faces! what an expression of countenance! what wretched beings!" (Shelley, as reported by Hogg, *circa* 1811.)—"A newspaper never found its
way to his rooms the whole period of his residence at Oxford;
but, when waiting in a bookseller's shop, or at an inn, he would
sometimes, although rarely, permit his eye to be attracted by a
murder or a storm. If it chanced to stray to a political article,
after reading a few lines he invariably threw it aside to a great
distance; and he started from his seat, his face flushing, and
strode about muttering broken sentences, the purport of which
was always the same—his extreme dissatisfaction at the want of
candour and fairness and the monstrous disingenuousness which
politicians manifest in speaking of the characters and measures
of their rivals." (Hogg, *circa* 1811.)—"Never have I seen him
read a newspaper." (Medwin, *circa* 1821.)

"I was about to enter Covent Garden when an Irish labourer
whom I met, bearing an empty hod, accosted me somewhat
roughly, and asked why I had run against him. I told him
briefly that he was mistaken. He discoursed for some time with
the vehemence of a man who considers himself injured or in-
sulted; and he concluded, being emboldened by my long
silence, with a cordial invitation just to push him again. Several
persons not very unlike in costume had gathered round him, and
appeared to regard him with sympathy. When he paused, I
addressed to him slowly and quietly, and (it should seem) with
great gravity, these words, as nearly as I can recollect them:
'I have put my hand into the hamper, I have looked upon the
sacred barley, I have eaten out of the drum, I have drunk and
was well pleased; I have said κόγξ ὄμπαξ, and it is finished.'—
'Have you, sir?' inquired the astonished Irishman; and his
ragged friends instantly pressed round him with—'Where is
the hamper, Paddy?' 'What barley?' and the like. I turned

therefore to the right, leaving the astounded neophyte, whom I had thus planted, to expound the mystic words of initiation as he could to his inquisitive companions. I marvelled at the ingenuity of Orpheus—if he were indeed the inventor of the Eleusinian mysteries—that he was able to devise words that (imperfectly as I had repeated them, and in the tattered fragment that has reached us) were able to soothe people so savage and barbarous. 'Κὸγξ ὄμπαξ, and it is finished!' exclaimed Shelley, crowing with enthusiastic delight at my whimsical adventure [afterwards narrated to him]. A thousand times, as he strode about the house, and in his rambles out of doors, would he stop, and repeat aloud the mystic words of initiation; but always with an energy of manner, and a vehemence of tone and of gesture, that would have prevented the ready acceptance which a calm passionless delivery had once procured for them. How often would he throw down his book, clasp his hands, and, starting from his seat, cry suddenly with a thrilling voice, ' I have said κὸγξ ὄμπαξ, and it is finished!'" (Hogg, *circa* 1811.)

"To be always in a hurry was Bysshe's grand and first rule of conduct. His second canon of practical wisdom—and this he esteemed hardly less important than the former—was to make a mystery of everything, to treat as a profound secret matters manifest, patent, and fully known to everybody. A lively fancy, which imagined difficulties and created obstacles where none existed, was the true cause of a course of dealing that was troublesome and injurious to himself, and to all connected with him." (Hogg, *circa* 1811.)

"I am determined to apply myself to a study that is hateful and disgusting to my very soul, but which is above all other studies necessary for him who would be listened to as a mender of antiquated abuses—I mean that record of crimes and miseries, history." (Shelley, 1812.)—"I am unfortunately little skilled in English history; and the interest which it excites in me is so feeble that I find it a duty to attain merely to that general knowledge of it which is indispensable." (Ditto, 1818.)

"He took strange caprices, unfounded frights and dislikes, vain apprehensions and panic terrors, and therefore he absented himself from formal and sacred engagements. He was unconscious and oblivious of times, places, persons, and seasons. When he was caught, the king of beauty and fancy would too commonly bolt. His flight from society was usually surreptitious and stealthy; but I have observed him to start up hastily, to declare publicly that his presence was imperatively required

elsewhere on matters of moment, and to retreat with as much
noise and circumstance as an army breaking up its camp."
(Hogg, *circa* 1813.)—" Amongst the persons who called on him
at Bishopgate was one whom he tried hard to get rid of, but
who forced himself on him in every possible manner.   He saw
him at a distance one day as he was walking down Egham Hill,
and instantly jumped through a hedge, ran across a field, and
laid himself down in a dry ditch.   Some men and women who
were haymaking in the field ran up to see what was the matter,
when he said to them : 'Go away, go away ! Don't you see it's
a bailiff ?' On which they left him, and he escaped discovery."
(Peacock, *circa* 1815.)—" One morning I was in Mrs. Williams's
drawing-room.   Shelley stood before us with a most woful expression. 'Mary says she will have a party ! There are English singers here, the Sinclairs: and she will ask them, and every
one she or you know—oh the horror ! For pity go to Mary,
and intercede for me.   I will submit to any other species of
torture than that of being bored to death by idle ladies and
gentlemen.'   After various devices, it was resolved that Ned
Williams should wait upon the lady, and see what he could do
to avert the threatened invasion of the poet's solitude.   Ned returned with a grave face.   'The lady,' commenced Ned, 'has
set her heart on having a party, and will not be baulked.'   But,
seeing the poet's despair, he added : ' It is to be limited to those
here assembled, and some of Count Gamba's family ; and, instead of a musical feast—as we have no souls—we are to have
a dinner.' The poet hopped off rejoicing; making a noise that
I should have thought whistling, but that he was ignorant of
that accomplishment. Shelley in society, not thinking of himself,
was as much at ease as in his own home ; omitting no occasion
of obliging those whom he came in contact with, readily con-
versing with all or any who addressed him, irrespective of age
or rank, dress or address."   (Trelawny, 1822.)

    " My greatest content would be utterly to desert all human
society.   I would retire with you and our child to a solitary
island in the sea ; would build a boat; and shut upon my retreat the floodgates of the world.   I would read no reviews, and
talk with no authors. If I dared trust my imagination, it would
tell me that there are one or two chosen companions beside
yourself whom I should desire. But to this I would not listen :
where two or three are gathered together, the devil is among
them.   And good far more than evil impulses, love far more
than hatred, has been to me, except as you have been its object,

the source of all sorts of mischief. So on this plan I would be alone; and would devote either to oblivion or to future generations the overflowings of a mind which, timely withdrawn from the contagion, should be kept fit for no baser object. The other side of the alternative (for a medium ought not to be adopted) is to form for ourselves a society of our own class, as much as possible, in intellect or in feelings, and to connect ourselves with the interests of that society. Our roots never struck so deeply as at Pisa." (Shelley to his wife, 1821.)

" I knew Shelley more intimately than any man, but I never could discern in him any more than two fixed principles. The first was a strong irrepressible love of liberty; of liberty in the abstract, and somewhat after the pattern of the ancient republics, without reference to the English constitution—respecting which he knew little and cared nothing, heeding it not at all. The second was an equally ardent love of toleration of all opinions, but more especially of religious opinions—of toleration complete, entire, universal, unlimited; and as a deduction and corollary from which latter principle he felt an intense abhorrence of persecution of every kind, public or private." (Hogg, *circa* 1814.)

" He was one day going to town with me in the Hampstead stage when our only companion was an old lady, who sat silent and still, after the English fashion. Shelley was fond of quoting a passage from *Richard the Second*, in the commencement of which the king, in the indulgence of his misery, exclaims,

> ' For heaven's sake, let us sit upon the ground,
> And tell sad stories of the death of kings.'

Shelley, who had been moved into the ebullition by something objectionable which he thought he saw in the face of our companion, startled her into a look of the most ludicrous astonishment by suddenly calling this passage to mind, and, in his enthusiastic tone of voice, addressing me by name with the first two lines. ' Hunt,' he exclaimed,

> ' For heaven's sake, let us sit upon the ground,
> And tell sad stories of the death of kings.'

The old lady looked on the coach-floor, as if expecting to see us take our seats accordingly." [1] (Leigh Hunt, 1817.)

" Shelley, in coming to our house that night, had found a

---

[1] The reader who wishes to judge whether some of Hogg's anecdotes should not be taken *cum grano salis*, may compare this temperate and authentic version of the matter with that in Hogg's *Life*, vol. ii. pp. 304-7.

woman lying near the top of the hill, in fits. It was a fierce
winter-night, with snow upon the ground; and winter loses
nothing of its fierceness at Hampstead. My friend, always the
promptest as well as most pitying on these occasions, knocked
at the first house he could reach, in order to have the woman
taken in. The invariable answer was that they could not do it.
Time flies; the poor woman is in convulsions—her son, a young
man, lamenting over her. At last my friend sees a carriage
driving up to a house at a little distance. He plants himself
in the way of an elderly person, who is stepping out of the carriage with his family. He tells his story: they only press on
the faster. 'Will you go and see her?' 'No sir; there's no
necessity for that sort of thing, depend on it. Impostors swarm
everywhere: the thing cannot be done. Sir, your conduct is
extraordinary.' 'Sir,' cried Shelley, assuming a very different
manner, and forcing the flourishing householder to stop out of
astonishment, 'I am sorry to say that *your* conduct is *not* extraordinary; and, if my own seems to amaze you, I will tell you
something which may amaze you a little more, and I hope will
frighten you. It is such men as you who madden the spirits
and the patience of the poor and wretched; and, if ever a con-
vulsion comes in this country (which is very probable), recollect
what I tell you :—You will have your house, that you refuse to
put the miserable woman into, burnt over your head!' 'God
bless me, sir! Dear me, sir!' exclaimed the poor frightened
man, and fluttered into his mansion. The woman was then
brought to our house, which was at some distance, and down a
bleak path (it was in the Vale of Health) ;[1] and Shelley and her
son were obliged to hold her till the doctor could arrive."
(Leigh Hunt, *circa* 1817.)

"When Shelley was staying in the villa of the Gisbornes, a
most droll incident occurred. It appears that the servants,
Giuseppe and Annunziata, who were man and wife, had been
left behind with the Shelleys. One evening there had sprung
up a thorough conjugal tempest; and Shelley, hearing Giuseppe
abusing his wife very savagely, and also ill-using her, rushed
upon him with a pistol, shouting, 'I'll shoot you, I'll shoot
you!' The startled fellow ran for his very life, Shelley after
him; till the former, coming to a shrubbery of laurels, managed
to slip under them. Shelley in his eagerness darting past him,
he in a few minutes found it possible to dodge back into the

---

[1] Mr. Thornton Hunt believes that Shelley carried the woman on his back for some
way down the Vale of Health, her son's strength having begun to fail him.

house unperceived. Shelley, seeing him no more, at last went back to the house ; where, to his unspeakable amaze, he found Giuseppe and Annunziata sitting together in the most amicable manner, addressing each other as 'Caro' and 'Carissima.' 'But were you not quarrelling even now?' exclaimed the perplexed poet. 'No, signor, we never quarrelled.' 'But I have been running after you in order to shoot you!' 'No, signor, you never ran after me, for I have been sitting here for the last hour or more. You must have fancied all this.' And—Giuseppe and Annunziata (who had both been considerably frightened) continuing to assure him that they had had no quarrel, and Mary Shelley, whom they had let into the secret, saying the same—Shelley was at last utterly mystified, and half inclined himself to believe that he must have fancied it." (Miss Mathilde Blind, 1820.) [1]

"He had never read *Wilhelm Meister*, but I have heard him say that he regulated his conduct towards his friends by a maxim which I found afterwards in the pages of Göthe : 'When we take people merely as they are, we make them worse; when we treat them as if they were what they should be, we improve them as far as they can be improved.'" (Mrs. Shelley, *circa* 1820.)

"Ready as Shelley always was with his purse or person to assist others, his purse had a limit, but his mental wealth seemed to have none ; for not only to Byron, but to any one disposed to try his hand at literature, Shelley was ever ready to give any amount of mental labour." (Trelawny, 1822.)

"The unmistakable quality of the verse would be evidence enough, under usual circumstances, not only of the kind and degree of .the intellectual but of the moral constitution of Shelley ; the whole personality of the poet shining forward from the poems, without much need of going further to seek it. The *Remains* [2]—produced within a period of ten years, and at a season of life when other men of at all comparable genius have hardly done more than prepare the eye for future sight, and the tongue for speech—present us with the complete enginery of a

---

[1] This amusing anecdote had not hitherto (1870) been in print, and is therefore all the more worthy of preservation here. Miss Blind, who has kindly imparted it to me (along with one or two other particulars), received it from a lady connected with the Gisborne family, whose informants were the servants themselves. The anecdote is of much value as illustrating the poet's haziness of mind in matters of fact—thus tending to show how readily he may sometimes, without meaning to deceive, have fancied things, and related them as realities.

[2] This term includes of course the entire poetical works of Shelley, and is not limited to the *Posthumous Poems* (comprising *Julian and Maddalo*, *The Witch of Atlas*, and a number of minor compositions).

poet, as signal in the excellence of its several adaptitudes as transcendent in the combination of effects :—examples, in fact, of the whole poet's function of beholding with an understanding keenness the universe, Nature and Man, in their actual state of perfection in imperfection,—of the whole poet's virtue of being untempted, by the manifold partial developments of beauty and good on every side, into leaving them the ultimates he found them, induced by the facility of the gratification of his own sense of those qualities, or by the pleasure of acquiescence in the shortcomings of his predecessors in art, and the pain of disturbing their conventionalisms. ' The whole poet's virtue,' I repeat, of looking higher than any manifestation yet made of both beauty and good, in order to suggest, from the utmost actual realization of the one, a corresponding capability in the other, and, out of the calm, purity, and energy, of Nature, to reconstitute and store up, for the forthcoming stage of man's being, a gift in repayment of that former gift, in which man's own thought and passion had been lavished by the poet on the else-incompleted magnificence of the sunrise, the else-uninterpreted mystery of the lake ; so drawing out, lifting up, and assimilating, this ideal of a future man, thus descried as possible, to the present reality of the poet's soul, already arrived at the higher state of development, and still aspirant to elevate and extend itself in conformity with its self-improving perceptions of, no longer the eventual Human, but the actual Divine.   In conjunction with which noble and rare powers came the subordinate power of delivering these attained results to the world in an embodiment of verse more closely answering to and indicative of the process of the informing spirit (failing as it occasionally does in art, only to succeed in highest art), with a diction more adequate to the task, in its natural and acquired richness, its material colour, and spiritual transparency (the whole being moved by and suffused with a music at once of the soul and the sense, expressive both of an external might of sincere passion, and an internal fitness and consonancy), than can be attributed to any other writer whose record is among us. . . . I pass from Shelley's minor excellences to his noblest and predominating characteristic.   This I call his simultaneous perception of Power and Love in the absolute, and of Beauty and Good in the concrete ; while he throws, from his poet's station between both, swifter, subtler, and more numerous films, for the connexion of each with each, than have been thrown by any modern artificer of whom I have knowledge,—proving how (as he says)

' The spirit of the worm beneath the sod
In love and worship blends itself with God.'

I would rather consider Shelley's poetry as a sublime fragmentary essay towards a presentment of the correspondency of the universe to Deity, of the natural to the spiritual, and of the actual to the ideal, than I would isolate and separately appraise the worth of many detachable portions which might be acknowledged as utterly perfect in a lower moral point of view, under the mere conditions of art." (Browning, 1851.)

" Shelley outsang all poets on record but some two or three throughout all time : his depths and heights of inner and outer music are as divine as Nature's, and not sooner exhaustible. He was the perfect singing-god ; his thoughts, words, deeds, all sang together. . . . . I do not think that justice has yet been done to Shelley, as to some among his peers, in all details and from every side. . . . . The *Lines written among the Euganean Hills* [are] no piece of spiritual sculpture, or painting-after-the-life of natural things. I do not pretend to assign it a higher or a lower place : I say simply that its place is not the same. It is a rhapsody of thought and feeling coloured by contact with Nature, but not born of the contact ; and such as it is all Shelley's work is, even when most vague and vast in its elemental scope of labour and of aim. A soul as great as the world lays hold on the things of the world ; on all life of plants and beasts and men—on all likeness of time and death, and good things and evil. His aim is rather to render the effect of a thing than a thing itself ; the soul and spirit of life rather than the living form, the growth rather than the thing grown. And herein he is unapproachable. . . . . If Shelley had lived, *The Cenci* would not now be the one great play, written in the great manner of Shakespeare's men, that our literature has seen since the time of these. The proof of power is here as sure and as clear as in Shelley's lyric work ; he has shown himself, what the dramatist must needs be, as able to face the light of hell as of heaven, to handle the fires of evil as to brighten the beauties of things. This latter work, indeed, he preferred, and wrought at it with all the grace and force of thought and word which give to all his lyrics the light of a divine life ; but his tragic truth and excellence are as certain and absolute as the sweetness and the glory of his songs. The mark of his hand, the trick of his voice, we can always recognize in their clear character and individual charm ; but the range is various, from the starry and heavenly heights to the tender and flowering fields

of the world, wherein he is god and lord. . . . The master-
singer of our modern race and age; the poet beloved above all
other poets, being beyond all other poets—in one word, and
the only proper word—divine." (Swinburne, 1869.)

XXXII.—SHELLEY'S OPINIONS.

It will be proper here to give a slight but not indefinite glance
at Shelley's opinions. I shall confine myself to three principal topics—1, the Existence or Nature of a Deity; 2, the
Immortality of the Soul; and 3, Political Institutions. The
reader will no doubt understand that I here enter into no controversy, and side with no disputant. To show that Shelley was
right or wrong theoretically—still less so morally—wrong in
being an atheist if he was one, or right in being a theist if he
was that—is no part of my function: I have no sort of wish to
" make him out " either one or the other, but solely to trace
which of the two he was. Personally, my firm conviction is that
he was entitled to hold his own speculative opinion, whatever it
may have been: and so I leave this aspect of the question.

Shelley, dying before he had completed thirty years of age,
was no doubt not at the end of his intellectual or speculative
tether. What he might have become it is of course impossible
to ascertain; what he had been in very early youth is now of
next to no consequence; what he had attained to by the close of
his life is the thing which it imports us to know. I shall therefore take as my starting-point the latest, and not the earliest,
indications that I can find, and trace backwards from that point
with lessening particularity; only premising that, in chrono-
logical sequence, he was mainly an adherent of the sceptical
system in his incipient manhood, or about the time of his
studentship at Oxford, afterwards of French materialism, as in
the notes to *Queen Mab,* and subsequently of the Berkeleyan or
Immaterial Philosophy. He became acquainted with Berkeley's writings at the instance of Southey, towards the beginning
of 1812; and they continued to germinate increasingly in his
mind from two or three years later. When he wrote the *Mont
Blanc* in 1816, he was obviously more of an Immaterialist than
a Materialist; and so with the *Ode to Heaven* (1819), *Sensitive
Plant* (1820), and other writings.

1. *The Existence or Nature of a Deity.* A Berkeleyan believes[1] that it is impossible to prove the existence of matter as

---

[1] I put these abstruse matters without any pretence to philosophical accuracy. If the
reader well versed in metaphysics perceives them to be badly put, he perceives no more
than I am quite prepared to learn.

anything else than a perception of the mind, *because* it is impossible to prove that the perception in question may not be communicated to the mind by an immediate operation of Deity, without the intervention of any actual matter. He further believes that matter can not only not be proved to exist, but *can* be proved not to exist. Thus, from the first of these two beliefs, a thorough Berkeleyan *cannot* be an atheist, for the argument itself presupposes a Deity. But it is conceivable that Shelley was not a thorough Berkeleyan : he may, as an Immaterialist, have stopped short at the nature of the human mind ; and may have thought that the perceptions of that mind, without either any operation of Deity thereon, or any actual matter, are our sole informants and criteria of phenomena. It therefore still remains to inquire whether or not Shelley became eventually a theist, and in what sense.

The latest indication I find on this subject is a dialogue between Shelley and Trelawny, related by the latter, and belonging probably to the Spring of 1822. Shelley is replying to Trelawny's inquiry " Why do you call yourself an atheist ? " and says : " I used it [the name atheist] to express my abhorrence of superstition : I took up the word, as a knight took up a gauntlet, in defiance of injustice." There is not much to be made out of this. If reported with verbatim accuracy, it implies that Shelley in 1822 was still wont to call himself an atheist ; and also that from first to last the term had been used for the purpose, not solely of definition, but partly of defiance.

In the year 1821 we meet with two phrases[1] which, taken on their own showing, would indicate belief in a God. In *Adonais* (vol. ii. p. 373)—

> "A quickening life from the Earth's heart has burst,
> As it has ever done, with change and motion,
> From the great morning of the world when first
> God dawned on chaos."

In *The Boat on the Serchio* (vol. iii. p. 171)—

> " All rose to do the task He set to each
> Who shaped us to His ends and not our own.
> The million rose to learn, and one to teach
> What none yet ever knew nor can be known."

---

[1] There is also a third phrase, in the *Defence of Poetry* : " A poem . . . . is the creation of actions according to the unchangeable forms of human nature as existing in the mind of the Creator, which is itself the image of all other mind." Here the word "Creator," having a capital initial letter (as printed in the *Essays and Letters*, vol. i. p. 12), seems at first sight to mean "Creative Deity," and, if it did so, the passage would be a very important one for our present purpose : but, on considering the entire clause and context, I can only infer that the " Creator " here spoken of is simply the human poet, ποιητής.

Of these phrases, the first certainly does not count for much : it may have little beyond a rhetorical or figurative significance, although properly it is an assertion of creative—or at any rate regulative—Deity. The second is more important. The poem is strictly personal to Shelley himself, and one can scarcely suppose he would put into it a theistic phrase if he steadfastly professed atheism. Still, one must hesitate before laying any very great stress, or putting any very sharply defined construction, on its terms.

We next (noting for what it may be worth the couplet from *Epipsychidion*—1821—quoted on p. 139) step back to the year 1819, and observe, in a letter to Leigh Hunt dated 27th September, an expression which counts for a good deal. "It would give me much pleasure to know Mr. Lloyd. Do you know, when I was in Cumberland, I got Southey to borrow a copy of Berkeley from him ; and I remember observing some pencil notes in it, probably written by Lloyd, which I thought particularly acute. One especially struck me as being the assertion of a doctrine of which even then I had long been persuaded, and on which I had founded much of my persuasions as regarded the imagined cause of the universe—' Mind cannot create, it can only perceive.'" To much the same effect, but more extended and ratiocinative, is a passage in an unfinished essay by Shelley *On Life*. Its date is not recorded, but I should presume it to be probably between 1815 and 1818, rather of the earlier than the later limit of date. I give in a condensed form the most important portion : "Nothing exists but as it is perceived. Pursuing the same thread of reasoning, the existence of distinct individual minds, similar to that which is employed in now questioning its own nature, is likewise found to be a delusion. Let it not be supposed that this doctrine conducts to the monstrous presumption that I, the person who now write and think, am that one mind. I am but a portion of it. The relations of *things* remain unchanged, by whatever system. Yet that the basis of things cannot be, as the popular philosophy alleges, Mind, is sufficiently evident. Mind, as far as we have any experience of its properties (and beyond that experience how vain is argument !) cannot create—it can only perceive. It is said also to be ' the cause.' But ' cause' is only a word expressing a certain state of the human mind with regard to the manner in which two thoughts are apprehended to be related to each other. It is infinitely improbable that the cause of mind—that is, of existence—is similar to mind." We shall probably not get beyond this in our endeavour to ascertain the bearing of Shelley's understanding with regard to the existence or nature of a Deity.   Clearly, when he wrote these lines, he did not believe in what is called "an Intelligent First Cause"—the God, self-existent from all eternity, of theologians.   At the same time, he did believe in a universal Mind, whereof he himself, the intellect or person Shelley, was a part; and he further believed that all we ordinarily call external objects, or matter, are but the sum of perceptions of the total Mind.   I must leave it to theosophists to decide whether this comes nearest to theism, atheism, or pantheism—I presume to the last.   I apprehend that from beginning to end—whether in *The Necessity of Atheism* or *The Boat on the Serchio*—Shelley's conception was equally and un-swervingly alien from the Personal God or Immediate Providence of the Jewish, Christian, Mahometan, and so many other religions.

2. *The Immortality of the Soul.*   As regards this question, we must primarily remember what we have just traced, viz. : That Shelley considered (at one stage of his speculations at any rate) that there are not, properly, separate minds, but that there is one universal mind informing many personalities ; also that the so-called Material Universe is in fact a mere perception of Universal Mind, which Mind must consequently be eternal—or at any rate must endure as long as any perception, commonly called any Material Universe, shall endure.   Therefore, in a certain sense, Shelley could not, at the same time with this belief, entertain a belief in the Mortality of the Soul, or of Mind.   To withdraw from the sum of mind that particular mind currently termed Shelley would, according to this view of the matter, be an extinction of soul in the same sense (and no other) as the absorption into the sand of a ladle-full of sea-water is an annihilation of the sea.

But "the Immortality of *the* Soul" is generally understood as meaning "the eternal separate self-consciousness of every individual soul."   Now it is plain that this doctrine is not necessarily involved in the hypothesis of Shelley as above expressed : he might, without self-contradiction, either add it to, or reject it from, his hypothesis.   He might, for instance, believe that the portions of mind individuated in Keats and Shelley on the earth would not, after the death of the body, continue eternally and separately to be, the one Keats, and the other Shelley.   What we have to investigate therefore is—How near did he approach to this phase of opinion?

The last intimation on this topic is of a date, 29th June 1822, very close indeed to Shelley's death: it occurs in a letter to some correspondent whose name is not given. "The destiny of man can scarcely be so degraded that he was born only to die; and, if such *should* be the case, delusions, especially the gross and preposterous ones of the existing religion, can scarcely be supposed to exalt it." Here, if we attach the ordinary meaning to the phrase "born only to die,"[1] we see clearly that Shelley's mind, at the very last, was in a state of suspense on this question: he thought it scarcely likely that the death of the body was lethal to the soul also, but he *knew* nothing about the matter, and did not profess to know anything. This is confirmatory of what Trelawny records, from the same conversation that we have already quoted, though here the opinion appears in a more distinctly negative shape—possibly more so than the poet would have been prepared deliberately and in written disquisition to maintain. As we have seen, he had said: "If old women's tales are true,[2] in another minute I might have been in another planet." *Trelawny:* "No, you would be mingled with the elements." *Shelley:* "My mind is at peace respecting nothing so much as the constitution and mysteries of the great system of things. My curiosity on this point never amounts to solicitude." *Trelawny:* "Do you believe in the immortality of the spirit?" *Shelley:* "Certainly not: how can I? We know nothing; we have no evidence. We cannot express our inmost thoughts: they are incomprehensible, even to ourselves." Another and seemingly later conversation contains this passage, spoken by Shelley. "With regard to the great question, the System of the Universe, I have no curiosity on the subject. I am content to see no farther into futurity than Plato and Bacon. My mind is tranquil: I have no fears, and some hopes. In our present gross material state, our faculties are clouded: when Death removes our clay coverings, the mystery will be solved." This is the language, not of confidence in either direction, but of uncertainty: it goes a little way, but *only* a little, towards confirming an expression in a letter from Byron to Moore, dated 6th March 1822, "Shelley believes in immortality." Again, in the notes

---

[1] I put in this qualifying clause because the context seems to me to raise some doubt. "Born only to die" would generally mean, "born to die, and not to live again after death;" but it might possibly mean, "born merely to die, without turning the present life to good account."

[2] This phrase, and the next ensuing question and answer, had never yet been in print. They are communicated to me by Mr. Trelawny, from his written memorandum of the conversation. The residue of the colloquy is in the *Recollections*.

to *Hellas*, written in 1821, we find (vol. ii. p. 417) a similar uncertainty. The poet comments on some expressions in his own verses, which might be supposed to imply a positive belief in immortal individual souls; he here explains that he has no idea of dogmatizing on the subject. He does, indeed, absolutely disbelieve the ordinary hypothesis of retributive punishment; but he has no distinct counter-belief with regard to "the condition of that futurity towards which we are all impelled by an inextinguishable thirst for immortality. Until better arguments can be produced than sophisms which disgrace the cause, this desire itself must remain the strongest and the only presumption that eternity is the inheritance of every thinking being." The general tenour of *Adonais* may seem to amount to the expression of a positive belief in the immortality of Keats as a separate individual soul: but we must be on our guard against poetic abstractions and (not to use the word disrespectfully) poetic machinery. We read, for instance, that Keats "is not dead," "hath awakened from the dream of life," "is made one with Nature;" his soul "beacons from the abode where the eternal are." If Shelley had thoroughly disbelieved the immortality of the soul, and had been writing in an expository strain, no doubt he would not and could not have used three of these expressions; but we cannot argue conversely, and say that, inasmuch as he did use the expressions, he must have thoroughly believed in immortality. The substructure is much too unsolid for such a superposition. I will quote one more testimony—that of Mrs. Shelley, in the Preface to the *Essays and Letters*. She refers to a fragmentary essay *On a Future State* written by her husband, and observes that the extant portion discusses the question merely on grounds of reasoning and analogy, which he himself would not have considered the sole grounds adducible. She then adds: "I cannot pretend to supply the deficiency, nor say what Shelley's views were. They were vague, certainly; yet as certainly regarded the country beyond the grave as one by no means foreign to our interests and hopes. Considering his individual mind as a unit divided from a mighty whole, to which it was united by restless sympathies and an eager desire for knowledge, he assuredly believed that hereafter, as now, he would form a portion of the whole—and a portion less imperfect, less suffering, than the shackles inseparable from humanity imposed on all who live beneath the moon." Mrs. Shelley also cites an extract from Shelley's diary, written when death seemed near him.   This must apparently be dated in 1814 : the essay *On a Future State*, perhaps about the same date, 1815 to 1818, as the fragment *On Life* previously cited.   As these dates are so far back, and as our enquiries have already yielded a tolerably plain result as to Shelley's views towards the close of his life, I shall say no more regarding those earlier writings, save that they do not alter the general result in question.   The essay, indeed, comes to much the same conclusion as the note on *Hellas*, and goes somewhat further in opposition to the hypothesis of immortality.

What, then, is the result?   I take it to be this : That Shelley regarded the aspiration of man after individual immortality as *some* presumption in favour of that, and he himself had the aspiration in a marked degree; but at the same time he considered it a mere presumption—unproved, incapable of proof, and exceedingly uncertain.   He found it difficult to *con*ceive that man is mortal, and alike difficult to *per*ceive that he is immortal.

3. *Political Institutions.*   There is not very much to be said in detail on this matter.   Shelley was an intense lover of freedom, and his ideal of freedom was a democratic republic.   In his *Ode to Liberty*, written in 1820, he expresses a longing that "the impious name of king" might be stamped into the dust ; and, wherever the people rose against oppression, or to secure to themselves an ampler share of liberty and power, Shelley's prompt and ardent sympathies were with them.   "He looked on political freedom," says Mrs. Shelley, "as the direct agent to effect the happiness of mankind."   He "loved and respected the people," and he worshiped the idea of equality.   Yet he was fully sensible, as several passages in his writings prove, of the difficulties and dangers which would attend a sudden transfer of power to the hands of the masses, ground down by oppression, and unprepared for self-government.   He especially deprecated anything like retaliation—any perpetuation of wrong and violence by the lately oppressed, uncontrolled, and in their turn oppressors.   There is, indeed, in a letter of Shelley's dated 1st September 1820, one ruthless passage.   "At Naples the constitutional party have declared to the Austrian minister that, if the Emperor should make war on them, their first action would be to put to death all the members of the royal family— a necessary and most just measure, where the forces of the combatants, as well as the merits of their respective causes, are so unequal.[1]   That kings should be everywhere the hostages for

---

[1] The Parisian Communists, in 1871, proceeded on much the same principle.

liberty were admirable." This, it will be observed, is advocated
as a measure of self-defence, not of retaliation; but, even in the
former aspect, it is quite contrary to the permanent and true
bent of Shelley's feelings, and must fairly be regarded as the
expression of excitement and impassioned perturbation, not of
deliberate judgment. Medwin, speaking of the last year or so
of Shelley's life, goes so far as to say that the poet "quoted
[and the biographer evidently means that he quoted with ac-
quiescence] the sentiment of the amiable Rousseau, that he
had rather behold the then state of things than the shedding of
a single drop" of blood.

I am satisfied, however, that Medwin lets-down Shelley's re-
publicanism too easy. He does indeed allow that "Shelley
used to say that a republic was the best form of government,
with disinterestedness, abnegation of self, and a Spartan virtue ;
but to produce which required the black bread and soup of the
Lacedæmonians, an equality of fortunes unattainable in the present factitious state of society, and only to be brought about by
an agrarian law, and a consequent baptism of blood." But to
say that "the poet was not so great a republican at heart as
Mrs. Shelley makes him out," and "and did not love a demo-
cracy," is rash ; and "that he was in some respects as aristocratic as Byron, and was far from despising the advantages of
birth and station," may be safely pronounced incorrect infer-
entially, if not literally. "No one was a truer admirer of our
triune constitution" is really a puerile assertion. There must
have been a very large number of admirers of our triune constitution—or else the latter was in a bad way—truer than the man
who denounced the kingly office, and the House of Commons
as it existed in his own time ; who, amid a miscellany of writings
bearing on political matters, found no word of praise to indite
concerning that constitution either in its essence or in its actual
development; whose utmost praise of British monarchy and
aristocracy consisted in terming them "symbols of the childhood of the public mind," not to be discarded in a trice.[1]
Besides, the reader has already seen, from Shelley himself and
from Hogg,[2] that the poet's interest in English history was extremely feeble, and that he "knew little and cared nothing"
about the British constitution.

---

[1] This phrase occurs at the close of the pamphlet on Reform by "The Hermit of
Marlow." There was also a later and longer book on Reform written by Shelley about
the end of 1819, but never yet published—which it ought to have been ere now.
[2] Pp. 133-5.

XXXIII.—MINOR WRITINGS OF SHELLEY.

The most important of Shelley's compositions, whether in poetry or in prose, have already been notified in this memoir; and, as for poetry, our edition contains (practically) everything of his that can be traced out. A few particulars, however, may not be unwelcome here as to his less-known writings. I shall name such only as have not been specified in the memoir, or elsewhere in this edition, and of these I shall set down *all* that I can find a record of.

1809. Towards the beginning of the year, a wild and extravagant romance about a witch, entitled *The Nightmare.* Shelley and Medwin, in alternate chapters, began this performance, but afterwards laid it aside for *The Wandering Jew.* In November, in the *Morning Chronicle*, appeared a letter signed " A.M., Oxon," upholding the candidateship of Lord Grenville as Chancellor of the University of Oxford. There is some ground for supposing that this was written by Mr. Timothy Shelley, with partial assistance from his son.

1810. According to Medwin, Shelley translated in this year a volume of German tales. Strong reason exists, however, for believing that Shelley did not as yet read German, and that his cousin's statement is therefore delusive.[1] At the end of the year he was projecting a novel, to be a deathblow to intolerance; apparently the same novel which we find him soon afterwards writing in conjunction with Hogg, in the form of letters. It was never completed.

1811. Shelley intended to include in the *Fragments of Margaret Nicholson* an apostrophe to the dagger of Brutus, and wrote it, but not in time; its composition may perhaps belong to 1811. He began an Oxford prize-poem, but left the University before it was finished. His introduction to Leigh Hunt arose from his offering to Mr. Rowland Hunter (a connection

---

[1] The "Newspaper Editor" (see p. 14) makes a rather unaccountable statement, however, which goes to confirm Medwin. He says that on a certain occasion, which must have been towards the end of 1811 or beginning of 1812, Shelley tried to dispose of "three tales, one original, the other two translations from the German"; and, failing to get a publisher, presented them to the Newspaper Editor. "They were of a very wild and romantic description, but full of energy." Towards 1822 the Editor lent the MS. to a friend, and after some months it was lost. In 1839 the Editor found that one of these tales had been printed in *The Novelist.* By this title he must, I suppose, designate *The Romancist and Novelist's Library*, which does contain reprints of *Zastrozzi* and *St. Irvyne.* But, as *St. Irvyne* had been published in the ordinary way in December 1810, and *Zastrozzi* earlier, it is puzzling to understand how Shelley could have offered either to a publisher towards the very end of 1811. Perhaps the statement as to the translations from the German is in like manner loose. Certainly in some respects the Newspaper Editor's reminiscences of Shelley were highly inexact, as I have already had occasion to show.

of Mrs. Hunt), for publication, a poem which his friend speaks of as unsuited to the firm. I find no further notice of this. He translated a treatise by Buffon. An *Essay on Love*, a short poem which he mentions in a letter of 1812 to Godwin, may perhaps also belong to the year 1811.

1812. He wrote and printed, but did not strictly publish, an indignant letter of some length to Lord Ellenborough, the judge who had sentenced a bookseller, Mr. Eaton, for publishing the Third Part of Paine's *Age of Reason:* some portions of this letter are inserted into the notes to *Queen Mab*, and the rest is in the *Shelley Memorials.* He projected translating the *Système de la Nature* written by Baron d'Holbach under the name of Mirabaud (whom he had also quoted in the same notes); but this idea was probably never put into execution, even by way of beginning. He compiled, and sent to Mr. Hookham with a view to publication, a work termed *Biblical Extracts:* a collection of passages from the Scriptures, embodying exalted moral truths and precepts, to the exclusion of dogma.

1813. He "translated an essay or treatise of some French philosopher on the Perfectibility of the Human Species;" and the two essays of Plutarch περὶ τῆς σαρκοφαγίας.

1814. From 28th July 1814 Shelley began keeping a diary. Mr. Garnett says it "accounts for every day of his life" thenceforward; which is only an apparent inconsistency with a statement made by Shelley himself in a letter of 26th January 1819 to Mr. Peacock, "I keep no journal." The reconciling explanation is that Shelley sometimes intermitted his journalizing, and then his wife kept it up.

1815. To this year we may perhaps roughly assign some of the prose compositions printed by Mrs. Shelley—*On Love, On the Punishment of Death*, and *Speculations on Morals;* the *Essay on Christianity* published in the *Shelley Memorials*, and some fragments of it in the *St. James's Magazine;* and that *On the Revival of Literature*, and *A System of Government by Furies* (a singular speculation), in the *Shelley Papers.* Mr. Trelawny tells me that Shelley said he had wished to write a Life of Christ, revoking the hasty afterthought (expressed in a note to *Queen Mab*, p. 236) "that Jesus was an ambitious man who aspired to the throne of Judæa;" but he added that he found the materials too deficient for reconstructing a Life having some solidity and authority. The *Essay on Christianity* may derive from this project, though what remains of it is doctrinal rather than biographical.

1816. *Remarks on Mandeville and Mr. Godwin.*

1817. Some observations *On Frankenstein.* Both these two last-mentioned productions are in the *Shelley Papers*, and had probably not been published elsewhere, though apparently written with a defined object.

1818. A criticism of Peacock's poem of *Rhododaphne*—now perhaps lost. The minor translations from Plato—*Ion, Menexenus*, and from *The Republic* —and the note *On a Passage in Crito*, may pertain to this year.

1819. The rhapsodic fragmentary tale named *The Coliseum* might, from its tone, be supposed a rather youthful production ; but it cannot be that, as Mrs. Shelley says that *The Assassins*, written in 1814, "was composed many years before." Probably then *The Coliseum* was a result of Shelley's stay in Rome in 1819 ; as well as the brief remarks on the Laocoon, and Bacchus and Ampelus, published by Medwin. The notes on sculptures in Florence given in the *Essays and Letters* belong to a later date in the same year ; and in November we find that Shelley had "just finished a letter of five sheets on Carlile's affair" (Richard Carlile the publisher). The "affair" was a prosecution for selling irreligious books, and some circumstances in the way it had been got up were peculiarly open to animadversion. The letter was intended for the *Examiner*, but was not, I understand, actually published.

1820. In March of this year Shelley was dictating to his wife a translation of Spinoza : the *Essay on Prophecy*, which Mr. Middleton gives as a very early original writing of Shelley's, is in fact, so Mr. Garnett has traced out, done into English from the *Tractatus Theologico-politicus*,—and this may probably be what Shelley was dictating in 1820. A letter of the poet dated 20th January 1821 says : " I was immeasurably amused by the quotation [in a paper by Archdeacon Hare] from Schlegel, about the way in which the popular faith is destroyed —first the Devil, then the Holy Ghost, then God the Father. I had written a Lucianic essay to prove the same thing." This must be the performance which Mrs. Shelley mentions by the title of *The Essay on Devils*, and of which Mr. Garnett says : " This amusing fragment was prepared for publication in 1839, with the rest of Shelley's prose works, but withdrawn." Whether its date was shortly before 1821, or some considerable while before, is not specified.

XXXIV.—AUTHORITIES.

A very brief reference to the principal authorities for the life of Shelley will close my notice. These I shall set forth in something like a descending scale of their practical importance for the biographer's purpose, irrespectively of their deservings in other regards.

1. The *Essays, Letters from Abroad, Translations, and Fragments*, edited by Mrs. Shelley.

2. The notices by Mrs. Shelley in her collected edition of the Poems, included in our issue.

3. Hogg's *Life of Shelley*, 2 vols., reaching only to the beginning of the year 1814. Some casual remarks have already been made on this truncated book, in the course of the present memoir. With all its defects, it is simply invaluable as the authority for the early career of Shelley, as a record of his tone of mind and character from a particular point of view, and as a masterly though excentric sample of biography.

4. The *Shelley Memorials*, edited by Lady Shelley, comes nearest to being a complete life of the poet, combining authenticity and method in the narrative portion, though only a rapid summary, with many interesting supplementary materials. It is clear that Shelley need not lack a creditable biographer on a full scale as long as the writer of the *Memorials* is there to undertake the office at need.

5. Trelawny's *Recollections of the Last Days of Shelley and Byron.* This excellent volume gives (so far as Shelley is concerned) simply what fell under Trelawny's personal observation, or was related thereto, in the last half-year or so of Shelley's life. For that brief period it is incomparably good, and shows a most affectionate, as well as vigorous and manly, appreciation of the poet's character and powers. Mr. Trelawny thinks (1877) of republishing it, with the addition of several interesting particulars—important or curious—most of which I have been privileged to see in MS.

6. Shelley's own Poems.

7. Medwin's *Life of Shelley*, 2 vols. This book, first published in 1847, is neither very strong-minded nor very accurate, but it has sunk unduly out of observation. Medwin had, on the whole, next to Mrs. Shelley and perhaps Mr. Hogg, the best opportunities of all the poet's biographers. The has used them with a light and slight touch, but with considerable sympathy, and to a readable result. Several matters not to be found elsewhere at first hand are in these volumes.

8. The three articles published by Mr. Peacock in *Fraser's Magazine* in 1858 and 1860 : the third of them consists of very valuable letters by Shelley himself. These articles are of course excellently written, and with a great deal of knowledge, and are indispensable as accompaniments to other records.

9. *Leigh Hunt's Autobiography*, 1860, embodies what he had said about Shelley in the far earlier work named *Lord Byron and some of his Contemporaries*. The record of Shelley is full of affectionate feeling, with quick though perhaps limited insight. The *Correspondence* of Leigh Hunt contains several letters from and to Shelley. Of the former, almost all are in the *Essays and Letters*.

10. *Shelley's Early Life, from Original Sources*, by Mr. Denis Florence MacCarthy, issued in 1872, enters most minutely and laboriously into all details affecting or bearing upon the poet's visit to Ireland in 1812, and brings to light the publication of his lost poem, the *Essay on the Existing State of Things*. In the course of this genuine labour of love Mr. MacCarthy corrects various errors made by preceding biographers, myself included.

11. The article by Mr. Thornton Hunt, entitled *Shelley, by One who knew him*, in the *Atlantic Monthly* for February 1863. There is much important matter in this brief notice, which is conspicuous for its outspoken and independent tone. It should by no means be overlooked by the biographer.

12. Mr. Kegan Paul's book, *William Godwin, his Friends and Contemporaries*, published in 1876, is more particular and authoritative than any other record regarding the details of Shelley's relations to the Godwin family.

13. Mr. Garnett's *Relics of Shelley*, and his article in *Macmillan's Magazine* for June 1860, stand alone within their own special sphere. The *Relics* consist principally of fragments of Shelley's poems, previously unpublished : there are also a few documents, and a very able discussion by Mr. Garnett regarding the separation from Harriet, and Mr. Peacock's account of that matter. The article in *Macmillan's Magazine* is founded principally on notices of Shelley which appeared in *Stockdale's Budget*, and which are now reprinted in full in the edition of Shelley published by Messrs. Chatto and Windus, compiled by Mr. R. H. Shepherd.

14. *Shelley and his Writings*, by Mr. C. S. Middleton, 2 vols., 1858. This is principally based on Medwin, Hogg, and the notes by Mrs. Shelley. The author had no personal know-

ledge of the poet; yet there are some few particulars, especially with regard to his writings, not to be found elsewhere.

15. The *Shelley Papers*, and the *Conversations of Lord Byron*, by Medwin. The biographical information contained in the former small volume is wholly, or very nearly, reproduced in the *Life of Shelley* by the same author.

16. Moore's *Life of Lord Byron* comprises, at first hand, a few points affecting Shelley as connected with his lordship.

17. *A Newspaper Editor's Reminiscences,* published in *Fraser's Magazine.* The number for June 1841 is the only one that contains any Shelleyan matter. I have already referred to these reminiscences; which, as far as they extend, are given in some detail, of not inconsiderable interest. The writer, however, was obviously very ignorant of Shelley's domestic position, and his confused dates mar the trustworthiness of his items. I do not know for certain who he may have been; probably (as a friend suggests to me) the " F " named in Hogg's book—vol. i. p. 374 and elsewhere.

18. Mr. G. Barnett's Smith's book, *Shelley, a Critical Biography* (1877), affords little information on matters of fact : two or three details should be noted hence, or at least enquired into.

My task here terminates. I have written of the immortal poet, and the man alike loveable and admirable, with one all-dominating desire—that of stating the exact truth, as far as I can ascertain or infer it, whatever may be its bearing. Any judgment pronounced upon Shelley ought to be that of a sympathizing and grateful as well as an equitable man ; sympathizing, for history records no more beautiful nature,—grateful, for how much do we not all owe him ! Our sympathy and gratitude entitle us to be fearless likewise ; and for myself I should have felt any slurring-over of dubious or censurable particulars to be so much derogation from my reverence for Shelley. The *meaning* of slurring-over (apart from motives of obligation and delicacy) is unmistakeable : it must imply that the person who adopts that course feels a little ashamed of his hero, and, to justify his professed admiration in the eyes of others, presents that hero to them as something slightly other than he really was. But I feel not at all ashamed of Shelley. He asks for no suppressions, he needs none, and from me he gets none. After everything has been stated, we find that the man Shelley was worthy to be the poet Shelley, and praise cannot reach higher than that; we find him to call forth the most eager and fervent homage, and to be one of the ultimate glories of our race and planet.